"Yes," answered Dolores. "I have almost finished—there is only half a page more to read over."

"And why do you read it over?" asked Inez. "Do you change what you have written? Do you not think now exactly as you did when you wrote?"

"No; I feel a great deal more—I want better words! And then it all seems so little, and so badly written, and I want to say things that no one ever said before, many, many things. He will laugh—no, not that! How could he? But my letter will seem childish to him. I know it will. I wish I had never written it I Do you think I had better give it to him, after all?"

"How can I tell?" asked Inez hopelessly. "You have never read it to me. I do not know what you have said to him."

"I have said that I love him as no man was ever loved before," answered Dolores, and the true words seemed to thrill with a life of their own as she spoke them.

Then she was silent for a moment, and looked down at the written pages without seeing them. Inez did not move, and seemed hardly to breathe. Then Dolores spoke again, pressing both her hands upon the paper before her unconsciously.

"I have told him that I love him, and shall love him for ever and ever," she said; "that I will live for him, die for him, suffer for him, serve him! I have told him all that and much more."

"More? That is much already. But he loves you, too. There is nothing you can promise which he will not promise, and keep, too, I think. But more! What more can you have said than that?"

"There is nothing I would not say if I could find words!"

There was a fullness of life in her voice which, to the other's uncertain tones, was as sunshine to moonlight.

"You will find words when you see him this evening," said Inez slowly. "And they will be better than anything you can write. Am I to give him your letter?"

Dolores looked at her sister quickly, for there was a little constraint in the accent of the last phrase.

"I do not know," she answered. "How can I tell what may happen, or how I shall see him first?"

"You will see him from the window presently. I can hear the guards forming already to meet him—and you—you will be able to see him from the window."

Inez had stopped and had finished her speech, as if something had choked her. She turned sideways in her chair when she had spoken, as if to listen better, for she was seated with her back to the light.

"I will tell you everything," said Maria Dolores softly. "It will be almost as if you could see him, too."

"Almost—"

Inez spoke the one word and broke off abruptly, and rose from her chair. In the familiar room she moved almost as securely as if she could see. She went to the window and listened. Dolores came and stood beside her.

"What is it, dear?" she asked. "What is the matter? What has hurt you? Tell me!"

"Nothing," answered the blind girl, "nothing, dear. I was thinking—how lonely I shall be when you and he are married, and they send me to a convent, or to our dismal old house in Valladolid."

A faint colour came into her pale face, and feeling it she turned away from Dolores; for she was not speaking the truth, or at least not half of it all.

"I will not let you go!" answered Dolores, putting one arm round her sister's waist. "They shall never take you from me. And if in many years from now we are married, you shall always be with us, and I will always take care of you as I do now."

Inez sighed and pressed her forehead and blind eyes to the cold window, almost withdrawing herself from the pressure of Dolores' arm. Down below there was tramping of heavy feet, as the companies of foot guards took their places, marching across the broad space, in their wrought steel caps and breastplates, carrying their tasselled halberds on their shoulders. An officer's voice gave sharp commands. The gust that had brought the rain had passed by, and a drizzling mist, caused by a sudden chill, now completely obscured the window.

"Can you see anything?" asked Inez suddenly, in a low voice. "I think I hear trumpets far away."

"I cannot see—there is mist on the glass, too. Do you hear the trumpets clearly?"

"I think I do. Yes—I hear them clearly now." She stopped. "He is coming," she added under her breath.

Dolores listened, but she had not the almost supernatural hearing of the blind, and could distinguish nothing but the tramping of the soldiers below, and her sister's irregular breathing beside her, as Inez held her breath again and again in order to catch the very faint and distant sound.

"Open the window," she said almost sharply, "I know I hear the trumpets."

Her delicate fingers felt for the bolts with almost feverish anxiety. Dolores helped her and opened the window wide. A strain of distant clarions sounding a triumphant march came floating across the wet city. Dolores started, and her face grew radiant, while her fresh lips opened a little as if to drink in the sound with the wintry air. Beside her, Inez grew slowly pale and held herself by the edge of the window frame, gripping it hard, and neither of the two girls felt any sensation of cold. Dolores' grey eyes grew wide and bright as she gazed fixedly towards the city where the avenue that led to the palace began, but Inez, bending a little, turned her ear in the same direction, as if she could not bear to lose a single note of the music that told her how Don John of Austria had come home in triumph, safe and whole, from his long campaign in the south.

Slowly it came nearer, strain upon strain, each more clear and loud and full of rejoicing. At first only the high-pitched clarions had sent their call to the window, but now the less shrill trumpets made rich harmonies to the melody, and the deep bass horns gave the marching time to the rest, in short full blasts that set the whole air shaking as with little peak of thunder. Below, the mounted officers gave orders, exchanged short phrases, cantered to their places, and came back again a moment later

In The Palace Of The King by F. Marion Crawford

Francis Marion Crawford was born on August 2nd, 1854 at Bagni di Lucca, Italy. An only son and a nephew to Julia Ward Howe, the American poet and writer of 'The Battle Hymn of the Republic'.

His education began at St Paul's School, Concord, New Hampshire, then to Cambridge University; University of Heidelberg; and the University of Rome.

In 1879 Crawford went to India, to study Sanskrit and then edited The Indian Herald. In 1881 he returned to America to continue his Sanskrit studies at Harvard University.

At this time in Boston he lived at his Aunt Julia house and in the company of his Uncle, Sam Ward. His family was concerned about his employment prospects. After a singing career as a baritone was ruled out, he was encouraged to write.

In December 1882 his first novel, 'Mr Isaacs', was an immediate hit which was amplified by 'Dr Claudius' in 1883.

In October 1884 he married Elizabeth Berdan. They went on to have two sons and two daughters.

Encouraged by his excellent start to a literary career he returned to Italy with Elizabeth to make a permanent home, principally in Sant' Agnello, where he bought the Villa Renzi that then became Villa Crawford.

In the late 1890s, he began to write his historical works: 'Ave Roma Immortalis' (1898), 'Rulers of the South' (1900) and 'Gleanings from Venetian History' (1905). The Saracinesca series is perhaps his best work. 'Saracinesca' was followed by 'Sant' Ilario' in 1889, 'Don Orsino' in 1892 and 'Corleone' in 1897, that being the first major treatment of the Mafia in literature.

Francis Marion Crawford died at Sorrento on Good Friday 1909 at Villa Crawford of a heart attack.

Index of Contents

CHAPTER I

Two young girls sat in a high though very narrow room of the old Moorish palace to which King Philip the Second had brought his court when he finally made Madrid his capital. It was in the month of November, in the afternoon, and the light was cold and grey, for the two tall windows looked due north, and a fine rain had been falling all the morning. The stones in the court were drying now, in patches, but the sky was like a smooth vault of cast lead, closing over the city that lay to the northward, dark, wet and still, as if its life had shrunk down under ground, away from the bitter air and the penetrating damp.

The room was scantily furnished, but the few objects it contained, the carved table, the high-backed chairs and the chiselled bronze brazier, bore the stamp of the time when art had not long been born again. On the walls there were broad tapestries of bold design, showing green forests populated by all sorts of animals in stiff attitudes, staring at one another in perpetual surprise. Below the tapestry a carved walnut wainscoting went round the room, and the door was panelled and flanked by fluted doorposts of the same dark wood, on which rested corbels fashioned into curling acanthus leaves, to hold up the cornice, which itself made a high shelf over the door. Three painted Italian vases, filled with last summer's rose leaves and carefully sealed lest the faint perfume should be lost, stood symmetrically on this projection, their contents slowly ripening for future use. The heap of white ashes, under which the wood coals were still alive in the big brazier, diffused a little warmth through the chilly room.

The two girls were sitting at opposite ends of the table. The one held a long goose-quill pen, and before her lay several large sheets of paper covered with fine writing. Her eyes followed the lines slowly, and from time to time she made a correction in the manuscript. As she read, her lips moved to form words, but she made no sound. Now and then a faint smile lent singular beauty to her face, and there was more light in her eyes, too; then it disappeared again, and she read on, carefully and intently, as if her soul were in the work.

She was very fair, as Spaniards sometimes are still, and were more often in those days, with golden hair and deep grey eyes; she had the high features, the smooth white throat, and the finely modelled ears that were the outward signs of the lordly Gothic race. When she was not smiling, her face was sad, and sometimes the delicate colour left her clear cheek and she grew softly pale, till she seemed almost delicate. Then the sensitive nostrils quivered almost imperceptibly, and the curving lips met closely as if to keep a secret; but that look came seldom, and for the most part her eyes were quiet and her mouth was kind. It was a face that expressed devotion, womanly courage, and sensitiveness rather than an active and dominating energy. The girl was indeed a full-grown woman, more than twenty years of age, but the early bloom of girlhood was on her still, and if there was a little sadness in the eyes, a man could guess well enough that it rose from the heart, and had but one simple source, which was neither a sudden grief nor a long-hidden sorrow, but only youth's one secret—love. Maria Dolores de Mendoza knew all of fear for the man she loved, that any woman could know, and much of the hope that is love's early life; but she knew neither the grief, nor the disappointment, nor the shame for another, nor for herself, nor any of the bitterness that love may bring. She did not believe that such things could be wrung from hearts that were true and faithful; and in that she was right. The man to whom she had given her heart and soul and hope had given her his, and if she feared for him, it was not lest he should forget her or his own honour. He was a man among men, good and true; but he was a soldier, and a leader, who daily threw his life to the battle, as Douglas threw the casket that held the Bruce's heart into the thick of the fight, to win it back, or die. The man she loved was Don John of Austria, the son of the great dead Emperor Charles the Fifth, the uncle of dead Don Carlos and the half brother of King Philip of Spain—the man who won glory by land and sea, who won back Granada a second time from the Moors, as bravely as his great grandfather Ferdinand had won it, but less cruelly, who won Lepanto, his brother's hatred and a death by poison, the foulest stain in Spanish history.

It was November now, and it had been June of the preceding year when he had ridden away from Madrid to put down the Moriscoes, who had risen savagely against the hard Spanish rule. He had left Dolores de Mendoza an hour before he mounted, in the freshness of the early summer morning, where they had met many a time, on a lonely terrace above the King's apartments. There were roses there, growing almost wild in great earthen jars, where some Moorish woman had planted them in older days, and Dolores could go there unseen with her blind sister, who helped her faithfully, on pretence of taking the poor girl thither to breathe the sweet quiet air. For Inez was painfully sensitive of her affliction, and suffered, besides blindness, all that an over-sensitive and imaginative being can feel.

She was quite blind, with no memory of light, though she had been born seeing, as other children. A scarlet fever had destroyed her sight. Motherless from her birth, her father often absent in long campaigns, she had been at the mercy of a heartless nurse, who had loved the fair little Dolores and had secretly tormented the younger child, as soon as she was able to understand, bringing her up to believe that she was so repulsively ugly as to be almost a monster. Later, when the nurse was gone, and Dolores was a little older, the latter had done all she could to heal the cruel wound and to make her sister know that she had soft dark hair, a sad and gentle face, with eyes that were quite closed, and a delicate mouth that had a little half painful, half pathetic way of twitching when anything hurt her,—for she was easily hurt. Very pale always, she turned her face more upwards than do people who have sight, and being of good average woman's height and very slender and finely made, this gave her carriage an air of dignity that seemed almost pride when she was offended or wounded. But the first hurt had been deep and lasting, and she could never quite believe that she was not offensive to the eyes of those who saw her, still less that she was sometimes almost beautiful in a shadowy, spiritual way. The blind, of all their sufferings, often feel most keenly the impossibility of knowing whether the truth is told them about their own looks; and he who will try and realize what it is to have been always sightless will understand that this is not vanity, but rather a sort of diffidence towards which all people should be very kind. Of all necessities of this world, of all blessings, of all guides to truth, God made light first. There are many sharp pains, many terrible sufferings and sorrows in life that come and wrench body and soul, and pass at last either into alleviation or recovery, or into the rest of death; but of those that abide a lifetime and do not take life itself, the worst is hopeless darkness. We call ignorance 'blindness,' and rage 'blindness,' and we say a man is 'blind' with grief.

Inez sat opposite her sister, at the other end of the table, listening. She knew what Dolores was doing, how during long months her sister had written a letter, from time to time, in little fragments, to give to the man she loved, to slip into his hand at the first brief meeting or to drop at his feet in her glove, or even, perhaps, to pass to him by the blind girl's quick fingers. For Inez helped the lovers always, and Don John was very gentle with her, talking with her when he could, and even leading her sometimes when she was in a room she did not know. Dolores knew that she could only hope to exchange a word with him when he came back, and that the terrace was bleak and wet now, and the roses withered, and that her father feared for her, and might do some desperate thing if he found her lover talking with her where no one could see or hear. For old Mendoza knew the world and the court, and he foresaw that sooner or later some royal marriage would be made for Don John of Austria, and that even if Dolores were married to him, some tortuous means would be found to annul her marriage, whereby a great shame would darken his house. Moreover, he was the King's man, devoted to Philip body and soul, as his sovereign, ready to give his life ten times for his sovereign's word, and thinking it treason to doubt a royal thought or motive. He was a rigid old man, a Spaniard of Spain's great days, fearless, proud, intolerant, making Spain's honour his idol, capable of gentleness only to his children, and loving them dearly, but with that sort of severity and hardness in all questions where his authority was concerned which can make a father's true affection the most intolerable burden to a girl of heart, and which, where a son is its object, leads sooner or later to fierce quarrels and lifelong estrangement. And so it had happened now. For the two girls had a brother much older than they, Rodrigo; and he had borne to be treated like a boy until he could bear no more, and then he had left his father's house in anger to find out his own fortune in the world, as many did in his day,—a poor gentleman seeking distinction in an army of men as brave as himself, and as keen to win honour on every field. Then, as if to oppose his father in everything, he had attached himself to Don John, and was spoken of as the latter's friend, and Mendoza feared lest his son should help Don John to a marriage with Dolores. But in this he was mistaken, for Rodrigo was as keen, as much a Spaniard, and as much devoted to the honour of his name as his father could be; and though he looked upon Don John as the very ideal of what a soldier and a prince should be, he would have cut off his own right hand rather than let it give his leader the letter Dolores had been writing so long; and she knew this and feared her brother, and tried to keep her secret from him.

Inez knew all, and she also was afraid of Rodrigo and of her father, both for her sister's sake and her own. So, in that divided house, the father was against the son, and the daughters were allied against them both, not in hatred, but in terror and because of Dolores' great love for Don John of Austria.

As they sat at the table it began to rain again, and the big drops beat against the windows furiously for a few minutes. The panes were round and heavy, and of a greenish yellow colour, made of blown glass, each with a sort of knob in the middle, where the iron blowpipe had been separated from the hot mass. It was impossible to see through them at all distinctly, and when the sky was dark with rain they admitted only a lurid glare into the room, which grew cold and colourless again when the rain ceased. Inez had been sitting motionless a long time, her elbow on the table, her chin resting upon her loosely clasped white hands, her blind face turned upward, listening to the turning of the pages and to the occasional scratching of her sister's pen. She sighed, moved, and let her hands fall upon the table before her in a helpless, half despairing way, as she leaned back in the big carved chair. Dolores looked up at once, for she was used to helping her sister in her slightest needs and to giving her a ready sympathy in every mood.

"What is it?" she asked quickly. "Do you want anything, dear?"

"Have you almost finished?"

The girl's voice would almost have told that she was blind. It was sweet and low, but it lacked life; though not weak, it was uncertain in strength and full of a longing that could never be satisfied, but that often seemed to come within possible reach of satisfaction. There was in the tones, too, the perpetual doubt of one from whom anything might be hidden by silence, or by the least tarn of words. Every passing hope and fear, and every pleasure and pain, were translated into sound by its quick changes. It trusted but could not always quite promise to believe; it swelled and sank as the sensitive heart beat faster or slower. It came from a world without light, in which only sound had meaning, and only touch was certainty.

to make some final arrangement—their splendid gold-inlaid corslets and the rich caparisons of their horses looking like great pieces of jewelry that moved hither and thither in the thin grey mist, while the dark red and yellow uniforms of the household guards surrounded the square on three sides with broad bands of colour. Dolores could see her father, who commanded them and to whom the officers came for orders, sitting motionless and erect on his big black horse—a stern figure, with close-cut grey beard, clad all in black saving his heavily gilded breastplate and the silk sash he wore across it from shoulder to sword knot. She shrank back a little, for she would not have let him see her looking down from an upper window to welcome the returning visitor.

"What is it? Do you see him? Is he there?" Inez asked the questions in a breath, as she heard her sister move.

"No—our father is below on his horse. He must not see us." And she moved further into the embrasure.

"You will not be able to see," said Inez anxiously. "How can you tell me—I mean, how can you see, where you are?"

Dolores laughed softly, but her laugh trembled with the happiness that was coming so soon.

"Oh, I see very well," she answered. "The window is wide open, you know."

"Yes—I know."

Inez leaned back against the wall beside the window, letting her hand drop in a hopeless gesture. The sample answer had hurt her, who could never see, by its mere thoughtlessness and by the joy that made her sister's voice quaver. The music grew louder and louder, and now there came with it the sound of a great multitude, cheering, singing the march with the trumpets, shouting for Don John; and all at once as the throng burst from the street to the open avenue the voices drowned the clarions for a moment, and a vast cry of triumph filled the whole air.

"He is there! He is there!" repeated Inez, leaning towards the window and feeling for the stone sill.

But Dolores could not hear for the shouting. The clouds had lifted to the westward and northward; and as the afternoon sun sank lower they broke away, and the level rays drank up the gloom of the wintry day in an instant. Dolores stood motionless before the window, undazzled, like a statue of ivory and gold in a stone niche. With the light, as the advancing procession sent the people before it, the trumpets rang high and clear again, and the bright breastplates of the trumpeters gleamed like dancing fire before the lofty standard that swayed with the slow pace of its bearer's horse. Brighter and nearer came the colours, the blazing armour, the standard, the gorgeous procession of victorious men-at-arms; louder and louder blew the trumpets, higher and higher the clouds were lifted from the lowering sun. Half the people of Madrid went before, the rest flocked behind, all cheering or singing or shouting. The stream of colour and light became a river, the river a flood, and in the high tide of a young victor's glory Don John of Austria rode onward to the palace gate. The mounted trumpeters parted to each side before him, and the standard-bearer ranged his horse to the left, opposite the banner of the King, which held the right, and Don John, on a grey Arab mare, stood out alone at the head of his men, saluting his royal brother with lowered sword and bent head. A final blast from the trumpets sounded full and high, and again and again the shout of the great throng went up like thunder and echoed from the palace walls, as King Philip, in his balcony above the gate, returned the salute with his hand, and bent a little forward over the stone railing.

Dolores de Mendoza forgot her father and all that he might say, and stood at the open window, looking down. She had dreamed of this moment; she had seen visions of it in the daytime; she had told herself again and again what it would be, how it must be; but the reality was beyond her dreams and her visions and her imaginings, for she had to the full what few women have in any century, and what few have ever had in the blush of maidenhood,—the sight of the man she loved, and who loved her with all his heart, coming home in triumph from a hard-fought war, himself the leader and the victor, himself in youth's first spring, the young idol of a warlike nation, and the centre of military glory.

When he had saluted the King he sat still a moment on his horse and looked upward, as if unconsciously drawn by the eyes that, of all others, welcomed him at that moment; and his own met them instantly and smiled, though his face betrayed nothing. But old Mendoza, motionless in his saddle, followed the look, and saw; and although he would have praised the young leader with the best of his friends, and would have fought under him and for him as well as the bravest, yet at that moment he would gladly have seen Don John of Austria fall dead from his horse before his eyes.

Don John dismounted without haste, and advanced to the gate as the King disappeared from the balcony above. He was of very graceful figure and bearing, not short, but looking taller than he really was by the perfection of his proportions. The short reddish brown hair grew close and curling on his small head, but left the forehead high, while it set off the clear skin and the mobile features. A very small moustache shaded his lip without hiding the boyish mouth, and at that time he wore no beard. The lips, indeed, smiled often, and the expression of the mouth was rather careless and good-humoured than strong. The strength of the face was in the clean-cut jaw, while its real expression was in the deep-set, fiery blue eyes, that could turn angry and fierce at one moment, and tender as a woman's the next.

He wore without exaggeration the military dress of his time,—a beautifully chiselled corslet inlaid with gold, black velvet sleeves, loose breeches of velvet and silk, so short that they did not descend half way to the knees, while his legs were covered by tight hose and leather boots, made like gaiters to clasp from the knee to the ankle and heel. Over his shoulder hung a short embroidered cloak, and his head covering was a broad velvet cap, in which were fastened the black and yellow plumes of the House of Austria.

As he came near to the gate, many friends moved forward to greet him, and he gave his hand to all, with a frank smile and words of greeting. But old Mendoza did not dismount nor move his horse a step nearer. Don John, looking round before he went in, saw the grim face, and waved his hand to Dolores' father; but the old man pretended that he saw nothing, and made no answering gesture. Some one in the crowd of courtiers laughed lightly. Old Mendoza's face never changed; but his knees must have pressed the saddle suddenly, for his black horse stirred uneasily, and tried to rear a little. Don John stopped short, and his eyes hardened and grew very light before the smile could fade from his lips, while he tried to find the face of the man whose laugh he had heard. But that was impossible, and his look was grave and stern as he went in under the great gate, the multitude cheering after him.

From her high window Dolores had seen and heard also, for she had followed every movement he made and every change of his expression, and had faithfully told her sister what she saw, until the laugh came, short and light, but cutting. And Inez heard that, too, for she was leaning far forward upon the broad stone sill to listen for the sound of Don John's voice. She drew back with a springing movement, and a sort of cry of pain.

"Some one is laughing at me!" she cried. "Some one is laughing because I am trying to see!"

Instantly Dolores drew her sister to her, kissing her tenderly, and soothing her as one does a frightened child.

"No, dear, no! It was not that—I saw what it was. Nobody was looking at you, my darling. Do you know why some one laughed? It hurt me, too. He smiled and waved his hand to our father, who took no notice of him. The laugh was for that—and for me, because the man knew well enough that our father does not mean that we shall ever marry. Do you see, dear? It was not meant for you."

"Did he really look up at us when you said so?" asked Inez, in a smothered voice.

"Who? The man who laughed?"

"No. I mean—"

"Don John? Yes. He looked up to us and smiled—as he often does at me—with his eyes only, while his face was quite grave. He is not changed at all, except that he looks more determined, and handsomer, and braver, and stronger than ever! He does each time I see him!"

But Inez was not listening.

"That was worth living for—worth being blind for," she said suddenly, "to hear the people shout and cheer for him as he came along. You who can see it all do not understand what the sound means to me. For a moment—only for a moment—I saw light—I know I saw a bright light before my eyes. I am not dreaming. It made my heart beat, and it made my head dizzy. It must have been light. Do you think it could be, Dolores?"

"I do not know, dear," answered the other gently.

But as the day faded and they sat together in the early dusk, Dolores looked long and thoughtfully at the blind face. Inez loved Don John, though she did not know it, and without knowing it she had told her sister.

CHAPTER II

When Don John had disappeared within the palace the people lingered a little while, hoping that something might happen which would be worth seeing, and then, murmuring a little in perfectly unreasonable disappointment, they slowly dispersed. After that old Mendoza gave his orders to the officers of the guards, the men tramped away, one detachment after another, in a regular order; the cavalry that had ridden up with Don John wheeled at a signal from the trumpets, and began to ride slowly back to the city, pressing hard upon the multitude, and before it was quite dark the square before the palace was deserted again. The sky had cleared, the pavement was dry again, and the full moon was rising. Two tall sentinels with halberds paced silently up and down in the shadow.

Dolores and her sister were still sitting in the dark when the door opened, and a grey-haired servant in red and yellow entered the room, bearing two lighted wax candles in heavy bronze candlesticks, which he set upon the table. A moment later he was followed by old Mendoza, still in his breastplate, as he had dismounted, his great spurs jingling on his heavy boots, and his long basket-hilted sword trailing on the marble pavement. He was bareheaded now, and his short hair, smooth and grizzled, covered his energetic head like a close-fitting skull cap of iron-grey velvet. He stood still before the table, his bony right hand resting upon it and holding both his long gloves. The candlelight shone upward into his dark face, and gleamed yellow in his angry eyes.

Both the girls rose instinctively as their father entered; but they stood close together, their hands still linked as if to defend each other from a common enemy, though the hard man would have given his life for either of them at any moment since they had come into the world. They knew it, and trembled.

"You have made me the laughing-stock of the court," he began slowly, and his voice shook with anger. "What have you to say in your defence?"

He was speaking to Dolores, and she turned a little pale. There was something so cruelly hard in his tone and bearing that she drew back a little, not exactly in bodily fear, but as a brave man may draw back a step when another suddenly draws a weapon upon him. Instantly Inez moved forward, raising one white hand in protest, and turning her blind face to her father's gleaming eyes.

"I am not speaking to you," he said roughly, "but you," he went on, addressing Dolores, and the heavy table shook under his hand. "What devil possessed you that you should shame me and yourself, standing at your window to smile at Don John, as if he were the Espadero at a bull fight and you the beauty of the ring—with all Madrid there to look on, from his Majesty the King to the beggar in the road? Have you no modesty, no shame, no blood that can blush? And if not, have you not even so much woman's sense as should tell you that you are ruining your name and mine before the whole world?"

"Father! For the sake of heaven do not say such words—you must not! You shall not!"

Dolores' face was quite white now, as she gently pushed Inez aside and faced the angry man. The table was between them.

"Have I said one word more than the very truth?" asked Mendoza. "Does not the whole court know that you love Don John of Austria—"

"Let the whole world know it!" cried the girl bravely. "Am I ashamed to love the best and bravest man that breathes?"

"Let the whole world know that you are willing to be his toy, his plaything—"

"His wife, sir!" Dolores' voice was steady and clear as she interrupted her father. "His wife," she repeated proudly; "And to-morrow, if you and the King will not hinder us. God made you my father, but neither God nor man has given you the right to insult me, and you shall not be unanswered, so long as I have strength and breath to speak. But for you, I should be Don John of Austria's wife to-day—and then, then his 'toy,' his 'plaything'—yes, and his slave and his servant—what you will! I love him, and I would work for him with my hands, as I would give my blood and my life for his, if God would grant me that happiness and grace, since you will not let me be his wife!"

"His wife!" exclaimed Mendoza, with a savage sneer. "His wife—to be married to-day and cast off to-morrow by a turn of the pen and the twisting of a word that would prove your marriage void, in order that Don John may be made the husband of some royal widowed lady, like Queen Mary of the Scots! His wife!" He laughed bitterly.

"You have an exalted opinion of your King, my father, since you suppose that he would permit such deeds in Spain!"

Dolores had drawn herself up to her full height as she spoke, and she remained motionless as she awaited the answer to what she had said. It was long in coming, though Mendoza's dark eyes met hers unflinchingly, and his lips moved more than once as if he were about to speak. She had struck a blow that was hard to parry, and she knew it. Inez stood beside her, silent and breathing hard as she listened.

"You think that I have nothing to say," he began at last, and his tone had changed and was more calm. "You are right, perhaps. What should I say to you, since you have lost all sense of shame and all thought of respect or obedience? Do you expect that I shall argue with you, and try to convince you that I am right, instead of forcing you to respect me and yourself? Thank Heaven, I have never yet questioned my King's thoughts, nor his motives, nor his supreme right to do whatsoever may be for the honour and glory of Spain. My life is his, and all I have is his, to do with it all as he pleases, by grace of his divine right. That is my creed and my law—and if I have failed to bring you up in the same belief, I have committed a great sin, and it will be counted against me hereafter, though I have done what I could, to the best of my knowledge."

Mendoza lifted his sheathed sword and laid his right hand upon the cross-bar of the basket hilt.

"God—the King—Spain!" he said solemnly, as he pressed his lips to it once for each article of his faith.

"I do not wish to shake your belief," said Dolores coldly. "I daresay that is impossible!"

"As impossible as it is to make me change my determination," answered Mendoza, letting his long sword rest on the pavement again.

"And what may your determination be?" asked the girl, still facing him.

Something in his face forewarned her of near evil and danger, as he looked at her long without answering. She moved a little, so as to stand directly in front of Inez. Taking an attitude that was almost defiant, she began to speak rapidly, holding her hands behind her and pressing herself back against her sister to attract the latter's attention; and in her hand she held the letter she had written to Don John, folded into the smallest possible space, for she had kept it ready in the wrist of her tight sleeve, not knowing what might happen any moment to give her an opportunity of sending it.

"What have you determined?" she asked again, and then went on without waiting for a reply. "In what way are you going to exhibit your power over me? Do you mean to take me away from the court to live in Valladolid again? Are you going to put me in the charge of some sour old woman who will never let me out of her sight from morning till morning?" She had found her sister's hand behind hers and had thrust the letter into the fingers that closed quickly upon it. Then she laughed a little, almost gaily. "Do you think that a score of sour old duennas could teach me to forget the man I love, or could prevent me from sending him a message every day if I chose? Do you think you could hinder Don John of Austria, who came back an hour ago from his victory the idol of all Spain, the favourite of the people—brave, young, powerful, rich, popular, beloved far more than the King himself, from seeing me every day if he chose, so long as he were not away in war? And then—I will ask you something more—do you think that father, or mother, or king, or law, or country has power to will away the love of a woman who loves with all her heart and soul and strength? Then answer me and tell me what you have determined to do with me, and I will tell you my determination, too, for I have one of my own, and shall abide by it, come what may, and whatsoever you may do!"

She paused, for she had heard Inez softly close the door as she went out. The letter at least was safe, and if it were humanly possible, Inez would find a means of delivering it; for she had all that strange ingenuity of the blind in escaping observation which it seems impossible that they should possess, but of which every one who has been much with them is fully aware. Mendoza had seen Inez go out, and was glad that she was gone, for her blind face sometimes disturbed him when he wished to assert his authority.

"Yes," he said, "I will tell you what I mean to do, and it is the only thing left to me, for you have given me no choice. You are disobedient and unruly, you have lost what little respect you ever had—or showed—for me. But that is not all. Men have had unruly daughters before, and yet have married them well, and to men who in the end have ruled them. I do not speak of my affection for you both, since you have none for me. But now, you are going beyond disobedience and lawlessness, for you are ruining yourself and disgracing me, and I will neither permit the one nor suffer the other." His voice rose harshly. "Do you understand me? I intend to protect my name from you, and yours from the world, in the only way possible. I intend to send you to Las Huelgas to-morrow morning. I am in earnest, and unless you consent to give up this folly and to marry as I wish, you shall stay there for the rest of your natural life. Do you understand? And until to-morrow morning you shall stay within these doors. We shall see whether Don John of Austria will try to force my dwelling first and a convent of holy nuns afterwards. You will be safe from him, I give you my word of honour,—the word of a Spanish gentleman and of your father. You shall be safe forever. And if Don John tries to enter here to-night, I will kill him on the threshold. I swear that I will."

He ceased speaking, turned, and began to walk up and down the small room, his spurs and sword clanking heavily at every step. He had folded his arms, and his head was bent low.

A look of horror and fear had slowly risen in Dolores' face, for she knew her father, and that he kept his word at every risk. She knew also that the King held him in very high esteem, and was as firmly opposed to her marriage as Mendoza himself, and therefore ready to help him to do what he wished. It had never occurred to her that she could be suddenly thrust out of sight in a religious institution, to be kept there at her father's pleasure, even for her whole life. She was too young and too full of life to have thought of such a possibility. She had indeed heard that such things could be done, and had been done, but she had never known such a case, and had never realized that she was so completely at her father's mercy. For the first time in her life she felt real fear, and as it fell upon her there came the sickening conviction that she could not resist it, that her spirit was broken all at once, that in a moment more she would throw herself at her father's feet and implore mercy, making whatever promise he exacted, yet making it falsely, out of sheer terror, in an utter degradation and abasement of all moral strength, of which she had never even dreamed. She grew giddy as she felt it coming upon her, and the lights of the two candles moved strangely. Already she saw herself on her knees, sobbing with fear, trying to take her father's hand, begging forgiveness, denying her love, vowing submission and dutiful obedience in an agony of terror. For on the other side she saw the dark corridors and gloomy cells of Las Huelgas, the veiled and silent nuns, the abomination of despair that was before her till she should die and escape at last,—the faint hope which would always prevent her from taking the veil herself, yet a hope fainter and fainter, crossed by the frightful uncertainty in which she should be kept by those who guarded her. They would not even tell her whether the man she loved were alive or dead, she could never know whether he had given up her love, himself in despair, or whether, then, as years went by, he would not lose the thread that took him back to the memory of her, and forget—and love again.

But then her strong nature rose again, and the vision of fear began to fade as her faith in his love denied the last thought with scorn. Many a time, when words could tell no more, and seemed exhausted just when trust was strongest, he had simply said, "I love you, as you love me," and somehow the little phrase meant all, and far more than the tender speeches that sometimes formed themselves so gracefully, and yet naturally and simply, because they, too, came straight from the heart. So now, in her extreme need, the plain words came back to her in his voice, "I love you, as you love me," with a sudden strength of faith in him that made her live again, and made fear seem impossible. While her father slowly paced the floor in silence, she thought what she should do, and whether there could be anything which she would not do, if Don John of Austria were kept a prisoner from her; and she felt sure that she could overcome every obstacle and laugh at every danger for the hope of getting to him. If she would, so would he, since he loved her as she loved him. But for all the world, he would not have her throw herself upon her father's mercy and make false promises and sob out denials of her love, out of fear. Death would be better than that.

"Do as you will with me, since you have the power," she said at last, quite calmly and steadily.

Instantly the old man stopped in his walk, and turned towards her, almost as if he himself were afraid now. To her amazement she saw that his dark eyes were moist with tears that clung but half shed to the rugged lids and rough lashes. He did not speak for some moments, while she gazed at him in wonder, for she could not understand. Then all at once he lifted his brown hands and covered his face with a gesture of utter despair.

"Dolores! My child, my little girl!" he cried, in a broken voice.

Then he sat down, as it overcome, clasped his hands on the hilt of his sword, and rested his forehead against them, rocking himself with a barely perceptible motion. In twenty years, Dolores had never understood, not even guessed, that the hard man, ever preaching of wholesome duty and strict obedience, always rebuking, never satisfied, ill pleased almost always, loved her with all his heart, and looked upon her as the very jewel of his soul. She guessed it now, in a sudden burst of understanding; but it was so new, so strange, that she could not have told what she felt. There was at best no triumph at the thought that, of the two, he had broken down first in the contest. Pity came first, womanly, simple and kind, for the harsh nature that was so wounded at last. She came to his side, and laid one hand upon his shoulder, speaking softly.

"I am very, very sorry that I have hurt you," she said, and waited for him to speak, pressing his shoulder with a gentle touch.

He did not look up, and still he rocked himself gently, leaning on his sword. The girl suffered, too, to see him suffering so. A little while ago he had been hard, fierce, angry, cruel, threatening her with a living death that had filled her with horror. It had seemed quite impossible that there could be the least tenderness in him for any one—least of all for her.

"God be merciful to me," he said at length in very low tones. "God forgive me if it is my fault—you do not love me—I am nothing to you but an unkind old man, and you are all the world to me, child!"

He raised his head slowly and looked into her face. She was startled at the change in his own, as well as deeply touched by what he said. His dark cheeks had grown grey, and the tears that would not quite fall were like a glistening mist under the lids, and almost made him look sightless. Indeed, he scarcely saw her distinctly. His clasped hands trembled a little on the hilt of the sword he still held.

"How could I know?" cried Dolores, suddenly kneeling down beside him. "How could I guess? You never let me see that you were fond of me—or I have been blind all these years—"

"Hush, child!" he said. "Do not hurt me any more—it must have been my fault."

He grew more calm, and though his face was very grave and sad, the natural dark colour was slowly coming back to it now, and his hands were steady again. The girl was too young, and far too different from him, to understand his nature, but she was fast realizing that he was not the man he had always seemed to her.

"Oh, if I had only known!" she cried, in deep distress. "If I had only guessed, I would have been so different! I was always frightened, always afraid of you, since I can remember—I thought you did not care for us and that we always displeased you—how could we know?"

Mendoza lifted one of his hands from the sword hilt, and took hers, with as much gentleness as was possible to him. His eyes became clear again, and the profound emotion he had shown subsided to the depths whence it had risen.

"We shall never quite understand each other," he said quietly. "You cannot see that it is a man's duty to do what is right for his children, rather than to sacrifice that in order to make them love him."

It seemed to Dolores that there might be a way open between the two, but she said nothing, and left her hand in his, glad that he was kind, but feeling, as he felt, that there could never be any real understanding between them. The breach had existed too long, and it was far too wide.

"You are headstrong, my dear," he said, nodding at each word. "You are very headstrong, if you will only reflect."

"It is not my head, it is my heart," answered Dolores. "And besides," she added with a smile, "I am your daughter, and you are not of a very gentle and yielding disposition, are you?"

"No," he answered with hesitation, "perhaps not." Then his face relaxed a little, and he almost smiled too.

It seemed as if the peace were made and as if thereafter there need not be trouble again. But it was even then not far off, for it was as impossible for Mendoza to yield as it would have been for Dolores to give up her love for Don John. She did not see this, and she fancied that a real change had taken place in his disposition, so that he would forget that he had threatened to send her to Las Huelgas, and not think of it again.

"What is done cannot be undone," he said, with renewed sadness. "You will never quite believe that you have been everything to me during your life. How could you not be, my child? I am very lonely. Your mother has been dead nearly eighteen years, and Rodrigo—"

He stopped short suddenly, for he had never spoken his son's name in the girl's hearing since Rodrigo had left him to follow his own fortunes.

"I think Rodrigo broke my heart," said the old man, after a short pause, controlling his voice so that it sounded dry and indifferent. "And if there is anything left of it, you will break the rest."

He rose, taking his hand from hers, and turning away, with the roughness of a strong, hard man, who has broken down once under great emotion and is capable of any harshness in his fear of yielding to it again. Dolores started slightly and drew back. In her the kindly impression was still strong, but his tone and manner wounded her.

"You are wrong," she said earnestly. "Since you have shown me that you love me, I will indeed do my best not to hurt you or displease you. I will do what I can—what I can."

She repeated the last words slowly and with unconscious emphasis. He turned his face to her again instantly.

"Then promise me that you will never see Don John of Austria again, that you will forget that you ever loved him, that you will put him altogether out of your thoughts, and that you will obediently accept the marriage I shall make for you."

The words of refusal to any such obedience as that rose to the girl's lips, ready and sharp. But she would not speak them this time, lest more angry words should answer hers. She looked straight at her father's eyes, holding her head proudly high for a moment. Then, smiling at the impossibility of what he asked, she turned from him and went to the window in silence. She opened it wide, leaned upon the stone sill and looked out. The moon had risen much higher now, and the court was white.

She had meant to cut short the discussion without rousing anger again, but she could have taken no worse way to destroy whatever was left of her father's kindlier mood. He did not raise his voice now, as he followed her and spoke.

"You refuse to do that?" he said, with an already ominous interrogation in his tone.

"You ask the impossible," she answered, without looking round. "I have not refused, for I have no will in this, no choice. You can do what you please with me, for you have power over my outward life—and if you lacked it, the King would help you. But you have no power beyond that, neither over my heart nor over my soul. I love him—I have loved him long, and I shall love him till I die, and beyond that, forever and ever, beyond everything—beyond the great to-morrow of God's last judgment! How can I put him out of my thoughts, then? It is madness to ask it of me."

She paused a moment, while he stood behind her, getting his teeth and slowly grinding the heel of one heavy boot on the pavement.

"And as for threatening me," she continued, "you will not kill Don John, nor even try to kill him, for he is the King's brother. If I can see him this evening, I will—and there will be no risk for him. You would not murder him by stealth, I suppose? No! Then you will not attack him at all, and if I can see him, I will—I tell you so, frankly. To-morrow or the next day, when the festivities they have for him are over, and you yourself are at liberty, take me to Las Huelgas, if you will, and with as little scandal as possible. But when I am there, set a strong guard of armed men to keep me, for I shall escape unless you do. And I shall go to Don John. That is all I have to say. That is my last word."

"I gave you mine, and it was my word of honour," said Mendoza. "If Don John tries to enter here, to see you, I will kill him. To-morrow, you shall go to Las Huelgas."

Dolores made no answer and did not even turn her head. He left her and went out. She heard his heavy tread in the hall beyond, and she heard a bolt slipped at the further door. She was imprisoned for the night, for the entrance her father had fastened was the one which cut off the portion of the apartment in which the sisters lived from the smaller part which he had reserved for himself. These rooms, from which there was no other exit, opened, like the sitting-room, upon the same hall.

When Dolores knew that she was alone, she drew back from the window and shut it. It had served its purpose as a sort of refuge from her father, and the night air was cold. She sat down to think, and being in a somewhat desperate mood, she smiled at the idea of being locked into her room, supperless, like a naughty child. But her face grew grave instantly as she tried to discover some means of escape. Inez was certainly not in the apartment—she must have gone to the other end of the palace, on pretence of seeing one of the court ladies, but really in the hope of giving Don John the letter. It was more than probable that she would not be allowed to enter when she came back, for Mendoza would distrust her. That meant that Dolores could have no communication with any one outside her rooms during the evening and night, and she knew her father too well to doubt that he would send her to Las Huelgas in the morning, as he had sworn to do. Possibly he would let her serving-woman come to her to prepare what she needed for the journey, but even that was unlikely, for he would suspect everybody.

The situation looked hopeless, and the girl's face grew slowly pale as she realized that after all she might not even exchange a word with Don John before going to the convent—she might not even be able to tell him whither they were sending her, and Mendoza might keep the secret for years—and she would never be allowed to write, of course.

She heard the further door opened again, the bolt running back with a sharp noise. Then she heard her father's footsteps and his voice calling to Inez, as he went from room to room. But there was no answer, and presently he went away, bolting the door a second time. There could be no more doubt about it now. Dolores was quite alone. Her heart beat heavily and slowly. But it was not over yet. Again the bolt slipped in the outer hall, and again she heard the heavy steps. They came straight towards the door. He had perhaps changed his mind, or he had something more to say; she held her breath, but he did not come in. As if to make doubly sure, he bolted her into the little room, crossed the hall a last time, and bolted it for the night, perfectly certain that Dolores was safely shut off from the outer world.

For some minutes she sat quite still, profoundly disturbed, and utterly unable to find any way out of her difficulty, which was, indeed, that she was in a very secure prison.

Then again there was a sound at the door, but very soft this time, not half as loud in her ears as the beating of her own heart. There was something ghostly in it, for she had heard no footsteps. The bolt moved very slowly and gently—she had to strain her ears to hear it move. The sound ceased, and another followed it—that of the door being cautiously opened. A moment later Inez was in the room—turning her head anxiously from side to side to hear Dolores' breathing, and so to find out where she was. Then as Dolores rose, the blind girl put her finger to her lips, and felt for her sister's hand.

"He has the letter," she whispered quickly. "I found him by accident, very quickly. I am to say to you that after he has been some time in the great hall, he will slip away and come here. You see our father will be on duty and cannot come up."

Dolores' hand trembled violently.

"He swore to me that he would kill Don John if he came here," she whispered. "He will do it, if it costs his own life! You must find him again—go quickly, dear, for the love of Heaven!" Her anxiety increased. "Go—go, darling—do not lose a moment—he may come sooner—save him, save him!"

"I cannot go," answered Inez, in terror, as she understood the situation. "I had hidden myself, and I am locked in with you. He called me, but I kept quiet, for I knew he would not let me stay." She buried her face in her hands and sobbed aloud in an agony of fear.

Dolores' lips were white, and she steadied herself against a chair.

CHAPTER III

Dolores stood leaning against the back of the chair, neither hearing nor seeing her sister, conscious only that Don John was in danger and that she could not warn him to be on his guard. She had not believed herself when she had told her father that he would not dare to lift his hand against the King's half brother. She had said the words to give herself courage, and perhaps in a rush of certainty that the man she loved was a match for other men, hand to hand, and something more. It was different now. Little as she yet knew of human nature, she guessed without reasoning that a man who has been angry, who has wavered and given way to what he believes to be weakness, and whose anger has then burst out again, is much more dangerous than before, because his wrath is no longer roused against another only, but also against himself. More follies and crimes have been committed in that second tide of passion than under a first impulse. Even if Mendoza had not fully meant what he had said the first time, he had meant it all, and more, when he had last spoken. Once more the vision of fear rose before Dolores' eyes, nobler now; because it was fear for another and not for herself, but therefore also harder to conquer.

Inez had ceased from sobbing now, and was sitting quietly in her accustomed seat, in that attitude of concentrated expectancy of sounds which is so natural to the blind, that one can almost recognize blindness by the position of the head and body without seeing the face. The blind rarely lean back in a chair; more often the body is quite upright, or bent a little forward, the face is slightly turned up when there is total silence, often turned down when a sound is already heard distinctly; the knees are hardly ever crossed, the hands are seldom folded together, but are generally spread out, as if ready to help the hearing by the sense of touch—the lips are slightly parted, for the blind know that they hear by the mouth as well as with their ears—the expression of the face is one of expectation and extreme attention, still, not placid, calm, but the very contrary of indifferent. It was thus that Inez sat, as she often sat for hours, listening, always and forever listening to the speech of things and of nature, as well as for human words. And in listening, she thought and reasoned patiently and continually, so that the slightest sounds had often long and accurate meanings for her. The deaf reason little or ill, and are very suspicious; the blind, on the contrary, are keen, thoughtful, and ingenious, and are distrustful of themselves rather than of others. Inez sat quite still, listening, thinking, and planning a means of helping her sister.

But Dolores stood motionless as if she were paralyzed, watching the picture that she could not chase away. For she saw the familiar figure of the man she loved coming down the gloomy corridor, alone and unarmed, past the deep embrasures through which the moonlight streamed, straight towards the oak door at the end; and then, from one of the windows another figure stood out, sword in hand, a gaunt man with a grey beard, and there were few words, and an uncertain quick confounding of shadows with a ray of cold light darting hither and thither, then a fall, and then stillness. As soon as it was over, it began again, with little change, save that it grew more distinct, till she could see Don John's white face in the moonlight as he lay dead on the pavement of the corridor.

It became intolerable at last, and she slowly raised one hand and covered her eyes to shut out the sight.

"Listen," said Inez, as Dolores stirred. "I have been thinking. You must see him to-night, even if you are not alone with him. There is only one way to do that; you must dress yourself for the court and go down to the great hall with the others and speak to him—then you can decide how to meet to-morrow."

"Inez—I have not told you the rest! To-morrow I am to be sent to Las Huelgas, and kept there like a prisoner." Inez uttered a low cry of pain.

"To a convent!" It seemed like death.

Dolores began to tell her all Mendoza had said, but Inez soon interrupted her. There was a dark flush in the blind girl's face.

"And he would have you believe that he loves you?" she cried indignantly. "He has always been hard, and cruel, and unkind, he has never forgiven me for being blind—he will never forgive you for being young! The King! The King before everything and every one—before himself, yes, that is well, but before his children, his soul, his heart—he has no heart! What am I saying—" She stopped short.

"And yet, in his strange way, he loves us both," said Dolores. "I cannot understand it, but I saw his face when there were tears in his eyes, and I heard his voice. He would give his life for us."

"And our lives, and hearts, and hopes to feed his conscience and to save his own soul!"

Inez was trembling with anger, leaning far forward, her face flushed, one slight hand clenched, the other clenching it hard. Dolores was silent. It was not the first time that Inez had spoken in this way, for the blind girl could be suddenly and violently angry for a good cause. But now her tone changed.

"I will save you," she said suddenly, "but there is no time to be lost. He will not come back to our rooms now, and he knows well enough that Don John cannot come here at this hour, so that he is not waiting for him. We have this part of the place to ourselves, and the outer door only is bolted now. It will take you an hour to dress—say three-quarters of an hour. As soon as you get out, you must go quickly round the palace to the Duchess Alvarez. Our father will not go there, and you can go down with her, as usual—but tell her nothing. Our father will be there, and he will see you, but he will not care to make an open scandal in the court. Don John will come and speak to you; you must stay beside the Duchess of course—but you can manage to exchange a few words."

Dolores listened intently, and her face brightened a little as Inez went on, only to grow sad and hopeless again a moment later. It was all an impossible dream.

"That would be possible if I could once get beyond the door of the hall," she said despondently. "It is of no use, dear! The door is bolted."

"They will open it for me. Old Eudaldo is always within hearing, and he will do anything for me. Besides, I shall seem to have been shut in by mistake, do you see? I shall say that I am hungry, thirsty, that I am cold, that in locking you in our father locked me in, too, because I was asleep. Then Eudaldo will open the door for me. I shall say that I am going to the Duchess's."

"Yes—but then?"

"You will cover yourself entirely with my black cloak and draw it over your head and face. We are of the same height—you only need to walk as I do—as if you were blind—across the hall to the left. Eudaldo will open the outer door for you. You will just nod to thank him, without speaking, and when you are outside, touch the wall of the corridor with your left hand, and keep close to it. I always do, for fear of running against some one. If you meet any of the women, they will take you for me. There is never much light in the corridor, is there? There is one oil lamp half way down, I know, for I always smell it when I pass in the evening."

"Yes, it is almost dark there—it is a little lamp. Do you really think this is possible?"

"It is possible, not sure. If you hear footsteps in the corridor beyond the corner, you will have time to slip into one of the embrasures. But our father will not come now. He knows that Don John is in his own apartments with many people. And besides, it is to be a great festival to-night, and all the court people and officers, and the Archbishop, and all the rest who do not live in the palace will come from the city, so that our father will have to command the troops and give orders for the guards to march out, and a thousand things will take his time. Don John cannot possibly come here till after the royal supper, and if our father can come away at all, it will be at the same time. That is the danger."

Dolores shivered and saw the vision in the corridor again.

"But if you are seen talking with Don John before supper, no one will suppose that in order to meet him you would risk coming back here, where you are sure to be caught and locked up again. Do you see?"

"It all depends upon whether I can get out," answered Dolores, but there was more hope in her tone. "How am I to dress without a maid?" she asked suddenly.

"Trust me," said Inez, with a laugh. "My hands are better than a serving-woman's eyes. You shall look as you never looked before. I know every lock of your hair, and just how it should be turned and curled and fastened in place so that it cannot possibly get loose. Come, we are wasting time. Take off your slippers as I have done, so that no one shall hear us walking through the hall to your room, and bring the candles with you if you choose—yes, you need them to pick out the colours you like."

"If you think it will be safer in the dark, it does not matter," said Dolores. "I know where everything is."

"It would be safer," answered Inez thoughtfully. "It is just possible that he might be in the court and might see the light in your window, whereas if it burns here steadily, he will suspect nothing. We will bolt the door of this room, as I found it. If by any possibility he comes back, he will think you are still here, and will probably not come in."

"Pray Heaven he may not!" exclaimed Dolores, and she began to go towards the door.

Inez was there before her, opening it very cautiously.

"My hands are lighter than yours," she whispered.

They both passed out, and Inez slipped the bolt back into its place with infinite precaution.

"Is there light here?" she asked under her breath.

"There is a very small lamp on the table. I can just see my door."

"Put it out as we pass," whispered Inez. "I will lead you if you cannot find your way."

They moved cautiously forward, and when they reached the table, Dolores bent down to the small wick and blew out the flame. Then she felt her sister's hand taking hers and leading her quickly to the other door. The blind girl was absolutely noiseless in her movements, and Dolores had the strange impression that she was being led by a spirit through the darkness. Inez stopped a moment, and then went slowly on; they had entered the room though Dolores had not heard the door move, nor did she hear it closed behind her again. Her own room was perfectly dark, for the heavy curtain that covered the window was drawn; she made a step alone, and cautiously, and struck her knee against a chair.

"Do not move," whispered Inez. "You will make a noise. I can dress you where you stand, or if you want to find anything, I will lead you to the place where it is. Remember that it is always day for me."

Dolores obeyed, and stood still, holding her breath a little in her intense excitement. It seemed impossible that Inez could do all she promised without making a mistake, and Dolores would not have been a woman had she not been visited just then by visions of ridicule. Without light she was utterly helpless to do anything for herself, and she had never before then fully realized the enormous misfortune with which her sister had to contend. She had not guessed, either, what energy and quickness of thought Inez possessed, and the sensation of being advised, guided, and helped by one she had always herself helped and protected was new.

They spoke in quick whispers of what she was to wear and of how her hair was to be dressed, and Inez found what was wanted without noise, and almost as quickly as Dolores could have done in broad daylight, and placed a chair for her, making her sit down in it, and began to arrange her hair quickly and skilfully. Dolores felt the spiritlike hands touching her lightly and deftly in the dark—they were very slight and soft, and did not offend her with a rough movement or a wrong turn, as her maid's sometimes did. She felt her golden hair undone, and swiftly drawn out and smoothed without catching, or tangling, or hurting her at all, in a way no woman had ever combed it, and the invisible hands gently divided it, and turned it upon her head, slipping the hairpins into the right places as if by magic, so that they were firm at the first trial, and there was a faint sound of little pearls tapping each other, and Dolores felt the small string laid upon her hair and fastened in its place,—the only ornament a young girl could wear for a headdress,—and presently it was finished, and Inez gave a sigh of satisfaction at her work, and lightly felt her sister's head here and there to be sure that all was right. It felt as if soft little birds were just touching the hair with the tips of their wings as they fluttered round it. Dolores had no longer any fear of looking ill dressed in the blaze of light she was to face before long. The dressing of her hair was the most troublesome part, she knew, and though she could not have done it herself, she had felt that every touch and turn had been perfectly skilful.

"What a wonderful creature you are!" she whispered, as Inez bade her stand up.

"You have beautiful hair," answered the blind girl, "and you are beautiful in other ways, but to-night you must be the most beautiful of all the court, for his sake—so that every woman may envy you, and every man envy him, when they see you talking together. And now we must be quick, for it has taken a long time, and I hear the soldiers marching out again to form in the square. That is always just an hour and a half before the King goes into the hall. Here—this is the front of the skirt."

"No—it is the back!"

Inez laughed softly, a whispering laugh that Dolores could scarcely hear.

"It is the front," she said. "You can trust me in the dark. Put your arms down, and let me slip it over your head so as not to touch your hair. No—hold your arms down!"

Dolores had instinctively lifted her hands to protect her headdress. Then all went quickly, the silence only broken by an occasional whispered word and by the rustle of silk, the long soft sound of the lacing as Inez drew it through the eyelets of the bodice, the light tapping of her hands upon the folds and gatherings of the skirt and on the puffed velvet on the shoulders and elbows.

"You must be beautiful, perfectly beautiful to-night," Inez repeated more than once.

She herself did not understand why she said it, unless it were that Dolores' beauty was for Don John of Austria, and that nothing in the whole world could be too perfect for him, for the hero of her thoughts, the sun of her blindness, the immeasurably far-removed deity of her heart. She did not know that it was not for her sister's sake, but for his, that she had planned the escape and was taking such infinite pains that Dolores might look her best. Yet she felt a deep and delicious delight in what she did, like nothing she had ever felt before, for it was the first time in her life that she had been able to do something that could give him pleasure; and, behind that, there was the belief that he was in danger, that she could no longer go to him nor warn him now, and that only Dolores herself could hinder him from coming unexpectedly against old Mendoza, sword in hand, in the corridor.

"And now my cloak over everything," she said. "Wait here, for I must get it, and do not move!"

Dolores hardly knew whether Inez left the room or not, so noiselessly did the girl move. Then she felt the cloak laid upon her shoulders and drawn close round her to hide her dress, for skirts were short in those days and easily hidden. Inez laid a soft silk handkerchief upon her sister's hair, lest it should be disarranged by the hood which she lightly drew over all, assuring herself that it would sufficiently hide the face.

"Now come with me," she whispered. I will lead you to the door that is bolted and place you just where it will open. Then I will call Eudaldo and speak to him, and beg him to let me out. If he does, bend your head and try to walk as I do. I shall be on one side of the door, and, as the room is dark, he cannot possibly see me. While he is opening the outer door for you, I will slip back into my own room. Do you understand? And remember to hide in an embrasure if you hear a man's footsteps. Are you quite sure you understand?"

"Yes; it will be easy if Eudaldo opens. And I thank you, dear; I wish I knew how to thank you as I ought! It may have saved his life—"

"And yours, too, perhaps," answered Inez, beginning to lead her away. "You would die in the convent, and you must not come back—you must never come back to us here—never till you are married. Good-by, Dolores—dear sister. I have done nothing, and you have done everything for me all your life. Good-by—one kiss—then we must go, for it is late."

With her soft hands she drew Dolores' head towards her, lifted the hood a little, and kissed her tenderly. All at once there were tears on both their faces, and the arms of each clasped the other almost desperately.

"You must come to me, wherever I am," Dolores said.

"Yes, I will come, wherever you are. I promise it."

Then she disengaged herself quickly, and more than ever she seemed a spirit as she went before, leading her sister by the hand. They reached the door, and she made Dolores stand before the right hand panel, ready to slip out, and once more she touched the hood to be sure it hid the face. She listened a moment. A harsh and regular sound came from a distance, resembling that made by a pit-saw steadily grinding its way lengthwise through a log of soft pine wood.

"Eudaldo is asleep," said Inez, and even at this moment she could hardly suppress a half-hysterical laugh. "I shall have to make a tremendous noise to wake him. The danger is that it may bring some one else,—the women, the rest of the servants."

"What shall we do?" asked Dolores, in a distressed whisper.

She had braced her nerves to act the part of her sister at the dangerous moment, and her excitement made every instant of waiting seem ten times its length. Inez did not answer the question at once. Dolores repeated it still more anxiously.

"I was trying to make up my mind," said the other at last. "You could pass Eudaldo well enough, I am sure, but it might be another matter if the hall were full of servants, as it is certain that our father has given a general order that you are not to be allowed to go out. We may wait an hour for the man to wake."

Dolores instinctively tried the door, but it was solidly fastened from the outside. She felt hot and cold by turns as her anxiety grew more intolerable. Each minute made it more possible that she might meet her father somewhere outside.

"We must decide something!" she whispered desperately. "We cannot wait here."

"I do not know what to do," answered Inez. "I have done all I can; I never dreamt that Eudaldo would be asleep. At least, it is a sure sign that our father is not in the house."

"But he may come at any moment! We must, we must do something at once!"

"I will knock softly," said Inez. "Any one who hears it will suppose it is a knock at the hall door. If he does not open, some one will go and wake him up, and then go away again so as not to be seen."

She clenched her small hand, and knocked three times. Such a sound could make not the slightest impression upon Eudaldo's sound sleep, but her reasoning was good, as well as ingenious. After waiting a few moments, she knocked again, more loudly. Dolores held her breath in the silence that followed. Presently a door was opened, and a woman's voice was heard, low but sharp.

"Eudaldo, Eudaldo! Some one is knocking at the front door!"

The woman probably shook the old man to rouse him, for his voice came next, growling and angry.

"Witch! Hag! Mother of malefactors! Let me alone—I am asleep. Are you trying to tear my sleeve off with your greasy claws? Nobody is knocking; you probably hear the wine thumping in your ears!"

The woman, who was the drudge and had been cleaning the kitchen, was probably used to Eudaldo's manner of expressing himself, for she only laughed.

"Wine makes men sleep, but it does not knock at doors," she answered. "Some one has knocked twice. You had better go and open the door."

A shuffling sound and a deep yawn announced that Eudaldo was getting out of his chair. The two girls heard him moving towards the outer entrance. Then they heard the woman go away, shutting the other door behind her, as soon as she was sure that Eudaldo was really awake. Then Inez called him softly.

"Eudaldo? Here—it was I that knocked—you must let me out, please—come nearer."

"Doña Inez?" asked the old man, standing still.

"Hush!" answered the girl. "Come nearer." She waited, listening while he approached. "Listen to me," she continued. "The General has locked me in, by mistake. He did not know I was here when he bolted the door. And I am hungry and thirsty and very cold, Eudaldo—and you must let me out, and I will run to the Duchess Alvarez and stay with her little girl. Indeed, Eudaldo, the General did not mean to lock me in, too."

"He said nothing about your ladyship to me," answered the servant doubtfully. "But I do not know—" he hesitated.

"Please, please, Eudaldo," pleaded Inez, "I am so cold and lonely here—"

"But Doña Dolores is there, too," observed Eudaldo.

Dolores held her breath and steadied herself against the panel.

"He shut her into the inner sitting-room. How could I dare to open the door! You may go in and knock—she will not answer you."

"Is your ladyship sure that Doña Dolores is within?" asked Eudaldo, in a more yielding tone.

"Absolutely, perfectly sure!" answered Inez, with perfect truth. "Oh, do please let me out."

Slowly the old man drew the bolt, while Dolores' heart stood still, and she prepared herself for the danger; for she knew well enough that the faithful old servant feared his master much more than he feared the devil and all evil spirits, and would prevent her from passing, even with force, if he recognized her.

"Thank you, Eudaldo—thank you!" cried Inez, as the latch turned. "And open the front door for me, please," she said, putting her lips just where the panel was opening.

Then she drew back into the darkness. The door was wide open now, and Eudaldo was already shuffling towards the entrance. Dolores went forward, bending her head, and trying to affect her sister's step. No distance had ever seemed so long to her as that which separated her from the hall door which Eudaldo was already opening for her. But she dared not hasten her step, for though Inez moved with perfect certainty in the house, she always walked with a certain deliberate caution, and often stopped to listen, while crossing a room. The blind girl was listening now, with all her marvellous hearing, to be sure that all went well till Dolores should be outside. She knew exactly how many steps there were from where she stood to the entrance, for she had often counted them.

Dolores must have been not more than three yards from the door, when Inez started involuntarily, for she heard a sound from without, far off—so far that Dolores could not possibly have heard it yet, but unmistakable to the blind girl's keener ear. She listened intently—there were Dolores' last four steps to the open doorway, and there were others from beyond, still very far away in the vaulted corridors, but coming nearer. To call her sister back would have made all further attempt at escape hopeless—to let her go on seemed almost equally fatal—Inez could have shrieked aloud. But Dolores had already gone out, and a moment later the heavy door swung back to its place, and it was too late to call her. Like an immaterial spirit, Inez slipped away from the place where she stood and went back to Dolores' room, knowing that Eudaldo would very probably go and knock where he supposed her sister to be a prisoner, before slipping the outer bolt again. And so he did, muttering an imprecation upon the little lamp that had gone out and left the small hall in darkness. Then he knocked, and spoke through the door, offering to bring her food, or fire, and repeating his words many times, in a supplicating tone, for he was devoted to both the sisters, though terror of old Mendoza was the dominating element in his existence.

At last he shook his head and turned despondently to light the little lamp again; and when he had done that, he went away and bolted the door after him, convinced that Inez had gone out and that Dolores had stayed behind in the last room.

When she had heard him go away the last time, the blind girl threw herself upon Dolores' bed, and buried her face in the down cushion, sobbing bitterly in her utter loneliness; weeping, too, for something she did not understand, but which she felt the more painfully because she could not understand it, something that was at once like a burning fire and an unspeakable emptiness craving to be filled, something that longed and feared, and feared longing, something that was a strong bodily pain but which she somehow knew might have been the source of all earthly delight,—an element detached from thought and yet holding it, above the body and yet binding it, touching the soul and growing upon it, but filling the soul itself with fear and unquietness, and making her heart cry out within her as if it were not hers and were pleading to be free. So, as she could not understand that this was love, which, as she had heard said, made women and men most happy, like gods and goddesses, above their kind, she lay alone in the darkness that was always as day to her, and wept her heart out in scalding tears.

In the corridor outside, Dolores made a few steps, remembering to put out her left hand to touch the wall, as Inez had told her to do; and then she heard what had reached her sister's ears much sooner. She stood still an instant, strained her eyes to see in the dim light of the single lamp, saw nothing, and heard the sound coming nearer. Then she quickly crossed the corridor to the nearest embrasure to hide herself. To her horror she realized that the light of the full moon was streaming in as bright as day, and that she could not be hid. Inez knew nothing of moonlight.

She pressed herself to the wall, on the side away from her own door, making herself as small as she could, for it was possible that whoever came by might pass without turning his head. Nervous and exhausted by all she had felt and been made to feel since the afternoon, she held her breath and waited.

The regular tread of a man booted and spurred came relentlessly towards her, without haste and without pause. No one who wore spurs but her father ever came that way. She listened breathlessly to the hollow echoes, and turned her eyes along the wall of the embrasure. In a moment she must see his gaunt figure, and the moonlight would be white on his short grey beard.

CHAPTER IV

Dolores knew that there was no time to reflect as to what she should do, if her father found her hiding in the embrasure, and yet in those short seconds a hundred possibilities flashed through her disturbed thoughts. She might slip past him and run for her life down the corridor, or she might draw her hood over her face and try to pretend that she was some one else,—but he would recognize the hood itself as belonging to Inez,—or she might turn and lean upon the window-sill, indifferently, as if she had a right to be there, and he might take her for some lady of the court, and pass on. And yet she could not decide which to attempt, and stood still, pressing herself against the wall of the embrasure, and quite forgetful of the fact that the bright moonlight fell unhindered through all the other windows upon the pavement, whereas she cast a shadow from the one in which she was standing, and that any one coming along the corridor would notice it and stop to see who was there.

There was something fateful and paralyzing in the regular footfall that was followed instantly by the short echo from the vault above. It was close at hand now she was sure that at the very next instant she should see her father's face, yet nothing came, except the sound, for that deceived her in the silence and seemed far nearer than it was. She had heard horrible ghost stories of the old Alcazar, and as a child she had been frightened by tales of evil things that haunted the corridors at night, of wraiths and goblins and Moorish wizards who dwelt in secret vaults, where no one knew, and came out in the dark, when all was still, to wander in the moonlight, a terror to the living. The girl felt the thrill of unearthly fear at the roots of her hair, and trembled, and the sound seemed to be magnified till it reëchoed like thunder, though it was only the noise of an advancing footfall, with a little jingling of spurs.

But at last there was no doubt. It was close to her, and she shut her eyes involuntarily. She heard one step more on the stones, and then there was silence. She knew that her father had seen her, had stopped before her, and was looking at her. She knew how his rough brows were knitting themselves together, and that even in the pale moonlight his eyes were fierce and angry, and that his left hand was resting on the hilt of his sword, the bony brown fingers tapping the basket nervously. An hour earlier, or little more, she had faced him as bravely as any man, but she could not face him now, and she dared not open her eyes.

"Madam, are you ill, or in trouble?" asked a young voice that was soft and deep.

She opened her eyes with a sharp cry that was not of fear, and she threw back her hood with one hand as the looked.

Don John of Austria was there, a step from her, the light full on his face, bareheaded, his cap in his hand, bending a little towards her, as one does towards a person one does not know, but who seems to be in distress and to need help. Against the whiteness without he could not see her face, nor could he recognize her muffled figure.

"Can I not help you, Madam?" asked the kind voice again, very gravely.

Then she put out her hands towards him and made a step, and as the hood fell quite back with the silk kerchief, he saw her golden hair in the silver light. Slowly and in wonder, and still not quite believing, he moved to meet her movement, took her hands in his, drew her to him, turned her face gently, till he saw it well. Then he, too, uttered a little sound that was neither a word nor a syllable nor a cry—a sound that was half fierce with strong delight as his lips met hers, and his hands were suddenly at her waist lifting her slowly to his own height, though he did not know it, pressing her closer and closer to him, as if that one kiss were the first and last that ever man gave woman.

A minute passed, and yet neither he nor she could speak. She stood with her hands clasped round his neck, and her head resting on his breast just below the shoulder, as if she were saying tender words to the heart she heard beating so loud through the soft black velvet. She knew that it had never beaten in battle as it was beating now, and she loved it because it knew her and welcomed her; but her own stood still, and now and then it fluttered wildly, like a strong young bird in a barred cage, and then was quite still again. Bending his face a little, he softly kissed her hair again and again, till at last the kisses formed themselves into syllables and words, which she felt rather than heard.

"God in heaven, how I love you—heart of my heart—life of my life—love of my soul!"

And again he repeated the same words, and many more like them, with little change, because at that moment he had neither thought nor care for anything else in the world, not for life nor death nor kingdom nor glory, in comparison with the woman he loved. He could not hear her answers, for she spoke without words to his heart, hiding her face where she heard it throbbing, while her lips pressed many kisses on the velvet.

Then, as thought returned, and the first thought was for him, she drew back a little with a quick movement, and looked up to him with frightened and imploring eyes.

"We must go!" she cried anxiously, in a very low voice. "We cannot stay here. My father is very angry—he swore on his word of honour that he would kill you if you tried to see me to-night!"

Don John laughed gently, and his eyes brightened. Before she could speak again, he held her close once more, and his kisses were on her cheeks and her eyes, on her forehead and on her hair, and then again upon her lips, till they would have hurt her if she had not loved them so, and given back every one. Then she struggled again, and he loosed his hold.

"It is death to stay here," she said very earnestly.

"It is worse than death to leave you," he answered. "And I will not," he added an instant later, "neither for the King, nor for your father, nor for any royal marriage they may try to force upon me."

She looked into his eyes for a moment, before she spoke, and there was deep and true trust in her own.

"Then you must save me," she said quietly. "He has vowed that I shall be sent to the convent of Las Huelgas to-morrow morning. He locked me into the inner room, but Inez helped me to dress, and I got out under her cloak."

She told him in a few words what she had done and had meant to do, in order to see him, and how she had taken his step for her father's. He listened gravely, and she saw his face harden slowly in an expression she had scarcely ever seen there. When she had finished her story he was silent for a moment.

"We are quite safe here," he said at last, "safer than anywhere else, I think, for your father cannot come back until the King goes to supper. For myself, I have an hour, but I have been so surrounded and pestered by visitors in my apartments that I have not found time to put on a court dress—and without vanity, I presume that I am a necessary figure at court this evening. Your father is with Perez, who seems to be acting as master of ceremonies and of everything else, as well as the King's secretary—they have business together, and the General will not have a moment. I ascertained that, before coming here, or I should not have come at this hour. We are safe from him here, I am sure."

"You know best," answered Dolores, who was greatly reassured by what he said about Mendoza.

"Let us sit down, then. You must be tired after all you have done. And we have much to say to each other."

"How could I be tired now?" she asked, with a loving smile; but she sat down on the stone seat in the embrasure, close to the window.

It was just wide enough for two to sit there, and Don John took his place beside her, and drew one of her hands silently to him between both his own, and kissed the tips of her fingers a great many times. But he felt that she was watching his face, and he looked up and saw her eyes—and then, again, many seconds passed before either could speak. They were but a boy and girl together, loving each other in the tender first love of early youth, for the victor of the day, the subduer of the Moors, the man who had won back Granada, who was already High Admiral of Spain, and who in some ten months from that time was to win a decisive battle of the world at Lepanto, was a stripling of twenty-three summers—and he had first seen Dolores when he was twenty and she seventeen, and now it was nearly two years since they had met.

He was the first to speak, for he was a man of quick and unerring determinations that led to actions as sudden as they were bold and brilliant, and what Dolores had told him of her quarrel with her father was enough to rouse his whole energy at once. At all costs she must never be allowed to pass the gates of Las Huelgas. Once within the convent, by the King's orders, and a close prisoner, nothing short of a sacrilegious assault and armed violence could ever bring her out into the world again. He knew that, and that he must act instantly to prevent it, for he knew Mendoza's character also, and had no doubt but that he would do what he threatened. It was necessary to put Dolores beyond his reach at once, and beyond the King's also, which was not an easy matter within the walls of the King's own palace, and on such a night. Don John had been but little at the court and knew next to nothing of its intrigues, nor of the mutual relations of the ladies and high officers who had apartments in the Alcazar. In his own train there were no women, of course. Dolores' brother Rodrigo, who had fought by his side at Granada, had begged to be left behind with the garrison, in order that he might not be forced to meet his father. Doña Magdalena Quixada, Don John's adoptive mother, was far away at Villagarcia. The Duchess Alvarez, though fond of Dolores, was Mistress of the Robes to the young Queen, and it was not to be hoped nor expected that she should risk the danger of utter ruin and disgrace if it were discovered that she had hidden the girl against the King's wishes. Yet it was absolutely necessary that Dolores should be safely hidden within an hour, and that she should be got out of the palace before morning, and if possible conveyed to Villagarcia. Don John saw in a moment that there was no one to whom he could turn.

Again he took Dolores' hand in his, but with a sort of gravity and protecting authority that had not been in his touch the first time. Moreover, he did not kiss her fingers now, and he resolutely looked at the wall opposite him. Then, in a low and quiet voice, he laid the situation before her, while she anxiously listened.

"You see," he said at last, "there is only one way left. Dolores, do you altogether trust me?"

She started a little, and her fingers pressed his hand suddenly.

"Trust you? Ah, with all my soul!"

"Think well before you answer," he said. "You do not quite understand—it is a little hard to put it clearly, but I must. I know you trust me in many ways, to love you faithfully always, to speak truth to you always, to defend you always, to help you with my life when you shall be in need. You know that I love you so, as you love me. Have we not often said it? You wrote it in your letter, too—ah, dear, I thank you for that. Yes, I have read it—I have it here, near my heart, and I shall read it again before I sleep—"

Without a word, and still listening, she bent down and pressed her lips to the place where her letter lay. He touched her hair with his lips and went on speaking, as she leaned back against the wall again.

"You must trust me even more than that, my beloved," he said. "To save you, you must be hidden by some one whom I myself can trust—and for such a matter there is no one in the palace nor in all Madrid—no one to whom I can turn and know that you will be safe—not one human being, except myself."

"Except yourself!" Dolores loved the words, and gently pressed his hand.

"I thank you, dearest heart—but do you know what that means? Do you understand that I must hide you myself, in my own apartments, and keep you there until I can take you out of the palace, before morning?"

She was silent for a few moments, turning her face away from him. His heart sank.

"No, dear," he said sadly, "you do not trust me enough for that—I see it—what woman could?"

Her hand trembled and started in his, then pressed it hard, and she turned her face quite to him.

"You are wrong," she said, with a tremor in her voice. "I love you as no man was ever loved by any woman, far beyond all that all words can say, and I shall love you till I die, and after that, for ever—even if I can never be your wife. I love you as no one loves in these days, and when I say that it is as you love me, I mean a thousand fold for every word. I am not the child you left nearly two years ago. I am a woman now, for I have thought and seen much since then—and I love you better and more than then. God knows, there is enough to see and to learn in this court—that should be hidden deep from honest women's sight! You and I shall have a heaven on this earth, if God grants that we may be joined together—for I will live for you, and serve you, and smooth all trouble out of your way—and ask nothing of you but your love. And if we cannot marry, then I will live for you in my heart, and serve you with my soul, and pray Heaven that harm may never touch you. I will pray so fervently that God must hear me. And so will you pray for me, as you would fight for me, if you could. Remember, if you will, that when you are in battle for Spain, your sword is drawn for Spain's honour, and for the honour of every Christian Spanish woman that lives—and for mine, too!"

The words pleased him, and his free hand was suddenly clenched.

"You would make cowards fight like wolves, if you could speak to them like that!" he said.

"I am not speaking to cowards," she answered, with a loving smile. "I am speaking to the man I love, to the best and bravest and truest man that breathes—and not to Don John of Austria, the victorious leader, but to you, my heart's love, my life, my all, to you who are good and brave and true to me, as no man ever was to any woman. No—" she laughed happily, and there were tears in her eyes—"no, there are no words for such love as ours."

"May I be all you would have me, and much more," he said fervently, and his voice shook in the short speech.

"I am giving you all I have, because it is not belief, it is certainty. I know you are all that I say you are, and more too. And I trust you, as you mean it, and as you need my trust to save me. Take me where you will. Hide me in your own room if you must, and bolt and bar it if need be. I shall be as safe with you as I should be with my mother in heaven. I put my hands between yours."

Again he heard her sweet low laughter, full of joy and trust, and she laid her hands together between his and looked into his eyes, straight and clear. Then she spoke softly and solemnly.

"Into your hands I put my life, and my faith, and my maiden honour, trusting them all to you alone in this world, as I trust them to God."

Don John held her hands tightly for a moment, still looking into her eyes as if he could see her soul there, giving itself to his keeping. But he swore no great oath, and made no long speech; for a man who has led men to deeds of glory, and against whom no dishonourable thing was ever breathed, knows that his word is good.

"You shall not regret that you trust me, and you will be quite safe," he said.

She wanted no more. Loving as she did, she believed in him without promises, yet she could not always believe that he quite knew how she loved him.

"You are dearer to me than I knew," he said presently, breaking the silence that followed. "I love you even more, and I thought it could never be more, when I found you here a little while ago—because you do really trust me."

"You knew it," the said, nestling to him. "But you wanted me to tell you. Yes—we are nearer now."

"Far nearer—and a world more dear," he answered. "Do you know? In all these months I have often and often again wondered how we should meet, whether it would be before many people, or only with your sister Inez there—or perhaps alone. But I did not dare hope for that."

"Nor I. I have dreamt of meeting you a hundred times—and more than that! But there was always some one in the way. I suppose that if we had found each other in the court and had only been able to say a few words, it would have been a long time before we were quite ourselves together—but now, it seems as if we had never been parted at all, does it not?"

"As if we could never be parted again," he answered softly.

For a little while there was silence, and though there was to be a great gathering of the court, that night, all was very still where the lovers sat at the window, for the throne room and the great halls of state were far away on the other side of the palace, and the corridor looked upon a court through which few persons had to pass at night. Suddenly from a distance there came the rhythmical beat of the Spanish drums, as some detachment of troops marched by the outer gate. Don John listened.

"Those are my men," he said. "We must go, for now that they are below I can send my people on errands with orders to them, until I am alone. Then you must come in. At the end of my apartments there is a small room, beyond my own. It is furnished to be my study, and no one will expect to enter it at night. I must put you there, and lock the door and take the key with me, so that no one can go in while I am at court—or else you can lock it on the inside, yourself. That would be better, perhaps," he added rather hurriedly.

"No," said the girl quietly. "I prefer that you should have the key. I shall feel even safer. But how can I get there without being seen? We cannot go so far together without meeting some one."

He rose, and she stood up beside him.

"My apartments open upon the broad terrace on the south side," he said. "At this time there will be only two or three officers there, and my two servants. Follow me at a little distance, with your hood over your face, and when you reach the sentry-box at the corner where I turn off, go in. There will be no sentinel there, and the door looks outward. I shall send away every one, on different errands, in five minutes. When every one is gone I will come for you. Is that clear?"

"Perfectly." She nodded, as if she had made quite sure of what he had explained. Then she put up her hands, as if to say good-by. "Oh, if we could only stay here in peace!" she cried.

He said nothing, for he knew that there was still much danger, and he was anxious for her. He only pressed her hands and then led her away. They followed the corridor together, side by side, to the turning. Then he whispered to her to drop behind, and she let him go on a dozen paces and followed him. The way was long, and ill lighted at intervals by oil lamps hung from the vault by small chains; they cast a broad black shadow beneath them, and shed a feeble light above. Several times persons passed them, and Dolores' heart beat furiously. A court lady, followed by a duenna and a serving-woman, stopped with a winning smile, and dropped a low courtesy to Don John, who lifted his cap, bowed, and went on. They did not look at Dolores. A man in a green cloth apron and loose slippers, carrying five lighted lamps in a greasy iron tray, passed with perfect indifference, and without paying the least attention to the victor of Granada. It was his business to carry lamps in that part of the palace—he was not a human being, but a lamplighter. They went on, down a short flight of broad steps, and then through a wider corridor where the lights were better, though the night breeze was blowing in and made them flicker and flare.

A corporal's guard of the household halberdiers came swinging down at a marching step, coming from the terrace beyond. The corporal crossed his halberd in salute, but Don John stopped him, for he understood at once that a sentry had been set at his door.

"I want no guard," he said. "Take the man away."

"The General ordered it, your Highness," answered the man, respectfully.

"Request your captain to report to the General that I particularly desire no sentinel at my door. I have no possessions to guard except my reputation, and I can take care of that myself." He laughed good-naturedly.

The corporal grinned—he was a very dark, broad-faced man, with high cheek bones, and ears that stuck out. He faced about with his three soldiers, and followed Don John to the terrace—but in the distance he had seen the hooded figure of a woman.

Not knowing what to do, for she had heard the colloquy, Dolores stood still a moment, for she did not care to pass the soldiers as they came back. Then she turned and walked a little way in the other direction, to gain time, and kept on slowly. In less than a minute they returned, bringing the sentinel with them. She walked slowly and counted them as they went past her—and then she started as if she had been stung, and blushed scarlet under her hood, for she distinctly heard the big corporal laugh to himself when he had gone by. She knew, then, how she trusted the man she loved.

When the soldiers had turned the corner and were out of sight, she ran back to the terrace and hid herself in the stone sentry-box just outside, still blushing and angry. On the side of the box towards Don John's apartment there was a small square window just at the height of her eyes, and she looked through it, sure that her face could not be seen from without. She looked from mere curiosity, to see what sort of men the officers were, and Don John's servants; for everything connected with him or belonging to him in any way interested her most intensely. Two tall captains came out first, magnificent in polished breastplates with gold shoulder straps and sashes and gleaming basket-hilted swords, that stuck up behind them as their owners pressed down the hilts and strutted along, twisting their short black moustaches in the hope of meeting some court lady on their way. Then another and older man passed, also in a soldier's dress, but with bent head, apparently deep in thought. After that no one came for some time—then a servant, who pulled something out of his pocket and began to eat it, before he was in the corridor.

Then a woman came past the little window. Dolores saw her as distinctly as she had seen the four men. She came noiselessly and stealthily, putting down her foot delicately, like a cat. She was a lady, and she wore a loose cloak that covered all her gown, and on her head a thick veil, drawn fourfold across her face. Her gait told the girl that she was young and graceful—something in the turn of the head made her sure that she was beautiful, too—something in the whole figure and bearing was familiar. The blood sank from Dolores' cheeks, and she felt a chill slowly rising to her heart. The lady entered the corridor and went on quickly, turned, and was out of sight.

Then all at once, Dolores laughed to herself, noiselessly, and was happy again, in spite of her danger. There was nothing to disturb her, she reflected. The terrace was long, there were doubtless other apartments beyond Don John's, though she had not known it. The lady had indeed walked cautiously, but it might well be that she had reasons for not being seen there, and that the further rooms were not hers. The Alcazar was only an old Moorish castle, after all, restored and irregularly enlarged, and altogether very awkwardly built, so that many of the apartments could only be reached by crossing open terraces.

When Don John came to get her in the sentry-box, Dolores' momentary doubt was gone, though not all her curiosity. She smiled as she came out of her hiding-place and met his eyes—clear and true as her own. She even hated herself for having thought that the lady could have come from his apartment at all. The light was streaming from his open door as he led her quickly towards it. There were three windows beyond it, and there the terrace ended. She looked at the front as they were passing, and counted again three windows between the open door and the corner where the sentry-box stood.

"Who lives in the rooms beyond you?" she asked quickly.

"No one—the last is the one where you are to be." He seemed surprised.

They had reached the open door, and he stood aside to let her go in.

"And on this side?" she asked, speaking with a painful effort.

"My drawing-room and dining-room," he answered.

She paused and drew breath before she spoke again, and she pressed one hand to her side under her cloak.

"Who was the lady who came from here when all the men were gone?" she asked, very pale.

CHAPTER V

Don John was a man not easily taken off his guard, but he started perceptibly at Dolores' question. He did not change colour, however, nor did his eyes waver; he looked fixedly into her face.

"No lady has been here," he answered quietly.

Dolores doubted the evidence of her own senses. Her belief in the man she loved was so great that his words seemed at first to have destroyed and swept away what must have been a bad dream, or a horrible illusion, and her face was quiet and happy again as she passed him and went in through the open entrance. She found herself in a vestibule from which doors opened to the right and left. He turned in the latter direction, leading the way into the room.

It was his bedchamber. Built in the Moorish manner, the vaulting began at the height of a man's head, springing upward in bold and graceful curves to a great height. The room was square and very large, and the wall below the vault was hung with very beautiful tapestries representing the battle of Pavia, the surrender of Francis the First, and a sort of apotheosis of the Emperor Charles, the father of Don John. There were two tall windows, which were quite covered by curtains of a dark brocade, in which the coats of Spain and the Empire were woven in colours at regular intervals; and opposite them, with the head to the wall, stood a vast curtained bedstead with carved posts twice a man's height. The vaulting had been cut on that side, in order that the foot of the bed might stand back against the wall. The canopy had coats of arms at the four corners, and the curtains were of dark green corded silk, heavily embroidered with gold thread in the beautiful scrolls and arabesques of the period of the Renascence. A carved table, dark and polished, stood half way between the foot of the bedstead and the space between the windows, where a magnificent kneeling-stool with red velvet cushions was placed under a large crucifix. Half a dozen big chairs were ranged against the long walls on each side of the room, and two commodious folding chairs with cushions of embossed leather were beside the table. Opposite the door by which Dolores had entered, another communicated with the room beyond. Both were carved and ornamented with scroll work of gilt bronze, but were without curtains. Three or four Eastern, rugs covered the greater part of the polished marble pavement, which here and there reflected the light of the tall wax torches that stood on the table in silver candlesticks, and on each side of the bed upon low stands. The vault above the tapestried walls was very dark blue, and decorated with gilded stars in relief. Dolores thought the room gloomy, and almost funereal. The bed looked like a catafalque, the candles like funeral torches, and the whole place breathed the magnificent discomfort of royalty, and seemed hardly intended for a human habitation.

Dolores barely glanced at it all, as her companion locked the first door and led her on to the next room. He knew that he had not many minutes to spare, and was anxious that she should be in her hiding-place before his servants came back. She followed him and went in. Unlike the bedchamber, the small study was scantily and severely furnished. It contained only a writing-table, two simple chairs, a straight-backed divan covered with leather, and a large chest of black oak bound with ornamented steel work. The window was curtained with dark stuff, and two wax candles burned steadily beside the writing-materials that were spread out ready for use.

"This is the room," Don John said, speaking for the first time since they had entered the apartments.

Dolores let her head fall back, and began to loosen her cloak at her throat without answering him. He helped her, and laid the long garment upon the divan. Then he turned and saw her in the full light of the candles, looking at him, and he uttered an exclamation.

"What is it?" she asked almost dreamily.

"You are very beautiful," he answered in a low voice. "You are the most beautiful woman I ever saw."

The merest girl knows the tone of a man whose genuine admiration breaks out unconsciously in plain words, and Dolores was a grown woman. A faint colour rose in her cheek, and her lips parted to smile, but her eyes were grave and anxious, for the doubt had returned, and would not be thrust away. She had seen the lady in the cloak and veil during several seconds, and though Dolores, who had been watching the men who passed, had not actually seen her come out of Don John's apartments, but had been suddenly aware of her as she glided by, it seemed out of the question that she should have come from any other place. There was neither niche nor embrasure between the door and the corridor, in which the lady could have been hidden, and it was hardly conceivable that she should have been waiting outside for some mysterious purpose, and should not have fled as soon as she heard the two officers coming out, since she evidently wished to escape observation. On the other hand, Don John had quietly denied that any woman had been there, which meant at all events that he had not seen any one. It could mean nothing else.

Dolores was neither foolishly jealous nor at all suspicious by nature, and the man was her ideal of truthfulness and honour. She stood looking at him, resting one hand on the table, while he came slowly towards her, moving almost unconsciously in the direction of her exquisite beauty, as a plant lifts itself to the sun at morning. He was near to her, and he stretched out his arms as if to draw her to him. She smiled then, for in his eyes she forgot her trouble for a moment, and she would have kissed him. But suddenly his face grew grave, and he set his teeth, and instead of taking her into his arms, he took one of her hands and raised it to his lips, as if it had been the hand of his brother's wife, the young Queen.

"Why?" she asked in surprise, and with a little start.

"You are here under my protection," he answered. "Let me have my own way."

"Yes, I understand. How good you are to me!" She paused, and then went on, seating herself upon one of the chairs by the table as she spoke. "You must leave me now," she said. "You must lock me in and keep the key. Then I shall know that I am safe; and in the meantime you must decide how I am to escape—it will not be easy." She stopped again. "I wonder who that woman was!" she exclaimed at last.

"There was no woman here," replied Don John, as quietly and assuredly as before.

He was leaning upon the table at the other side, with both hands resting upon it, looking at her beautiful hair as she bent her head.

"Say that you did not see her," she said, "not that she was not here, for she passed me after all the men, walking very cautiously to make no noise; and when she was in the corridor she ran—she was young and light-footed. I could not see her face."

"You believe me, do you not?" asked Don John, bending over the table a little, and speaking very anxiously.

She turned her face up instantly, her eyes wide and bright.

"Should I be here if I did not trust you and believe you?" she asked almost fiercely. "Do you think—do you dare to think—that I would have passed your door if I had supposed that another woman had been here before me, and had been turned out to make room for me, and would have stayed here—here in your room—if you had not sent her away? If I had thought that, I would have left you at your door forever. I would have gone back to my father. I would have gone to Las Huelgas to-morrow, and not to be a prisoner, but to live and die there in the only life fit for a broken-hearted woman. Oh, no! You dare not think that,—you who would dare anything! If you thought that, you could not love me as I love you,—believing, trusting, staking life and soul on your truth and faith!"

The generous spirit had risen in her eyes, roused not against him, but by all his question might be made to mean; and as she met his look of grateful gladness her anger broke away, and left only perfect love and trust behind it.

"A man would die for you, and wish he might die twice," he answered, standing upright, as if a weight had been taken from him and he were free to breathe.

She looked up at the pale, strong features of the young fighter, who was so great and glorious almost before the down had thickened on his lip; and she saw something almost above nature in his face,—something high and angelic, yet manly and well fitted to face earthly battles. He was her sun, her young god, her perfect image of perfection, the very source of her trust. It would have killed her to doubt him. Her whole soul went up to him in her eyes; and as he was ready to die for her, she knew that for him she would suffer every anguish death could hold, and not flinch.

Then she looked down, and suddenly laughed a little oddly, and her finger pointed towards the pens and paper.

"She has left something behind," she said. "She was clever to get in here and slip out again without being seen."

Don John looked where she pointed, and saw a small letter folded round the stems of two white carnations, and neatly tied with a bit of twisted silk. It was laid between the paper and the bronze inkstand, and half hidden by the broad white feather of a goose-quill pen, that seemed to have been thrown carelessly across the flowers. It lay there as if meant to be found, only by one who wrote, and not to attract too much attention.

"Oh!" he exclaimed, in a rather singular tone, as he saw it, and a boyish blush reddened his face.

Then he took the letter and drew out the two flowers by the blossoms very carefully. Dolores watched him. He seemed in doubt as to what he should do; and the blush subsided quickly, and gave way to a look of settled annoyance. The carnations were quite fresh, and had evidently not been plucked more than an hour. He held them up a moment and looked at them, then laid them down again and took the note. There was no writing on the outside. Without opening it he held it to the flame of the candle, but Dolores caught his wrist.

"Why do you not read it?" she asked quickly.

"Dear, I do not know who wrote it, and I do not wish to know anything you do not know also."

"You have no idea who the woman is?" Dolores looked at him wonderingly.

"Not the very least," he answered with a smile.

"But I should like to know so much!" she cried. "Do read it and tell me. I do not understand the thing at all."

"I cannot do that." He shook his head. "That would be betraying a woman's secret. I do not know who it is, and I must not let you know, for that would not be honourable."

"You are right," she said, after a pause. "You always are. Burn it."

He pushed the point of a steel erasing-knife through the piece of folded paper and held it over the flame. It turned brown, crackled and burst into a little blaze, and in a moment the black ashes fell fluttering to the table.

"What do you suppose it was?" asked Dolores innocently, as Don John brushed the ashes away.

"Dear—it is very ridiculous—I am ashamed of it, and I do not quite know how to explain it to you." Again he blushed a little. "It seems strange to speak of it—I never even told my mother. At first I used to open them, but now I generally burn them like this one."

"Generally! Do you mean to say that you often find women's letters with flowers in them on your table?"

"I find them everywhere," answered Don John, with perfect simplicity. "I have found them in my gloves, tied into the basket hilt of my sword—often they are brought to me like ordinary letters by a messenger who waits for an answer. Once I found one on my pillow!"

"But"—Dolores hesitated—"but are they—are they all from the same person?" she asked timidly. Don John laughed, and shook his head.

"She would need to be a very persistent and industrious person," he answered. "Do you not understand?"

"No. Who are these women who persecute you with their writing? And why do they write to you? Do they want you to help them?"

"Not exactly that;" he was still smiling. "I ought not to laugh, I suppose. They are ladies of the court sometimes, and sometimes others, and I—I fancy that they want me to—how shall I say?—to begin by writing them letters of the same sort."

"What sort of letters?"

"Why—love letters," answered Don John, driven to extremity in spite of his resistance.

"Love letters!" cried Dolores, understanding at last. "Do you mean to say that there are women whom you do not know, who tell you that they love you before you have ever spoken to them? Do you mean that a lady of the court, whom you have probably never even seen, wrote that note and tied it up with flowers and risked everything to bring it here, just in the hope that you might notice her? It is horrible! It is vile! It is shameless! It is beneath anything!"

"You say she was a lady—you saw her. I did not. But that is what she did, whoever she may be."

"And there are women like that—here, in the palace! How little I know!"

"And the less you learn about the world, the better," answered the young soldier shortly.

"But you have never answered one, have you?" asked Dolores, with a scorn that showed how sure she was of his reply.

"No." He spoke thoughtfully. "I once thought of answering one. I meant to tell her that she was out of her senses, but I changed my mind. That was long ago, before I knew you—when I was eighteen."

"Ever since you were a boy!"

The look of wonder was not quite gone from her face yet, but she was beginning to understand more clearly, though still very far from distinctly. It did not occur to her once that such things could be temptations to the brilliant young leader whom every woman admired and every man flattered, and that only his devoted love for her had kept him out of ignoble adventures since he had grown to be a man. Had she seen that, she would have loved him even better, if it were possible. It was all, as she had said, shameless and abominable. She had thought that she knew much of evil, and she had even told him so that evening, but this was far beyond anything she had dreamt of in her innocent thoughts, and she instinctively felt that there were lower depths of degradation to which a woman could fall, and of which she would not try to guess the vileness and horror.

"Shall I burn the flowers, too?" asked Don John, taking them in his hand.

"The flowers? No. They are innocent and fresh. What have they to do with her? Give them to me."

He raised them to his lips, looking at her, and then held them out. She took them, and kissed them, as he had done, and they both smiled happily. Then she fastened them in her hair.

"No one will see me to-night but you," she said. "I may wear flowers in my hair like a peasant woman!"

"How they make the gold gleam!" he exclaimed, as he looked. "It is almost time that my men came back," he said sadly. "When I go down to the court, I shall dismiss them. After the royal supper I shall try and come here again and see you. By that time everything will be arranged. I have thought of almost everything already. My mother will provide you with everything you need. To-morrow evening I can leave this place myself to go and see her, as I always do."

He always spoke of Doña Magdalena Quixada as his mother—he had never known his own.

Dolores rose from her seat, for he was ready to go.

"I trust you in everything," she said simply. "I do not need to know how you will accomplish it all—it is enough to know that you will. Tell Inez, if you can—protect her if my father is angry with her."

He held out his hand to take hers, and she was going to give it, as she had done before. But it was too little. Before he knew it she had thrown her arms round his neck, and was kissing him, with little cries and broken words of love. Then she drew back suddenly.

"I could not help it," she said. "Now lock me in. No—do not say good-by—even for two hours!"

"I will come back as soon as I can," he answered, and with a long look he left her, closed the door and locked it after him, leaving her alone.

She stood a few moments looking at the panels as if her sight could pierce them and reach him on the other side, and she tried to hold the last look she had seen in his eyes. Hardly two minutes had elapsed before she heard voices and footsteps in the bedchamber. Don John spoke in short sentences now and then to his servants, and his voice was commanding though it was kindly. It seemed strange to be so near him in his life; she wondered whether she should some day always be near him, as she was now, and nearer; she blushed, all alone. So many things had happened, and he and she had found so much to say that nothing had been said at all of what was to follow her flight to Villagarcia. She was to leave for the Quixadas' house before morning, but Quixada and his wife could not protect her against her father, if he found out where she was, unless she were married. After that, neither Mendoza nor any one else, save the King himself, would presume to interfere with the liberty of Don John of Austria's wife. All Spain would rise to protect her—she was sure of that. But they had said nothing about a marriage and had wasted time over that unknown woman's abominable letter. Since she reasoned it out to herself, she saw that in all probability the ceremony would take place as soon as Don John reached Villagarcia. He was powerful enough to demand the necessary permission of the Archbishop, and he would bring it with him; but no priest, even in the absence of a written order, would refuse to marry him if he desired it. Between the real power he possessed and the vast popularity he enjoyed, he could command almost anything.

She heard his voice distinctly just then, though she was not listening for it. He was telling a servant to bring white shoes. The fact struck her because she had never seen him wear any that were not black or yellow. She smiled and wished that she might bring him his white shoes and hang his order of the Golden Fleece round his neck, and breathe on the polished hilt of his sword and rub it with soft leather. She had seen Eudaldo furbish her father's weapons in that way since she had been a child.

It had all come so suddenly in the end. Shading her eyes from the candles with her hand, she rested one elbow on the table, and tried to think of what should naturally have happened, of what must have happened if the unknown voice among the courtiers had not laughed and roused her father's anger and brought all the rest. Don John would have come to the door, and Eudaldo would have let him in—because no one could refuse him anything and he was the King's brother. He would have spent half an hour with her in the little drawing-room, and it would have been a constrained meeting, with Inez near, though she would presently have left them alone. Then, by this time, she would have gone down with the Duchess Alvarez and the other maids of honour, and by and by she would have followed the Queen when she entered the throne room with the King and Don John; and she might not have exchanged another word with the latter for a whole day, or two days. But now it seemed almost certain that she was to be his wife within the coming week. He was in the next room.

"Do not put the sword away," she heard him say. "Leave it here on the table."

Of course; what should he do with a sword in his court dress? But if he had met her father in the corridor, coming to her after the supper, he would have been unarmed. Her father, on the contrary, being on actual duty, wore the sword of his rank, like any other officer of the guards, and the King wore a rapier as a part of his state dress.

She was astonished at the distinctness with which she heard what was said in the next room. That was doubtless due to the construction of the vault, as she vaguely guessed. It was true that Don John spoke very clearly, but she could hear the servants' subdued answers almost as well, when she listened. It seemed to her that he took but a very short time to dress.

"I have the key of that room," he said presently. "I have my papers there. You are at liberty till midnight. My hat, my gloves. Call my gentlemen, one of you, and tell them to meet me in the corridor."

She could almost hear him drawing on his gloves. One of the servants went out.

"Fadrique," said Don John, "leave out my riding-cloak. I may like to walk on the terrace in the moonlight, and it is cold. Have my drink ready at midnight and wait for me. Send Gil to sleep, for he was up last night."

There was a strange pleasure in hearing his familiar orders and small directions and in seeing how thoughtful he was for his servants. She knew that he had always refused to be surrounded by valets and gentlemen-in-waiting, and lived very simply when he could, but it was different to be brought into such close contact with his life. There was a wonderful gentleness in his ways that contrasted widely with her father's despotic manner and harsh tone when he gave orders. Mendoza believed himself the type and model of a soldier and a gentleman, and he maintained that without rigid discipline there could be no order and no safety at home or in the army. But between him and Don John there was all the difference that separates the born leader of men from the mere martinet.

Dolores listened. It was clear that Don John was not going to send Fadrique away in order to see her again before he went down to the throne room, though she had almost hoped he might.

On the contrary, some one else came. She heard Fadrique announce him.

"The Captain Don Juan de Escobedo is in waiting, your Highness," said the servant. "There is also Adonis."

"Adonis!" Don John laughed, not at the name, for it was familiar to him, but at the mere mention of the person who bore it and who was the King's dwarf jester, Miguel de Antona, commonly known by his classic nickname. "Bring Adonis here—he is an old friend."

The door opened again, and Dolores heard the well-known voice of the hunchback, clear as a woman's, scornful and full of evil laughter,—the sort of voice that is heard instantly in a crowd, though it is not always recognizable. The fellow came in, talking loud.

"Ave Cæsar!" he cried from the door. "Hail, conqueror! All hail, thou favoured of heaven, of man,— and of the ladies!"

"The ladies too?" laughed Don John, probably amused by the dwarfs antics. "Who told you that?"

"The cook, sir. For as you rode up to the gate this afternoon a scullery maid saw you from the cellar grating and has been raving mad ever since, singing of the sun, moon, and undying love, until the kitchen is more like a mad-house than this house would be if the Day of Judgment came before or after Lent."

"Do you fast in Lent, Adonis?"

"I fast rigidly three times a day, my lord conqueror,—no, six, for I eat nothing either just before or just after my breakfast, my dinner, and my supper. No monk can do better than that, for at those times I eat nothing at all."

"If you said your prayers as often as you fast, you would be in a good way," observed Don John.

"I do, sir. I say a short grace before and after eating. Why have you come to Madrid, my lord? Do you not know that Madrid is the worst, the wickedest, the dirtiest, vilest, and most damnable habitation devised by man for the corruption of humanity? Especially in the month of November? Has your lordship any reasonable reason for this unreason of coming here, when the streets are full of mud, and men's hearts are packed like saddle-bags with all the sins they have accumulated since Easter and mean to unload at Christmas? Even your old friends are shocked to see so young and honest a prince in such a place!"

"My old friends? Who?"

"I saw Saint John the Conqueror graciously wave his hand to a most highly respectable old nobleman this afternoon, and the nobleman was so much shocked that he could not stir an arm to return the salutation! His legs must have done something, though, for he seemed to kick his own horse up from the ground under him. The shock must have been terrible. As for me, I laughed aloud, which made both the old nobleman and Don Julius Caesar of Austria exceedingly angry. Get before me, Don Fadrique! I am afraid of the terror of the Moors,—and no shame to me either! A poor dwarf, against a man who tears armies to shreds,—and sends scullery maids into hysterics! What is a poor crippled jester compared with a powerful scullery maid or an army of heathen Moriscoes? Give me that sword, Fadrique, or I am a dead man!"

But Don John was laughing good-naturedly.

"So it was you, Adonis? I might have-known your voice, I should think."

"No one ever knows my voice, sir. It is not a voice, it is a freak of grammar. It is masculine, feminine, and neuter in gender, singular by nature, and generally accusative, and it is optative in mood and full of acute accents. If you can find such another voice in creation, sir, I will forfeit mine in the King's councils."

Adonis laughed now, and Dolores remembered the laughter she had heard from the window.

"Does his Majesty consult you on matters of state?" inquired Don John. "Answer quickly, for I must be going."

"It takes twice as long to tell a story to two men, as to tell it to one,—when you have to tell them different stories,"

"Go, Fadrique," said Don John, "and shut the door."

The dwarf, seeing the servant gone, beckoned Don John to the other side of the room.

"It is no great secret, being only the King's," he said. "His Majesty bids me tell your Serene Highness that he wishes to speak with you privately about some matters, and that he will come here soon after supper, and begs you to be alone."

"I will be here—alone."

"Excellent, sir. Now there is another matter of secrecy which is just the contrary of what I have told you, for it is a secret from the King. A lady laid a letter and two white carnations on your writing-table. If there is any answer to be taken, I will take it."

"There is none," answered Don John sternly, "Tell the lady that I burned the letter without reading it. Go, Adonis, and the next time you come here, do not bring messages from women. Fadrique!"

"Your Highness burned the letter without reading it?"

"Yes. Fadrique!"

"I am sorry," said the dwarf, in a low voice.

No more words were spoken, and in a few moments there was deep silence, for they were all gone, and Dolores was alone, locked into the little room.

CHAPTER VI

The great throne room of the palace was crowded with courtiers long before the time when the King and Queen and Don John of Austria were to appear, and the entries and halls by which it was approached were almost as full. Though the late November air was keen, the state apartments were at summer heat, warmed by thousands of great wax candles that burned in chandeliers, and in huge sconces and on high candelabra that stood in every corner. The light was everywhere, and was very soft and yellow, while the odour of the wax itself was perceptible in the air, and helped the impression that the great concourse was gathered in a wide cathedral for some solemn function rather than in a throne room to welcome a victorious soldier. Vast tapestries, dim and rich in the thick air, covered the walls between the tall Moorish windows, and above them the great pointed vaulting, ornamented with the fantastically modelled stucco of the Moors, was like the creamy crests of waves lashed into foam by the wind, thrown upright here, and there blown forward in swift spray, and then again breaking in the fall to thousands of light and exquisite shapes; and the whole vault thus gathered up the light of the candles into itself and shed it downward, distributing it into every corner and lighting every face in a soft and golden glow.

At the upper end, between two great doors that were like the gateways of an eastern city, stood the vacant throne, on a platform approached by three broad steps and covered with deep red cloth; and there stood magnificent officers of the guard in gilded corslets and plumed steel caps, and other garments of scarlet and gold, with their drawn swords out. But Mendoza was not there yet, for it was his duty to enter with the King's own guard, preceding the Majorduomo. Above the throne, a huge canopy of velvet, red and yellow, was reared up around the royal coat of arms.

To the right and left, on the steps, stood carved stools with silken cushions—those on the right for the chief ministers and nobles of the kingdom, those on the left for the great ladies of the court. These would all enter in the King's train and take their places. For the throng of courtiers who filled the floor and the entries there were no seats, for only a score of the highest and greatest personages were suffered to sit in the royal presence. A few, who were near the windows, rested themselves surreptitiously on the high mouldings of the pilasters, pushing aside the curtains cautiously, and seeming from a distance to be standing while they were in reality comfortably seated, an object of laughing envy and of many witticisms to their less fortunate fellow-courtiers. The throng was not so close but that it was possible to move in the middle of the hall, and almost all the persons there were slowly changing place, some going forward to be nearer the throne, others searching for their friends among their many acquaintances, that they might help the tedious hour to pass more quickly.

Seen from the high gallery above the arch of the great entrance the hall was a golden cauldron full of rich hues that intermingled in streams, and made slow eddies with deep shadows, and then little waves of light that turned upon themselves, as the colours thrown into the dyeing vat slowly seethe and mix together in rivulets of dark blue and crimson, and of splendid purple that seems to turn black in places and then is suddenly shot through with flashes of golden and opalescent light. Here and there also a silvery gleam flashed in the darker surface, like a pearl in wine, for a few of the court ladies were dressed all in white, with silver and many pearls, and diamonds that shed little rays of their own.

The dwarf Adonis had been there for a few moments behind the lattice which the Moors had left, and as he stood there alone, where no one ever thought of going, he listened to the even and not unmusical sound that came up from the great assembly—the full chorus of speaking voices trained never to be harsh or high, and to use chosen words, with no loud exclamations, laughing only to please and little enough out of merriment; and they would not laugh at all after the King and Queen came in, but would only murmur low and pleasant flatteries, the change as sudden as when the musician at the keys closes the full organ all at once and draws gentle harmonies from softer stops.

The jester had stood there, and looked down with deep-set, eager eyes, his crooked face pathetically sad and drawn, but alive with a swift and meaning intelligence, while the thin and mobile lips expressed a sort of ready malice which could break out in bitterness or turn to a kindly irony according as the touch that moved the man's sensitive nature was cruel or friendly. He was scarcely taller than a boy of ten years old, but his full-grown arms hung down below his knees, and his man's head, with the long, keen face, was set far forward on his shapeless body, so that in speaking with persons of ordinary stature he looked up under his brows, a little sideways, to see better. Smooth red hair covered his bony head, and grew in a carefully trimmed and pointed beard on his pointed chin. A loose doublet of crimson velvet hid the outlines of his crooked back and projecting breastbone, and the rest of his dress was of materials as rich, and all red. He was, moreover, extraordinarily careful of his appearance, and no courtier had whiter or more delicately tended hands or spent more time before the mirror in tying a shoulder knot, and in fastening the stiffened collar of white embroidered linen at the fashionable angle behind his neck.

He had entered the latticed gallery on his way to Don John's apartments with the King's message. A small and half-concealed door, known to few except the servants of the palace, opened upon it suddenly from a niche in one of the upper corridors. In Moorish days the ladies of the harem had been wont to go there unseen to see the reception of ambassadors of state, and such ceremonies, at which, even veiled, they could never be present.

He only stayed a few moments, and though his eyes were eager, it was by habit rather than because they were searching for any one in the crowd. It pleased him now and then to see the court world as a spectacle, as it delights the hard-worked actor to be for once a spectator at another's play. He was an integral part of the court himself, a man of whom most was often expected when he had the least to give, to whom it was scarcely permitted to say anything in ordinary language, but to whom almost any license of familiar speech was freely allowed. He was not a man, he was a tradition, a thing that had to be where it was from generation to generation; wherever the court had lived a jester lay buried, and often two and three, for they rarely lived an ordinary lifetime. Adonis thought of that sometimes, when he was alone, or when he looked down at the crowd of delicately scented and richly dressed men and women, every one called by some noble name, who would doubtless laugh at some jest of his before the night was over. To their eyes the fool was a necessary servant, because there had always been a fool at court; he was as indispensable as a chief butler, a chief cook, or a state coachman, and much more amusing. But he was not a man, he had no name, he had no place among men, he was not supposed to have a mother, a wife, a home, anything that belonged to humanity. He was well lodged, indeed, where the last fool had died, and richly clothed as the other had been, and he fed delicately, and was given the fine wines of France to drink, lest his brain should be clouded by stronger liquor and he should fail to make the court laugh. But he knew well enough that somewhere in Toledo or Valladolid the next court jester was being trained to good manners and instructed in the art of wit, to take the vacant place when he should die. It pleased him therefore sometimes to look down at the great assemblies from the gallery and to reflect that all those magnificent fine gentlemen and tenderly nurtured beauties of Spain were to die also, and that there was scarcely one of them, man or woman, for whose death some one was not waiting, and waiting perhaps with evil anxiety and longing. They were splendid to see, those fair women in their brocades and diamonds, those dark young princesses and duchesses in velvet and in pearls. He dreamed of them sometimes, fancying himself one of those Djin of the southern mountains of whom the Moors told blood-curdling tales, and in the dream he flew down from the gallery on broad, black wings and carried off the youngest and most beautiful, straight to his magic fortress above the sea.

They never knew that he was sometimes up there, and on this evening he did not wait long, for he had his message to deliver and must be in waiting on the King before the royal train entered the throne room. After he was gone, the courtiers waited long, and more and more came in from without. Now and then the crowd parted as best it might, to allow some grandee who wore the order of the Golden Fleece or of some other exalted order, to lead his lady nearer to the throne, as was his right, advancing with measured steps, and bowing gravely to the right and left as he passed up to the front among his peers. And just behind them, on one aide, the young girls, of whom many were to be presented to the King and Queen that night, drew together and talked in laughing whispers, gathering in groups and knots of three and four, in a sort of irregular rank behind their mothers or the elder ladies who were to lead them to the royal presence and pronounce their names. There was more light where they were gathered, the shadows were few and soft, the colours tender as the tints of roses in a garden at sunset, and from the place where they stood the sound of young voices came silvery and clear. That should have been Inez de Mendoza's place if she had not been blind. But Inez had never been willing to be there, though she had more than once found her way to the gallery where the dwarf had stood, and had listened, and smelled the odour of the wax candles and the perfumes that rose with the heated air.

It was long before the great doors on the right hand of the canopy were thrown open, but courtiers are accustomed from their childhood to long waiting, and the greater part of their occupation at court is to see and to be seen, and those who can do both and can take pleasure in either are rarely impatient. Moreover, many found an opportunity of exchanging quick words and of making sudden plans for meeting, who would have found it hard to exchange a written message, and who had few chances of seeing each other in the ordinary course of their lives; and others had waited long to deliver a cutting speech, well studied and tempered to hurt, and sought their enemies in the crowd with the winning smile a woman wears to deal her keenest thrust. There were men, too, who had great interests at stake and sought the influence of such as lived near the King, flattering every one who could possibly be of use, and coolly overlooking any who had a matter of their own to press, though they were of their own kin. Many officers of Don John's army were there, too, bright-eyed and bronzed from their campaigning, and ready to give their laurels for roses, leaf by leaf, with any lady of the court who would make a fair exchange—and of these there were not a few, and the time seemed short to them. There were also ecclesiastics, but not many, in sober black and violet garments, and they kept together in one corner and spoke a jargon of Latin and Spanish which the courtiers could not understand; and all who were there, the great courtiers and the small, the bishops and the canons, the stout princesses laced to suffocation and to the verge of apoplexy, and fanning themselves desperately in the heat, and their slim, dark-eyed daughters, cool and laughing—they were all gathered together to greet Spain's youngest and greatest hero, Don John of Austria, who had won back Granada from the Moors.

As the doors opened at last, a distant blast of silver trumpets rang in from without, and the full chorus of speaking voices was hushed to a mere breathing that died away to breathless silence during a few moments as the greatest sovereign of the age, and one of the strangest figures of all time, appeared before his court. The Grand Master of Ceremonies entered first, in his robe of office, bearing a long white staff. In the stillness his voice rang out to the ends of the hall:

"His Majesty the King! Her Majesty the Queen!"

Then came a score of halberdiers of the guard, picked men of great stature, marching in even steps, led by old Mendoza himself, in his breastplate and helmet, sword in hand; and he drew up the guard at one side in a rank, making them pass him so that he stood next to the door.

After the guards came Philip the Second, a tall and melancholy figure; and with him, on his left side, walked the young Queen, a small, thin figure in white, with sad eyes and a pathetic face—wondering, perhaps, whether she was to follow soon those other queens who had walked by the same King to the same court, and had all died before their time—Mary of Portugal, Mary of England, Isabel of Valois.

The King was one of those men who seem marked by destiny rather than by nature, fateful, sombre, almost repellent in manner, born to inspire a vague fear at first sight, and foreordained to strange misfortune or to extraordinary success, one of those human beings from whom all men shrink instinctively, and before whom they easily lose their fluency of speech and confidence of thought. Unnaturally still eyes, of an uncertain colour, gazed with a terrifying fixedness upon a human world, and were oddly set in the large and perfectly colourless face that was like an exaggerated waxen mask. The pale lips did not meet evenly, the lower one protruding, forced, outward by the phenomenal jaw that has descended to this day in the House of Austria. A meagre beard, so fair that it looked faded, accentuated the chin rather than concealed it, and the hair on the head was of the same undecided tone, neither thin nor thick, neither long nor short, but parted, and combed with the utmost precision about the large but very finely moulded ears. The brow was very full as well as broad, and the forehead high, the whole face too large, even for a man so tall, and disquieting in its proportions. Philip bent his head forward a little when at rest; when he looked about him it moved with something of the slow, sure motion of a piece of mechanism, stopping now and then, as the look in the eyes solidified to a stare, and then, moving again, until curiosity was satisfied and it resumed its first attitude, and remained motionless, whether the lips were speaking or not.

Very tall and thin, and narrow chested, the figure was clothed all in cream-coloured silk and silver, relieved only by the collar of the Golden Fleece, the solitary order the King wore. His step was ungraceful and slow, as if his thin limbs bore his light weight with difficulty, and he sometimes stumbled in walking. One hand rested on the hilt of his sword as he walked, and even under the white gloves the immense length of the fingers and the proportionate development of the long thumb were clearly apparent. No one could have guessed that in such a figure there could be much elasticity or strength, and yet, at rare moments and when younger, King Philip displayed such strength and energy and quickness as might well have made him the match of ordinary men. As a rule his anger was slow, thoughtful, and dangerous, as all his schemes were vast and far-reaching.

With the utmost deliberation, and without so much as glancing at the courtiers assembled, he advanced to the throne and sat down, resting both hands on the gilded arms of the great chair; and the Queen took her place beside him. But before he had settled himself, there was a low sound of suppressed delight in the hall, a moving of heads, a brightening of women's eyes, a little swaying of men's shoulders as they tried to see better over those who stood before them; and voices rose here and there above the murmur, though not loudly, and were joined by others. Then the King's waxen face darkened, though the expression did not change and the still eyes did not move, but as if something passed between it and the light, leaving it grey in the shadow. He did not turn to look, for he knew that his brother had entered the throne room and that every eye was upon him.

Don John was all in dazzling white—white velvet, white satin, white silk, white lace, white shoes, and wearing neither sword nor ornament of any kind, the most faultless vision of young and manly grace that ever glided through a woman's dream.

His place was on the King's right, and he passed along the platform of the throne with an easy, unhesitating step, and an almost boyish smile of pleasure at the sounds he heard, and at the flutter of excitement that was in the air, rather to be felt than otherwise perceived. Coming up the steps of the throne, he bent one knee before his brother, who held out his ungloved hand for him to kiss—and when that was done, he knelt again before the Queen, who did likewise. Then, bowing low as he passed back before the King, he descended one step and took the chair set for him in the place that was for the royal princes.

He was alone there, for Philip was again childless at his fourth marriage, and it was not until long afterwards that a son was born who lived to succeed him; and there were no royal princesses in Madrid, so that Don John was his brother's only near blood relation at the court, and since he had been acknowledged he would have had his place by right, even if he had not beaten the Moriscoes in the south and won back Granada.

After him came the high Ministers of State and the ambassadors in a rich and stately train, led in by Don Antonio Perez, the King's new favourite, a man of profound and evil intelligence, upon whom Philip was to rely almost entirely during ten years, whom he almost tortured to death for his crimes, and who in the end escaped him, outlived him, and died a natural death, in Paris, when nearly eighty. With these came also the court ladies, the Queen's Mistress of the Robes, and the maids of honour, and with the ladies was Doña Ana de la Cerda, Princess of Eboli and Melito and Duchess of

Pastrana, the wife of old Don Ruy Gomez de Silva, the Minister. It was said that she ruled her husband, and Antonio Perez and the King himself, and that she was faithless to all three.

She was not more than thirty years of age at that time, and she looked younger when seen in profile. But one facing her might have thought her older from the extraordinary and almost masculine strength of her small head and face, compact as a young athlete's, too square for a woman's, with high cheekbones, deep-set black eyes and eyebrows that met between them, and a cruel red mouth that always curled a little just when she was going to speak, and showed extraordinarily perfect little teeth, when the lips parted. Yet she was almost beautiful when she was not angry or in a hurtful mood. The dark complexion was as smooth as a perfect peach, and tinged with warm colour, and her eyes could be like black opals, and no woman in Spain or Andalusia could match her for grace of figure and lightness of step.

Others came after in the long train. Then, last of all, at a little distance from the rest, the jester entered, affecting a very dejected air. He stood still a while on the platform, looking about as if to see whether a seat had been reserved for him, and then, shaking his head sadly, he crouched down, a heap of scarlet velvet with a man's face, just at Don John's feet, and turning a little towards him, so as to watch his eyes. But Don John would not look at him, and was surprised that he should put himself there, having just been dismissed with a sharp reprimand for bringing women's messages.

The ceremony, if it can be called by that name, began almost as soon as all were seated. At a sign from the King, Don Antonio Perez rose and read out a document which he had brought in his hand. It was a sort of throne speech, and set forth briefly, in very measured terms, the results of the long campaign against the Moriscoes, according high praise to the army in general, and containing a few congratulatory phrases addressed to Don John himself. The audience of nobles listened attentively, and whenever the leader's name occurred, the suppressed flutter of enthusiasm ran through the hall like a breeze that stirs forest leaves in summer; but when the King was mentioned the silence was dead and unbroken. Don John sat quite still, looking down a little, and now and then his colour deepened perceptibly. The speech did not hint at any reward or further distinction to be conferred on him

When Perez had finished reading, he paused a moment, and the hand that held the paper fell to his side. Then he raised his voice to a higher key.

"God save his Majesty Don Philip Second!" be cried. "Long live the King!"

The courtiers answered the cheer, but moderately, as a matter of course, and without enthusiasm, repeating it three times. But at the last time a single woman's voice, high and clear above all the rest, cried out other words.

"God save Don John of Austria! Long live Don John of Austria!"

The whole multitude of men and women was stirred at once, for every heart was in the cheer, and in an instant, courtiers though they were, the King was forgotten, the time, the place, and the cry went up all at once, full, long and loud, shaming the one that had gone before it.

King Philip's hands strained at the arms of his great chair, and he half rose, as if to command silence; and Don John, suddenly pale, had half risen, too, stretching out his open hand in a gesture of deprecation, while the Queen watched him with timidly admiring eyes, and the dark Princess of Eboli's dusky lids drooped to hide her own, for she was watching him also, but with other thoughts.

For a few seconds longer, the cheers followed each other, and then they died away to a comparative silence. The dwarf rocked himself, his head between his knees, at Don John's feet.

"God save the Fool!" he cried softly, mimicking the cheer, and he seemed to shake all over, as he sat huddled together, swinging himself to and fro.

But no one noticed what he said, for the King had risen to his feet as soon as there was silence. He spoke in a muffled tone that made his words hard to understand, and those who knew him best saw that he was very angry. The Princess of Eboli's red lips curled scornfully as she listened, and unnoticed she exchanged a meaning glance with Antonio Perez; for he and she were allies, and often of late they had talked long together, and had drawn sharp comparisons between the King and his brother, and the plan they had made was to destroy the King and to crown Don John of Austria in his place; but the woman's plot was deeper, and both were equally determined that Don John should not marry without their consent, and that if he did, his marriage should not hold, unless, as was probable, his young wife should fall ill and die of a sickness unknown to physicians.

All had risen with the King, and he addressed Don John amidst the most profound silence.

"My brother," he said, "your friends have taken upon themselves unnecessarily to use the words we would have used, and to express to you their enthusiasm for your success in a manner unknown at the court of Spain. Our one voice, rendering you the thanks that are your due, can hardly give you great satisfaction after what you have heard just now. Yet we presume that the praise of others cannot altogether take the place of your sovereign's at such a moment, and we formally thank you for the admirable performance of the task entrusted to you, promising that before long your services shall be required for an even more arduous undertaking. It is not in our power to confer upon you any personal distinction or public office higher than you already hold, as our brother, and as High Admiral of Spain; but we trust the day is not far distant when a marriage befitting your rank may place you on a level with kings."

Don John had moved a step forward from his place and stood before the King, who, at the end of his short speech, put his long arms over his brother's shoulders, and proceeded to embrace him in a formal manner by applying one cheek to his and solemnly kissing the air behind Don John's head, a process which the latter imitated as nearly as he could. The court looked on in silence at the ceremony, ill satisfied with Philip's cold words. The King drew back, and Don John returned to his place. As he reached it the dwarf jester made a ceremonious obeisance and handed him a glove which he had dropped as he came forward. As he took it he felt that it contained a letter, which made a slight sound when his hand crumpled it inside the glove. Annoyed by the fool's persistence, Don John's eyes hardened as he looked at the crooked face, and almost imperceptibly he shook his head. But the dwarf was as grave as he, and slightly bent his own, clasping his hands in a gesture of supplication. Don John reflected that the matter must be one of importance this time, as Adonis would not otherwise have incurred the risk of passing the letter to him under the eyes of the King and the whole court.

Then followed the long and tedious procession of the court past the royal pair, who remained seated, while all the rest stood up, including Don John himself, to whom a master of ceremonies presented the persons unknown to him, and who were by far the more numerous. To the men, old and young, great or insignificant, he gave his hand with frank cordiality. To the women he courteously bowed his head. A full hour passed before it was over, and still he grasped the glove with the crumpled letter in his hand, while the dwarf stood at a little distance, watching in case it should fall; and as the Duchess Alvarez and the Princess of Eboli presented the ladies of Madrid to the young Queen, the Princess often looked at Don John and often at the jester from beneath her half-dropped lids. But she did not make a single mistake of names nor of etiquette, though her mind was much preoccupied with other matters.

The Queen was timidly gracious to every one; but Philip's face was gloomy, and his fixed eyes hardly seemed to see the faces of the courtiers as they passed before him, nor did he open his lips to address a word to any of them, though some were old and faithful servants of his own and of his father's.

In his manner, in his silence, in the formality of the ceremony, there was the whole spirit of the Spanish dominion. It was sombrely magnificent, and it was gravely cruel; it adhered to the forms of sovereignty as rigidly as to the outward practices of religion; its power extended to the ends of the world, and the most remote countries sent their homage and obeisance to its head; and beneath the dark splendour that surrounded its gloomy sovereigns there was passion and hatred and intrigue. Beside Don John of Austria stood Antonio Perez, and under the same roof with Dolores de Mendoza dwelt Ana de la Cerda, Princess of Eboli, and in the midst of them all Miguel de Antona, the King's fool.

CHAPTER VII

When the ceremony was over, and every one on the platform and steps of the throne moved a little in order to make way for the royal personages, making a slight momentary confusion, Adonis crept up behind Don John, and softly touched his sleeve to attract his attention. Don John looked round quickly, and was annoyed to see the dwarf there. He did not notice the fact that Doña Ana de la Cerda was watching them both, looking sideways without turning her head.

"It is a matter of importance," said the jester, in a low voice. "Read it before supper if you can."

Don John looked at him a moment, and turned away without answering, or even making a sign that he understood. The dwarf met Doña Ana's eyes, and grew slowly pale, till his face was a yellow mask; for he feared her.

The door on the other side of the throne was opened, and the King and Queen, followed by Don John, and preceded by the Master of Ceremonies, went out. The dwarf, who was privileged, went after them with his strange, rolling step, his long arms hanging down and swinging irregularly, as if they did not belong to his body, but were only stuffed things that hung loose from his shoulders.

As on all such state occasions, there were separate suppers, in separate apartments, one for the King, and one for the ministers of state and the high courtiers; thirdly, a vast collation was spread in a hall on the other side of the throne room for the many nobles who were but guests at the court and held no office nor had any special privileges. It was the custom at that time that the supper should last an hour, after which all reëntered the throne room to dance, except the King and Queen, who either retired to the royal apartments, or came back for a short time and remained standing on the floor of the hall, in order to converse with a few of the grandees and ambassadors.

The royal party supped in a sombre room of oval shape, dark with tapestries and splendid with gold. The King and Queen sat side by side, and Don John was placed opposite them at the table, of which the shape and outline corresponded on a small scale with those of the room. Four or five gentlemen, whose office it was, served the royal couple, receiving the dishes and wines from the hands of the chief butler; and he, with two other servants in state liveries, waited on Don John. Everything was most exactly ordered according to the unchangeable rules of the most formal court in Europe, not even excepting that of Rome.

Philip sat in gloomy silence, eating nothing, but occasionally drinking a little Tokay wine, brought with infinite precaution from Hungary to Madrid. As be said nothing, neither the Queen nor Don John could speak, it being ordained that the King must be the first to open his lips. The Queen, however, being young and of a good constitution in spite of her almost delicate appearance, began to taste everything that was set before her, glancing timidly at her husband, who took no notice of her, or pretended not to do so. Don John, soldier-like, made a sparing supper of the first thing that was offered to him, and then sat silently watching the other two. He understood very well that his brother wished to see him in private, and was annoyed that the Queen should make the meal last longer than necessary. The dwarf understood also, and smiled to himself in the corner where he stood waiting in case the King should wish to be amused, which on that particular evening seemed far from likely. But sometimes he turned pale and his lips twisted a little as if he were suffering great pain; for Don John had not yet read the letter that was hidden in his glove; and Adonis saw in the dark corners of the room the Princess of Eboli's cruel half-closed eyes, and he fancied he heard her deep voice, that almost always spoke very sweetly, telling him again and again that if Don John did not read her letter before he met the King alone that night, Adonis should before very long cease to be court jester, and indeed cease to be anything at all that 'eats and drinks and sleeps and wears a coat'—as Dante had said. What Doña Ana said she would do, was as good as done already, both then and for nine years from that time, but thereafter she paid for all her deeds, and more too. But this history is not concerned with those matters, being only the story of what happened in one night at the old Alcazar of Madrid.

King Philip sat a little bent in his chair, apparently staring at a point in space, and not opening his lips except to drink. But his presence filled the shadowy room, his large and yellowish face seemed to be all visible from every part of it, and his still eyes dominated everything and every one, except his brother. It was as if the possession of some supernatural and evil being were stealing slowly upon all who were there; as if a monstrous spider sat absolutely motionless in the midst of its web, drawing everything within reach to itself by the unnatural fascination of its lidless sight—as if the gentlemen in waiting were but helpless flies, circling nearer and nearer, to be caught at last in the meshes, and the Queen a bright butterfly, and Don John a white moth, already taken and soon to be devoured. The dwarf thought of this in his corner, and his blood was chilled, for three queens lay in their tombs in three dim cathedrals, and she who sat at table was the fourth who had supped with the royal Spider in his web. Adonis watched him, and the penetrating fear he had long known crept all through him like the chill that shakes a man before a marsh fever, so that he had to set his teeth with all his might, lest they should chatter audibly. As he looked, he fancied that in the light of the waxen torches the King's face turned by degrees to an ashy grey, and then more slowly to a shadowy yellow again, as he had seen a spider's ugly body change colour when the flies came nearer, and change again when one was entangled in the threads. He thought that the faces of all the people in the room changed, too, and that he saw in them the look that only near and certain death can bring, which is in the eyes of him who goes out with bound hands, at dawn, amongst other men who will see the rising sun shine on his dead face. That fear came on the dwarf sometimes, and he dreaded always lest at that moment the King should call to him and bid him sing or play with words. But this had never happened yet. There were others in the room, also, who knew something of that same terror, though in a less degree, perhaps because they knew Philip less well than the jester, who was almost always near him. But Don John sat quietly in his place, no more realizing that there could be danger than if he had been charging the Moors at the head of his cavalry, or fighting a man hand to hand with drawn swords.

But still the fear grew, and even the gentlemen and the servants wondered, for it had never happened that the King had not at last broken the silence at supper, so that all guessed trouble near at hand and peril for themselves. The Queen grew nervous and ceased to eat. She looked from Philip to Don John, and more than once seemed about to speak, but recollected herself and checked the words. Her hand shook and her thin young nostrils quivered now and then. Evil was gathering in the air, and she felt it approaching, though she could not tell whence it came. A sort of tension took possession of every one, like what people feel in southern countries when the southeast wind blows, or when, almost without warning, the fresh sea-breeze dies away to a dead calm and the blackness rises like a tide of pitch among the mountains of the coast, sending up enormous clouds above it to the pale sky, and lying quite still below; and the air grows lurid quickly, and heavy to breathe and sultry, till the tempest breaks in lightning and-thunder and drenching rain.

In the midst of the brewing storm the dwarf saw only the Spider in its web, illuminated by the unearthly glare of his own fear, and with it the frightened butterfly and the beautiful silver moth, that had never dreamed of danger. He shrank against the hangings, pressing backwards till he hurt his crooked back against the stone wall behind the tapestry, and could have shrieked with fear had not a greater fear made him dumb. He felt that the King was going to speak to him, and that he should not be able to answer him. A horrible thought suddenly seized him, and he fancied that the King had seen him slip the letter into Don John's glove, and would ask for it, and take it, and read it—and that would be the end. Thrills of torment ran through him, and he knew how it must feel to lie bound on the rack and to hear the executioner's hands on the wheel, ready to turn it again at the judge's word. He had seen a man tortured once, and remembered his face. He was sure that the King must have seen the letter, and that meant torment and death, and the King was angry also because the court had cheered Don John. It was treason, and he knew it—yet it would have been certain death, too, to refuse to obey Doña Ana. There was destruction on either side, and he could not escape. Don John had not read the writing yet, and if the King asked for it, he would probably give it to him without a thought, unopened, for he was far too simple to imagine that any one could accuse him of a treasonable thought, and too boyishly frank to fancy that his brother could be jealous of him—above all, he was too modest to suppose that there were thousands who would have risked their lives to set him on the throne of Spain. He would therefore give the King the letter unopened, unless, believing it to be a love message from some foolish woman, he chose to tear it up unread. The wretched jester knew that either would mean his own disgrace and death, and he quivered with agony from head to foot.

The lights moved up and down before his sight, the air grew heavier, the royal Spider took gigantic proportions, and its motionless eyes were lurid with evil It was about to turn to him; he felt it turning already, and knew that it saw him in his corner, and meant to draw him to it, very slowly. In a moment he should fall to the floor a senseless heap, out of deadly fear—it would be well if his fear really killed him, but he could not even hope for that. His hands gripped the hangings on each side of him as he shrank and crushed his deformity against the wall. Surely the King was taming his head. Yes—he was right. He felt his short hair rising on his scalp and unearthly sounds screamed in his ears. The terrible eyes were upon him now, but he could not move hand or foot—if he had been nailed to the wall to die, he could not have been so helpless.

Philip eyed him with cold curiosity, for it was not an illusion, and he was really looking steadily at the dwarf. After a long time, his protruding lower lip moved two or three times before he spoke. The jester should have come forward at his first glance, to answer any question asked him. Instead, his colourless lips were parted and tightly drawn back, and his teeth were chattering, do what he could to close them. The Queen and Don John followed the King's gaze and looked at the dwarf in surprise, for his agony was painfully visible.

"He looks as if he were in an ague," observed Philip, as though he were watching a sick dog.

He had spoken at last, and the fear of silence was removed. An audible sigh of relief was heard in the room.

"Poor man!" exclaimed the Queen. "I am afraid he is very ill!"

"It is more like—" began Don John, and then he checked himself, for he had been on the point of saying that the dwarfs fit looked more like physical fear than illness, for he had more than once seen men afraid of death; but he remembered the letter in his glove and thought the words might rouse Philip's suspicions.

"What was your Serene Highness about to say?" enquired the King, speaking coldly, and laying stress on the formal title which he had himself given Don John the right to use.

"As your Majesty says, it is very like the chill of a fever," replied Don John.

But it was already passing, for Adonis was not a natural coward, and the short conversation of the royal personages had broken the spell that held him, or had at least diminished its power. When he had entered the room he had been quite sure that no one except the Princess had seen him slip the letter into Don John's glove. That quieting belief began to return, his jaw became steady, and he relaxed his hold on the tapestries, and even advanced half a step towards the table.

"And now he seems better," said the King, in evident surprise. "What sort of illness is this, Fool? If you cannot explain it, you shall be sent to bed, and the physicians shall practise experiments upon your vile body, until they find out what your complaint is, for the advancement of their learning."

"They would advance me more than their science, Sire," answered Adonis, in a voice that still quaked with past fear, "for they would send me to paradise at once and learn nothing that they wished to know."

"That is probable," observed Don John, thoughtfully, for he had little belief in medicine generally, and none at all in the present case.

"May it please your Majesty," said Adonis, taking heart a little, "there are musk melons on the table."

"Well, what of that?" asked the King.

"The sight of melons on your Majesty's table almost kills me," answered the dwarf.

"Are you so fond of them that you cannot bear to see them? You shall have a dozen and be made to eat them all. That will cure your abominable greediness."

"Provided that the King had none himself, I would eat all the rest, until I died of a surfeit of melons like your Majesty's great-grandsire of glorious and happy memory, the Emperor Maximilian."

Philip turned visibly pale, for he feared illness and death as few have feared either.

"Why has no one ever told me that?" he asked in a muffled and angry voice, looking round the room, so that the gentlemen and servants shrank back a little.

No one answered his question, for though the fact was true, it had been long forgotten, and it would have been hard for any of those present to realize that the King would fear a danger so far removed. But the dwarf knew him well.

"Let there be no more melons," said Philip, rising abruptly, and still pale.

Don John had suppressed a smile, and was taken unawares when the King rose, so that in standing up instantly, as was necessary according to the rules, his gloves slipped from his knees, where he had kept them during supper, to the floor, and a moment passed before he realized that they were not in his hand. He was still in his place, for the King had not yet left his own, being engaged in saying a Latin grace in a low tone, He crossed himself devoutly, and an instant later Don John stooped down and picked up what he had dropped. Philip could not but notice the action, and his suspicions were instantly roused.

"What have you found?" he asked sharply, his eyes fixing themselves again.

"My gloves, Sire. I dropped them."

"And are gloves such precious possessions that Don John of Austria must stoop to pick them up himself?"

Adonis began to tremble again, and all his fear returned, so that he almost staggered against the wall. The Queen looked on in surprise, for she had not been Philip's wife many months. Don John was unconcerned, and laughed in reply to the question.

"It chances that after long campaigning these are the only new white gloves Don John of Austria possesses," he answered lightly.

"Let me see them," said the King, extending his hand, and smiling suddenly.

With some deliberation Don John presented one of the gloves to his brother, who took it and pretended to examine it critically, still smiling. He turned it over several times, while Adonis looked on, gasping for breath, but unnoticed.

"The other," said Philip calmly.

Adonis tried to suppress a groan, and his eyes were fixed on Don John's face. Would he refuse? Would he try to extract the letter from the glove under his brother's eyes? Would he give it up?

Don John did none of those things, and there was not the least change of colour in his cheek. Without any attempt at concealment he took the letter from its hiding-place, and held out the empty glove with his other hand. The King drew back, and his face grew very grey and shadowy with anger.

"What have you in your other hand?" he asked in a voice indistinct with passion.

"A lady's letter, Sire," replied Don John, unmoved.

"Give it to me at once!"

"That, your Majesty, is a request I will not grant to any gentleman in Spain."

He undid a button of his close-fitting doublet, thrust the letter into the opening and fastened the button again, before the King could speak. The dwarf's heart almost stood still with joy,—he could have crawled to Don John's feet to kiss the dust from his shoes. The Queen smiled nervously, between fear of the one man and admiration for the other.

"Your Serene Highness," answered Philip, with a frightful stare, "is the first gentleman of Spain who has disobeyed his sovereign."

"May I be the last, your Majesty," said Don John, with a courtly gesture which showed well enough that he had no intention of changing his mind.

The King turned from him coldly and spoke to Adonis, who had almost got his courage back a second time.

"You gave my message to his Highness, Fool?" he asked, controlling his voice, but not quite steadying it to a natural tone.

"Yes, Sire."

"Go and tell Don Antonio Perez to come at once to me in my own apartments."

The dwarf bent till his crooked back was high above his head, and he stepped backwards towards the door through which the servants had entered and gone out. When he had disappeared, Philip turned and, as if nothing had happened, gave his hand to the Queen to lead her away with all the prescribed courtesy that was her due. The servants opened wide the door, two gentlemen placed themselves on each side of it, the chief gentleman in waiting went before, and the royal couple passed out, followed at a little distance by Don John, who walked unconcernedly, swinging his right glove carelessly in his hand as he went. The four gentlemen walked last. In the hall beyond, Mendoza was in waiting with the guards.

A little while after they were all gone, Adonis came back from his errand, with his rolling step, and searched for the other glove on the floor, where the King had dropped it. He found it there at once and hid it in his doubtlet. No one was in the room, for the servants had disappeared as soon as they could. The dwarf went quickly to Don John's place, took a Venetian goblet full of untasted wine that stood there and drank it at a draught. Then he patted himself comfortably with his other hand and looked thoughtfully at the slices of musk melon that lay in the golden dish flanked by other dishes full of late grapes and pears.

"God bless the Emperor Maximilian!" he said in a devout tone. "Since he could not live for ever, it was a special grace of Providence that his death should be by melons."

Then he went away again, and softly closed the door behind him, after looking back once more to be sure that no one was there after all, and perhaps, as people sometimes do on leaving a place where they have escaped a great danger, fixing its details unconsciously in his memory, with something almost akin to gratitude, as if the lifeless things had run the risk with them and thus earned their lasting friendship. Thus every man who has been to sea knows how, when his vessel has been hove to in a storm for many hours, perhaps during more than one day, within a few miles of the same spot, the sea there grows familiar to him as a landscape to a landsman, so that when the force of the gale is broken at last and the sea subsides to a long swell, and the ship is wore to the wind and can lay her course once more, he looks astern at the grey water he has learned to know so well and feels that he should know it again if he passed that way, and he leaves it with a faint sensation of regret. So Adoris, the jester, left the King's supper-room that night, devoutly thanking Heaven that the Emperor Maximilian had died of eating too many melons more than a hundred and fifty years ago.

Meanwhile, the King had left the Queen at the door of her apartments, and had dismissed Don John in angry silence by a gesture only, as he went on to his study. And when there, he sent away his gentlemen and bade that no one should disturb him, and that only Don Antonio Perez, the new favourite, should be admitted. The supper had scarcely lasted half an hour, and it was still early in the evening when he found himself alone and was able to reflect upon what had happened, and upon what it would be best to do to rid himself of his brother, the hero and idol of Spain.

He did not admit that Don John of Austria could be allowed to live on, unmolested, as if he had not openly refused to obey an express command and as if he were not secretly plotting to get possession of the throne. That was impossible. During more than two years, Don John's popularity, not only with the people, but with the army, which was a much more serious matter, had been steadily growing; and with it and even faster than it, the King's jealousy and hatred had grown also, till it had become a matter of common discussion and jest among the soldiers when their officers were out of hearing.

But though it was without real cause, it was not without apparent foundation. As Philip slowly paced the floor of his most private room, with awkward, ungainly steps, stumbling more than once against a cushion that lay before his great armchair, he saw clearly before him the whole dimensions of that power to which he had unwillingly raised his brother. The time had been short, but the means used had been great, for they had been intended to be means of destruction, and the result was tremendous when they turned against him who used them. Philip was old enough to have been Don John's father, and he remembered how indifferent he had been to the graceful boy of twelve, whom they called Juan Quixada, when he had been brought to the old court at Valladolid and acknowledged as a son of the Emperor Charles. Though he was his brother, Philip had not even granted him the privilege of living in the palace then, and had smiled at the idea that he should be addressed as "Serene Highness." Even as a boy, he had been impatient to fight; and Philip remembered how he was always practising with the sword or performing wild feats of skill and strength upon half-broken horses, except when he was kept to his books by Doña Magdalena Quixada, the only person in the world whom he ever obeyed without question. Every one had loved the boy from the first, and Philip's jealousy had begun from that; for he, who was loved by none and feared by all, craved popularity and common affection, and was filled with bitter resentment against the world that obeyed him but refused him what he most desired.

Little more than ten years had passed since the boy had come, and he had neither died a natural death nor fallen in battle, and was grown up to young manhood, and was by far the greatest man in Spain. He had been treated as an inferior, the people had set him up as a god. He had been sent out to command expeditions that be might fail and be disgraced; but he had shown deeper wisdom than his elders, and had come back covered with honour; and now he had been commanded to fight out the final battle of Spain with the Moriscoes, in the hope that he might die in the fight, since he could not be dishonoured, and instead he had returned in triumph, having utterly subdued the fiercest warriors in Europe, to reap the ripe harvest of his military glory at an age when other men were in the leading-strings of war's school, and to be acclaimed a hero as well as a favourite by a court that could hardly raise a voice to cheer for its own King. Ten years had done all that. Ten more, or even five, might do the rest. The boy could not be without ambition, and there could be no ambition for him of which the object should be less than a throne. And yet no word had been breathed against him,—his young reputation was charmed, as his life was. In vain Philip had bidden Antonio Perez and the Princess of Eboli use all their wits and skill to prove that he was plotting to seize the crown. They answered that he loved a girl of the court, Mendoza's daughter, and that besides war, for war's sake, he cared for nothing in the world but Dolores and his adopted mother.

They spoke the truth, for they had reason to know it, having used every means in their power to find out whether he could be induced to quarrel with Philip and enter upon a civil war, which could have had but one issue, since all Spain would have risen to proclaim him king. He had been tempted by questions, and led into discussions in which it seemed certain that he must give them some hope. But they and their agents lost heart before the insuperable obstacle of the young prince's loyalty. It was simple, unaffected, and without exaggeration. He never drew his sword and kissed the blade, and swore by the Blessed Virgin to give his last drop of blood for his sovereign and his country. He never made solemn vows to accomplish ends that looked impossible. But when the charge sounded, he pressed his steel cap a little lower upon his brow, and settled himself in the saddle without any words and rode at death like the devil incarnate; and then men followed him, and the impossible was done, and that was all. Or he could wait and watch, and manoeuvre for weeks, until he had his foe in his hand, with a patience that would have failed his officers and his men, had they not seen him always ready and cheerful, and fully sure that although he might fail twenty times to drive the foe into the pen, he should most certainly succeed in the end,—as he always did.

Philip paced the chamber in deep and angry thought. If at that moment any one had offered to rid him of his brother, the reward would have been ready, and worth a murderer's taking. But the King had long cherished the scheme of marrying Don John to Queen Mary of Scotland,—whose marriage with Bothwell could easily be annulled—in order that his presumptuous ambition might be satisfied, and at the same time that he might make of his new kingdom a powerful ally of Spain against Elizabeth of England. It was for this reason that he had long determined to prevent his brother's marriage with Maria Dolores de Mendoza. Perez and Doña Ana de la Cerda, on the other hand, feared that if Don John were allowed to marry the girl he so devotedly loved, he would forget everything for her, give up campaigning, and settle to the insignificance of a thoroughly happy man. For they knew the world well from their own point of view. Happiness is often like sadness, for it paralyzes those to whose lot it falls; but pain and danger rouse man's strength of mind and body.

Yet though the King and his treacherous favourite had diametrically opposite intentions, a similar thought had crossed the minds of both, even before Don John had ridden up to the palace gate late on that afternoon, from his last camping ground outside the city walls. Both had reasoned that whoever was to influence a man so straightforward and fearless must have in his power and keeping the person for whom Don John would make the greatest sacrifice of his life; and that person, as both knew, was Dolores herself. Yet when Antonio Perez entered Philip's study, neither had guessed the other's thought.

CHAPTER VIII

The court had been still at supper when Adonis had summoned Don Antonio Perez to the King, and the Secretary, as he was usually called, had been obliged to excuse his sudden departure by explaining that the King had sent for him unexpectedly. He was not even able to exchange a word with Doña Ana, who was seated at another of the three long tables and at some distance from him. She understood, however, and looked after him anxiously. His leaving was not signal for the others, but it caused a little stir which unhinged the solemn formality of the supper. The Ambassador of the Holy Roman Empire presently protested that he was suffering from an unbearable headache, and the Princess of Eboli, next to whom he was seated, begged him not to stand upon ceremony, since

Perez was gone from the room, but to order his coach at once; she found it hot, she said, and would be glad to escape. The two rose together, and others followed their example, until the few who would have stayed longer were constrained to imitate the majority. When Mendoza, relieved at last from his duty, went towards the supper-room to take the place that was kept for him at one of the tables, he met Doña Ana in the private corridor through which the officers and ladies of the household passed to the state apartments. He stood still, surprised to see her there.

"The supper is over," she said, stopping also, and trying to scrutinize the hard old face by the dim light of the lamps. "May I have a word with you, General? Let us walk together to your apartments."

"It is far, Madam," observed Mendoza, who suspected at once that she wished to see Dolores.

"I shall be glad to walk a little, and breathe the air," she answered. "Your corridor has arches open to the air, I remember." She began to walk, and he was obliged to accompany her. "Yes," she continued indifferently, "we have had such changeable weather to-day! This morning it almost snowed, then it rained, then it, began to freeze, and now it feels like summer! I hope Dolores has not taken cold? Is she ill? She was not at court before supper."

"The weather is indeed very changeable," replied the General, who did not know what to say, and considered it beneath his dignity to lie except by order of the King.

"Yes—yes, I was saying so, was I not? But Dolores—is she ill? Please tell me." The Princess spoke almost anxiously.

"No, Madam, my daughters are well, so far as I know."

"But then, my dear General, it is strange that you should not have sent an excuse for Dolores' not appearing. That is the rule, you know. May I ask why you ventured to break it?" Her tone grew harder by degrees.

"It was very sudden," said Mendoza, trying to put her off. "I hope that your Grace will excuse my daughter."

"What was sudden?" enquired Doña Ana coldly. "You say she was not taken ill."

"Her—her not coming to court." Mendoza hesitated and pulled at his grey beard as they went along. "She fully intended to come," he added, with perfect truth.

Doña Ana walked more slowly, glancing sideways at his face, though she could hardly see it except when they passed by a lamp, for he was very tall, and she was short, though exquisitely proportioned.

"I do not understand," she said, in a clear, metallic voice. "I have a right to an explanation, for it is quite impossible to give the ladies of the court who live in the palace full liberty to attend upon the Queen or not, as they please. You will be singularly fortunate if Don Antonio Perez does not mention the matter to the King."

Mendoza was silent, but the words had their effect upon him, and a very unpleasant one, for they contained a threat.

"You see," continued the Princess, pausing as they reached a flight of steps which they would have to ascend, "every one acknowledges the importance of your services, and that you have been very poorly rewarded for them. But that is in a degree your own fault, for you have refused to make friends when you might, and you have little interest with the King."

"I know it," said the old soldier, rather bitterly. "Princess," he continued, without giving her time to say more, "this is a private matter, which concerns only me and my daughter. I entreat you to overlook the irregularity and not to question me further. I will serve you in any way in my power—"

"You cannot serve me in any way," answered Doña Ana cruelly. "I am trying to help you," she added, with a sudden change of tone. "You see, my dear General, you are no longer young. At your age, with your name and your past services, you should have been a grandee and a rich man. You have thrown away your opportunities of advancement, and you have contented yourself with an office which is highly honourable—but poorly paid, is it not? And there are younger men who court it for the honour alone, and who are willing to be served by their friends."

"Who is my successor?" asked Mendoza, bravely controlling his voice though he felt that he was ruined.

The skilful and cruel woman began to mount the steps in silence, in order to let him suffer a few moments, before she answered. Reaching the top, she spoke, and her voice was soft and kind.

"No one," she answered, "and there is nothing to prevent you from keeping your post as long as you like, even if you become infirm and have to appoint a deputy—but if there were any serious cause of complaint, like this extraordinary behaviour of Dolores—why, perhaps—"

She paused to give her words weight, for she knew their value.

"Madam," said Mendoza, "the matter I keep from you does not touch my honour, and you may know it, so far as that is concerned. But it is one of which I entreat you not to force me to speak."

Doña Ana softly passed her arm through his.

"I am not used to walking so fast," she said, by way of explanation. "But, my dear Mendoza," she went on, pressing his arm a little, "you do not think that I shall let what you tell me go further and reach any one else—do you? How can I be of any use to you, if you have no confidence in me? Are we not relatives? You must treat me as I treat you."

Mendoza wished that he could.

"Madam," he said almost roughly, "I have shut my daughter up in her own room and bolted the door, and to-morrow I intend to send her to a convent, and there she shall stay until she changes her mind, for I will not change mine"

"Oh!" ejaculated Doña Ana, with a long intonation, as if grasping the position of affairs by degrees. "I understand," she said, after a long time. "But then you and I are of the same opinion, my dear friend. Let us talk about this."

Mendoza did not wish to talk of the matter at all, and said nothing, as they slowly advanced. They had at last reached the passage that ended at his door, and he slackened his pace still more, obliging his companion, whose arm was still in his, to keep pace with him. The moonlight no longer shone in straight through the open embrasures, and there was a dim twilight in the corridor.

"You do not wish Dolores to marry Don John of Austria, then," said the Princess presently, in very low tones. "Then the King is on your side, and so am I. But I should like to know your reason for objecting to such a very great marriage."

"Simple enough, Madam. Whenever it should please his Majesty's policy to marry his brother to a royal personage, such as Queen Mary of Scotland, the first marriage would be proved null and void, because the King would command that it should be so, and my daughter would be a dishonoured woman, fit for nothing but a convent."

"Do you call that dishonour?" asked the Princess thoughtfully. "Even if that happened, you know that Don John would probably not abandon Dolores. He would keep her near him—and provide for her generously—"

"Madam!" cried the brave old soldier, interrupting her in sudden and generous anger, "neither man nor woman shall tell me that my daughter could ever fall to that!"

She saw that she had made a mistake, and pressed his arm soothingly.

"Pray, do not be angry with me, my dear friend. I was thinking what the world would say—no, let me speak! I am quite of your opinion that Dolores should be kept from seeing Don John, even by quiet force if necessary, for they will certainly be married at the very first opportunity they can find. But you cannot do such things violently, you know. You will make a scandal. You cannot take your daughter away from court suddenly and shut her up in a convent without doing her a great injury. Do you not see that? People will not understand that you will not let her marry Don John—I mean that most people would find it hard to believe. Yes, the world is bad, I know; what can one do? The world would say—promise me that you will not be angry, dear General! You can guess what the world would say."'

"I see—I see!" exclaimed the old man, in sudden terror for his daughter's good name. "How wise you are!"

"Yes," answered Doña Ana, stopping at ten paces from the door, "I am wise, for I am obliged to be. Now, if instead of locking Dolores into her room two or three hours ago, you had come to me, and told me the truth, and put her under my protection, for our common good, I would have made it quite impossible for her to exchange a word with Don John, and I would have taken such good care of her that instead of gossiping about her, the world would have said that she was high in favour, and would have begun to pay court to her. You know that I have the power to do that."

"How very wise you are!" exclaimed Mendoza again, with more emphasis.

"Very well. Will you let me take her with me now, my dear friend? I will console her a little, for I daresay she has been crying all alone in her room, poor girl, and I can keep her with me till Don John goes to Villagarcia. Then we shall see."

Old Mendoza was a very simple-hearted man, as brave men often are, and a singularly spotless life spent chiefly in war and austere devotion had left him more than ignorant of the ways of the world. He had few friends, chiefly old comrades of his own age who did not live in the palace, and he detested gossip. Had he known what the woman was with whom he was speaking, he would have risked Dolores' life rather than give her into the keeping of Doña Ana. But to him, the latter was simply the wife of old Don Ruy Gomez de Silva, the Minister of State, and she was the head of the Queen's household. No one would have thought of repeating the story of a court intrigue to Mendoza, but it was also true that every one feared Doña Ana, whose power was boundless, and no one wished to be heard speaking ill of her. To him, therefore, her proposition seemed both wise and kind.

"I am very grateful," he said, with some emotion, for he believed that she was helping him to save his fortune and his honour, as was perhaps really the case, though she would have helped him to lose both with equally persuasive skill could his ruin have served her. "Will you come in with me, Princess?" he asked, beginning to move towards the door.

"Yes. Take me to her room and leave me with her."

"Indeed, I would rather not see her myself this evening," said Mendoza, feeling his anger still not very far from the surface. "You will be able to speak more wisely than I should."

"I daresay," answered Doña Ana thoughtfully. "If you went with me to her, there might be angry words again, and that would make it much harder for me. If you will leave me at the door of her rooms, and then go away, I will promise to manage the rest. You are not sorry that you have told me, now, are you, my dear friend?"

"I am most grateful to you. I shall do all I can to be of service to you, even though you said that it was not in my power to serve you."

"I was annoyed," said Doña Ana sweetly. "I did not mean it—please forgive me."

They reached the door, and as she withdrew her hand from his arm, he took it and ceremoniously kissed her gloved fingers, while she smiled graciously. Then he knocked three times, and presently the shuffling of Eudaldo's slippers was heard within, and the old servant opened sleepily. On seeing the Princess enter first, he stiffened himself in a military fashion, for he had been a soldier and had fought under Mendoza when both were younger.

"Eudaldo," said the General, in the stern tone he always used when giving orders, "her Excellency the Princess of Eboli will take Doña Dolores to her own apartments this evening. Tell the maid to follow later with whatever my daughter needs, and do you accompany the ladies with a candle."

But at this Doña Ana protested strongly. There was moonlight, there were lamps, there was light everywhere, she said. She needed no one. Mendoza, who had no man-servant in the house but Eudaldo, and eked out his meagre establishment by making use of his halberdiers when he needed any one, yielded after very little persuasion.

"Open the door of my daughter's apartments," he said to Eudaldo. "Madam," he said, turning to the Princess, "I have the honour to wish you good-night. I am your Grace's most obedient servant. I must return to my duty."

"Good-night, my dear friend," answered Doña Ana, nodding graciously.

Mendoza bowed low, and went out again, Eudaldo closing the door behind him. He would not be at liberty until the last of the grandees had gone home, and the time he had consumed in accompanying the Princess was just what he could have spared for his supper. She gave a short sigh of relief as she heard his spurred heels and long sword on the stone pavement. He was gone, leaving Dolores in her power, and she meant to use that power to the utmost.

Eudaldo shuffled silently across the hall, to the other door, and she followed him. He drew the bolt.

"Wait here," she said quietly. "I wish to see Doña Dolores alone."

"Her ladyship is in the farther room, Excellency," said the servant, bowing and standing back.

She entered and closed the door, and Eudaldo returned to his big chair, to doze until she should come out.

She had not taken two steps in the dim room, when a shadow flitted between her and the lamp, and it was a most instantly extinguished. She uttered an exclamation of surprise and stood still. Anywhere save in Mendoza's house, she would have run back and tried to open the door as quickly as possible, in fear of her life, for she had many enemies, and was constantly on her guard. But she guessed that the shadowy figure she had seen was Dolores. She spoke, without hesitation, in a gentle voice.

"Dolores! Are you there?" she asked.

A moment later she felt a small hand on her arm.

"Who is it?" asked a whisper, which might have come from Dolores' lips for all Doña Ana could tell.

She had forgotten the existence of Inez, whom she had rarely seen, and never noticed, though she knew that Mendoza had a blind daughter.

"It is I—the Princess of Eboli," she answered in the same gentle tone.

"Hush! Whisper to me."

"Your father has gone back to his duty, my dear—you need not be afraid."

"Yes, but Eudaldo is outside—he hears everything when he is not asleep. What is it, Princess? Why are you here?"

"I wish to talk with you a little," replied Doña Ana, whispering now, to please the girl. "Can we not get a light? Why did you put out the lamp? I thought you were in another room."

"I was frightened. I did not know who you were. We can talk in the dark, if you do not mind. I will lead you to a chair. I know just where everything is in this room."

The Princess suffered herself to be led a few steps, and presently she felt herself gently pushed into a seat. She was surprised, but realizing the girl's fear of her father, she thought it best to humour her. So far Inez had said nothing that could lead her visitor to suppose that she was not Dolores. Intimate as the devoted sisters were, Inez knew almost as much of the Princess as Dolores herself; the two girls were of the same height, and so long as the conversation was carried on in whispers, there was no possibility of detection by speech alone. The quick-witted blind girl reflected that it was strange if Doña Ana had not seen Dolores, who must have been with the court the whole evening, and she feared some harm. That being the case, her first impulse was to help her sister if possible, but so long as she was a prisoner in Dolores' place, she could do nothing, and she resolved that the Princess should help her to escape.

Doña Ana began to speak quickly and fluently in the dark. She said that she knew the girl's position, and had long known how tenderly she loved Don John of Austria, and was loved by him. She sympathized deeply with them both, and meant to do all in her power to help them. Then she told how she had missed Dolores at court that night.

Inez started involuntarily and drew her breath quickly, but Doña Ana thought it natural that Dolores should give some expression to the disappointment she must have felt at being shut up a prisoner on such an occasion, when all the court was assembled to greet the man she loved.

Then the Princess went on to tell how she had met Mendoza and had come with him, and how with great difficulty she had learned the truth, and had undertaken Dolores' care for a few days; and how Mendoza had been satisfied, never suspecting that she really sympathized with the lovers. That was a state secret, but of course Dolores must know it. The King privately desired the marriage, she said, because he was jealous of his brother and wished that he would tire of winning battles and live quietly, as happy men do.

"Don John will tell you, when you see him," she continued. "I sent him two letters this evening. The first he burned unopened, because he thought it was a love letter, but he has read the second by this time. He had it before supper."

"What did you write to him?" asked Inez, whispering low.

"He will tell you. The substance was this: If he would only be prudent, and consent to wait two days, and not attempt to see you alone, which would make a scandal, and injure you, too, if any one knew it, the King would arrange everything at his own pleasure, and your father would give his consent. You have not seen Don John since he arrived, have you?" She asked the question anxiously.

"Oh no!" answered the blind girl, with conviction. "I have not seen him. I wish to Heaven I had!"

"I am glad of that," whispered the Princess. "But if you will come with me to my apartments, and stay with me till matters are arranged—well—I will not promise, because it might be dangerous, but perhaps you may see him for a moment."

"Really? Do you think that is possible?" In the dark Inez was smiling sadly.

"Perhaps. He might come to see me, for instance, or my husband, and I could leave you together a moment."

"That would be heaven!" And the whisper came from the heart.

"Then come with me now, my dear, and I will do my best," answered the Princess.

"Indeed I will! But will you wait one moment while I dress? I am in my old frock—it is hardly fit to be seen."

This was quite true; but Inez had reflected that dressed as she was she could not pass Eudaldo and be taken by him for her sister, even with a hood over her head. The clothes Dolores had worn before putting on her court dress were in her room, and Dolores' hood was there, too. Before the Princess could answer, Inez was gone, closing the door of the bedroom behind her. Doña Ana, a little taken by surprise again, was fain to wait where she was, in the dark, at the risk of hurting herself against the furniture. Then it struck her that Dolores must be dressing in the dark, for no light had come from the door as it was opened and shut. She remembered the blind sister then, and she wondered idly whether those who lived continually with the blind learned from them to move easily in the dark and to do everything without a light. The question did not interest her much, but while she was thinking of it the door opened again. A skirt and a bodice are soon changed. In a moment she felt her hand taken, and she rose to her feet.

"I am ready, Princess. I will open the door if you will come with me. I have covered my head and face," she added carelessly, though always whispering, "because I am afraid of the night air."

"I was going to advise you to do it in any case, my dear. It is just as well that neither of us should be recognized by any one in the corridors so far from my apartments."

The door opened and let in what seemed a flood of light by comparison with the darkness. The Princess went forward, and Eudaldo got upon his legs as quickly as he could to let the two ladies out, without looking at them as they crossed the hall. Inez followed her companion's footfall exactly, keeping one step behind her by ear, and just pausing before passing out. The old servant saw Dolores' dress and Dolores' hood, which he expected to see, and no more suspected anything than he had when, as he supposed, Inez, had gone out earlier.

But Inez herself had a far more difficult part to perform than her sister's. Dolores had gone out alone, and no one had watched her beyond the door, and Dolores had eyes, and could easily enough pretend that she could not see. It was another matter to be blind and to play at seeing, with a clever woman like the Princess at one's elbow, ready to detect the slightest hesitation. Besides, though she had got out of the predicament in which it had been necessary to place her, it was quite impossible to foresee what might happen when the Princess discovered that she had been deceived, and that catastrophe must happen sooner or later, and might occur at any moment. The Princess walked quickly, too, with a gliding, noiseless step that was hard to follow. Fortunately Inez was expected to keep to the left of a superior like her companion, and was accustomed to taking that side when she went anywhere alone in the palace. That made it easier, but trouble might come at one of the short flights of steps down and up which they would have to pass to reach the Princess's apartments. And then, once there, discovery must come, to a certainty, and then, she knew not what.

She had not run the risk for the sake of being shut up again. She had got out by a trick in order to help her sister, if she could find her, and in order to be at liberty the first thing necessary was to elude her companion. To go to the door of her apartments would be fatal, but she had not had time to think what she should do. She thought now, with all the concentration of her ingenuity. One chance presented itself to her mind at once. They most pass the pillar behind which was the concealed entrance to the Moorish gallery above the throne room, and it was not at all likely that Doña Ana should know of its existence, for she never came to that part of the palace, and if Inez lagged a little way behind, before they reached the spot, she could slip noiselessly behind the pillar and disappear. She could always trust herself not to attract attention when she had to open and shut a door.

The Princess spoke rarely, making little remarks now and then that hardly required an answer, but to which Inez answered in monosyllables, speaking in a low voice through the thick veil she had drawn over her mantle under her hood, on pretence of fearing the cold. She thought it a little safer to speak aloud in that way, lest her companion should wonder at her total silence.

She knew exactly where she was, for she touched each corner as she passed, and counted her steps between one well-known point and the next, and she allowed the Princess to gain a little as they neared the last turning before reaching the place where she meant to make the attempt. She hoped in this way, by walking quite noiselessly, and then stopping suddenly just before she reached the pillar, to gain half a dozen paces, and the Princess would take three more before she stopped also. Inez had noticed that most people take at least three steps before they stop, if any one calls them suddenly when they are walking fast. It seems to need as much to balance the body when its speed is checked. She noticed everything that could be heard.

She grew nervous. It seemed to her that her companion was walking more slowly, as if not wishing to leave her any distance behind. She quickened her own pace again, fearing that she had excited suspicion. Then she heard the Princess stop suddenly, and she had no choice but to do the same. Her heart began to beat painfully, as she saw her chance slipping from her. She waited for Doña Ana to speak, wondering what was the matter.

"I have mistaken the way," said the Princess, in a tone of annoyance. "I do not know where I am. We had better go back and turn down the main staircase, even if we meet some one. You see, I never come to this part of the palace."

"I think we are on the right corridor," said Inez nervously. "Let me go as far as the corner. There is a light there, and I can tell you in a moment." In her anxiety to seem to see, she had forgotten for the moment to muffle her voice in her veil.

They went on rapidly, and the Doña Ana did what most people do when a companion offers to examine the way,—she stood still a moment and hesitated, looking after the girl, and then followed her with the slow step with which a person walks who is certain of having to turn back. Inez walked lightly to the corner, hardly touching the wall, turned by the corner, and was out of sight in a moment. The Princess walked faster, for though she believed that Dolores trusted her, it seemed foolish to give the girl a chance. She reached the corner, where there was a lamp,—and she saw that the dim corridor was empty to the very end.

CHAPTER IX

The Princess was far from suspecting, even then, that she had been deceived about her companion's identity as well as tricked at the last, when Inez escaped from her. She would have laughed at the idea that any blind person could have moved as confidently as Inez, or could afterwards have run the length of the next corridor in what had seemed but an instant, for she did not know of the niche behind the pillar, and there were pilasters all along, built into the wall. The construction of the high, springing vault that covered the whole throne room required them for its solidity, and only the one under the centre of the arch was built as a detached pillar, in order to give access to the gallery. Seen from either end of the passage, it looked exactly like the rest, and few persons would have noticed that it differed from them, even in passing it.

Doña Ana stood looking in the direction she supposed the girl to have taken. An angry flush rose in her cheek, she bit her lips till they almost bled, and at last she stamped once before she turned away, so that her little slipper sent a sharp echo along the corridor. Pursuit was out of the question, of course, though she could run like a deer; some one might meet her at any turning, and in an hour the whole palace would know that she had been seen running at full speed after some unknown person. It would be bad enough if she were recognized walking alone at night at a distance from her own apartments. She drew her veil over her face so closely that she could hardly see her way, and began to retrace her steps towards the principal staircase, pondering as to what she should say to Mendoza when he discovered that she had allowed his daughter to escape. She was a woman of manlike intelligence and not easily unbalanced by a single reverse, however, and before she had gone far her mind began to work clearly. Dolores, she reasoned, would do one of two things. She would either go straight to Don John's apartments, wait for him, and then tell him her story, in the hope that he would protect her, or she would go to the Duchess Alvarez and seek protection there. Under no circumstances would she go down to the throne room without her court dress, for her mere appearance there, dressed as she was, would produce the most profound astonishment, and could do her no possible good. And as for her going to the Duchess, that was impossible, too. If she had run away from Doña Ana, she had done so because the idea of not seeing Don John for two days was intolerable, and she meant to try and see him at once. The Duchess was in all probability with the Queen, in the latter's private apartments, as Dolores would know. On the whole, it seemed far more likely that she had done the rashest thing that had suggested itself to her, and had gone directly to the man she loved,—a man powerful enough to protect her against all comers, at the present time, and quite capable of facing even the King's displeasure.

But the whole object of Doña Ana's manoeuvre had been to get possession of Dolores' person, as a means of strongly influencing Don John's actions, in order thus to lead him into a false position from which he should not be able to escape without a serious quarrel with King Philip, which would be the first step towards the execution of the plot elaborated by Doña Ana and Perez together. Anything which could produce an open difference between the brothers would serve to produce two parties in Spain, of which the one that would take Don John's side would be by far the stronger. His power would be suddenly much increased, an organized agitation would be made throughout the country to set him on the throne, and his popularity, like Cæsar's, would grow still more, when he refused the crown, as he would most certainly do. But just then King Philip would die suddenly of a fever, or a cold, or an indigestion, as the conspirators thought best. There would be no direct male heir to the throne but Don John himself, the acknowledged son of the Emperor Charles; and even Don John would then be made to see that he could only serve his country by ruling it, since it cried out for his rule and would have no other. It was a hard and dangerous thing to lead King Philip; it would be an easy matter to direct King John. An honest and unsuspicious soldier would be but as a child in such skilful hands. Doña Ana and Perez would rule Spain as they pleased, and by and by Don John should be chosen Emperor also by the Electors of the Holy Roman Empire, and the conspirators would rule the world, as Charles the Fifth had ruled it. There was no limit to their ambition, and no scruple would stand between them and any crime, and the stake was high and worth many risks.

The Princess walked slowly, weighing in the balance all there was to lose or gain. When she reached the head of the main staircase, she had not yet altogether decided how to act, and lest she should meet some one she returned, and walked up and down the lonely corridor nearly a quarter of an hour, in deep thought. Suddenly a plan of action flashed upon her, and she went quickly on her way, to act at once.

Don John, meanwhile, had read the letter she had sent him by the dwarf jester. When the King had retired into his own apartments, Don John found himself unexpectedly alone. Mendoza and the guard had filed into the antechamber, the gentlemen in waiting, being temporarily at liberty, went to the room leading out of it on one side, which was appropriated to their use. The sentries were set at the King's door, and Mendoza marched his halberdiers out again and off to their quarters, while the servants disappeared, and the hero of the day was left to himself. He smiled at his own surprise, recollecting that he should have ordered his own attendants to be in waiting after the supper, whereas he had dismissed them until midnight.

He turned on his heel and walked away to find a quiet place where he might read the paper which had suddenly become of such importance, and paused at a Moorish niche, where Philip had caused a sacred picture to be placed, and before which a hanging silver lamp shed a clear light.

The small sheet of paper contained but little writing. There were half a dozen sentences in a clear hand, without any signature—it was what has since then come to be called an anonymous letter. But it contained neither any threat, nor any evidence of spite; it set forth in plain language that if, as the writer supposed, Don John wished to marry Dolores de Mendoza, it was as necessary for her personal safety as for the accomplishment of his desires, that he should make no attempt to see her for at least two days, and that, if he would accept this advice, he should have the support of every noble and minister at court, including the very highest, with the certainty that no further hindrance would be set in his way; it added that the letter he had burned had contained the same words, and that the two flowers had been intended to serve as a signal which it was now too late to use. It would be sufficient if he told the bearer of the present letter that he agreed to take the advice it contained. His assent in that way would, of course, be taken by the writer to mean that he promised, on his word. That was all.

He did not like the last sentence, for it placed him in an awkward position, as a man of honour, since he had already seen Dolores, and therefore could not under any circumstances agree to take advice contrary to which he had already acted. The most he could now say to the dwarf would be that he could give no answer and would act as carefully as possible. For the rest, the letter contained nothing treasonable, and was not at all what he had expected and believed it to be. It appeared to be written in a friendly spirit, and with the exception of his own brother and Mendoza, he was not aware that he had an enemy in Spain, in which he was almost right. Nevertheless, bold and frank as he was by nature, he knew enough of real warfare to distrust appearances. The writer was attached to the King's person, or the letter might have been composed, and even written in an assumed hand, by the King himself, for Philip was not above using the methods of a common conspirator. The limitation of time set upon his prudence was strange, too. If he had not seen her and agreed to the terms, he would have supposed that Dolores was being kept out of his way during those two days, whereas in that time it would be possible to send her very far from Madrid, or to place her secretly in a convent where it would be impossible to find her. It flashed upon him that in shutting up Dolores that evening Mendoza had been obeying the King's secret orders, as well as in telling her that she was to be taken to Las Huelgas at dawn. No one but Philip could have written the letter— only the dwarf's fear of Philip's displeasure could have made him so anxious that it should be read at once. It was all as clear as daylight now, and the King and Mendoza were acting together. The first letter had been brought by a woman, who must have got out through the window of the study, which was so low that she could almost have stepped from it to the terrace without springing. She had watched until the officers and the servants had gone out and the way was clear. Nothing could have been simpler or easier.

He would have burnt the letter at the lamp before the picture, had he not feared that some one might see him do it, and he folded it again and thrust it back under his doublet. His face was grave as he turned away, for the position, as he understood it, was a very desperate one. He had meant to send Dolores to Villagarcia, but it was almost impossible that such a matter should remain unknown, and in the face of the King's personal opposition, it would probably ruin Quixada and his wife. He, on his side, might send Dolores to a convent, under an assumed name, and take her out again before she was found, and marry her. But that would be hard, too, for no places were more directly under the sovereign's control than convents and monasteries. Somewhere she must go, for she could not possibly remain concealed in his study more than three or four hours.

Suddenly he fancied that she might be in danger even now. The woman who had brought the first letter had of course left the window unfastened. She, or the King, or any one, might get in by that way, and Dolores was alone. They might have taken her away already. He cursed himself for not having looked to see that the window was bolted. The man who had won great battles felt a chill at his heart, and he walked at the best of his speed, careless whether he met any one or not. But no place is more deserted than the more distant parts of a royal palace when there is a great assembly in the state apartments. He met no one on his way, and entered his own door alone. Ten minutes had not elapsed since the King had left the supper-room, and it was almost at that moment that Doña Ana met Mendoza.

Dolores started to her feet as she heard his step in the next room and then the key in the lock, and as he entered her hands clasped themselves round his neck, and her eyes looked into his. He was very pale when he saw her at last, for the belief that she had been stolen away had grown with his speed, till it was an intolerable certainty.

"What is it? What has happened?" she cried anxiously. "Why are you so white? Are you ill?"

"I was frightened," he said simply. "I was afraid you were gone. Look here!"

He led her to the window, and drew the curtain to one side. The cool air rushed in, for the bolts were unfastened, and the window was ajar. He closed it and fastened it securely, and they both came back.

"The woman got out that way," he said, in explanation. "I understand it all now—and some one might have come back."

He told her quietly what had happened, and showed her the letter, which she read slowly to the end before she gave it back to him.

"Then the other was not a love letter, after all," she said, with a little laugh that had more of relief in it than amusement, though she did not know it herself.

"No," he answered gravely. "I wish I had read it. I should at least have shut the window before leaving you!"

Careless of any danger to herself, she sat looking up into his anxious face, her clasped hands lying in his and quite covered by them, as he stood beside her. There was not a trace of fear in her own face, nor indeed of any feeling but perfect love and confidence. Under the gaze of her deep grey eyes his expression relaxed for a moment, and grew like hers, so that it would have been hard to say which trusted the other the more.

"What does anything matter, since we are together now?" she asked. "I am with you, can anything happen to me?"

"Not while I am alive," he answered, but the look of anxiety for her returned at once. "You cannot stay here."

"No—you will take me away. I am ready—"

"I do not mean that. You cannot stay in this room, nor in my apartments. The King is coming here in a few minutes. I cannot tell what he may do—he may insist on seeing whether any one is here, listening, for he is very suspicious, and he only comes here because he does not even trust his own apartments. He may wish to open the door—"

"I will lock it on the inside. You can say that it is locked, and that you have not the key. If he calls men to open it, I will escape by the window, and hide in the old sentry-box. He will not stay talking with you till morning!"

She laughed, and he saw that she was right, simply because there was no other place where she could be even as safe as where she was. He slowly nodded as she spoke.

"You see," she cried, with another little laugh of happy satisfaction, "you must keep me here whether you will or not! You are really afraid—frightened like a boy! You! How men would stare if they could see you afraid!"

"It is true," he answered, with a faint smile.

"But I will give you courage!" she said. "The King cannot come yet. Perez can only have just gone to him, you say. They will talk at least half an hour, and it is very likely that Perez will persuade him not to come at all, because he is angry with you. Perhaps Perez will come instead, and he will be very smooth and flattering, and bring messages of reconciliation, and beg to make peace. He is very clever, but I do not like his face. He makes me think of a beautiful black fox! Even if the King comes himself, we have more than half an hour. You can stay a little while with me—then go into your room and sit down and read, as if you were waiting for him. You can read my letter over, and I will sit here and say all the things I wrote, over and over again, and you will know that I am saying them—it will be almost as if I were with you, and could say them quite close to you—like this—I love you!"

She had drawn his hand gently down to her while she was speaking, and she whispered the last words into his ear with a delicate little kiss that sent a thrill straight to his heart.

"You are not afraid any more now, are you?" she asked, as she let him go, and he straightened himself suddenly as a man drawing back from something he both fears and loves.

He opened and shut his hands quickly two or three times, as some nervous men do, as if trying to shake them clear from a spell, or an influence. Then he began to walk up and down, talking to her.

"I am at my wit's end," he said, speaking fast and not looking at her face, as he turned and turned again. "I cannot send you to Villagarcia—there are things that neither you nor I could do, even for each other, things you would not have me do for you, Dolores. It would be ruin and disgrace to my adopted mother and Quixada—it might be worse, for the King can call anything he pleases high treason. It is impossible to take you there without some one knowing it—can I carry you in my arms? There are grooms, coachmen, servants, who will tell anything under examination—under torture! How can I send you there?"

"I would not go," answered Dolores quietly.

"I cannot send you to a convent, either," he went on, for he had taken her answer for granted, as lovers do who trust each other. "You would be found in a day, for the King knows everything. There is only one place, where I am master—"

He stopped short, and grew very pale again, looking at the wall, but seeing something very far away.

"Where?" asked Dolores. "Take me there! Oh, take me where you are master—where there is no king but you, where we can be together all our lives, and no one can come between us!"

He stood motionless, staring at the wall, contemplating in amazement the vastness of the temptation that arose before him. Dolores could not understand, but she did what a loving women does when the man she loves seems to be in a great distress. She came and stood beside him, passing one arm through his and pressing it tenderly, without a word. There are times when a man needs only that to comfort him and give him strength. But even a woman does not always know them.

Very slowly he turned to her, almost as if he were trying to resist her eyes and could not. He took his arm from hers and his hands framed her face softly, and pushed the gold hair gently back on her forehead. But she grew frightened by degrees, for there was a look in his eyes she had never seen there, and that had never been in them before, neither in love nor in battle. His hands were quite cold, and his face was like a beautiful marble, but there was an evil something in it, as in a fallen angel's, a defiance of God, an irresistible strength to do harm, a terror such as no man would dare to meet.

"You are worth it," he said in a tone so different from his natural voice that Dolores started, and would have drawn back from him, but could not, for his hands held her, shaking a little fiercely.

"What? What is it?" she asked, growing more and more frightened—half believing that he was going mad.

"You are worth it," he repeated. "I tell you, you are worth that, and much more, and the world, and all the world holds for me, and all earth and heaven besides. You do not know how I love you—you can never guess—"

Her eyes grew tender again, and her hands went up and pressed his that still framed her face.

"As I love you—dear love!" she answered, wondering, but happy.

"No—not now. I love you more. You cannot guess—you shall see what I will do for your sake, and then you will understand."

He uttered an incoherent exclamation, and his eyes dazzled her as he seized her in his arms and pressed her to him so that she could have cried out. And suddenly he kissed her, roughly, almost cruelly, as if he meant to hurt her, and knew that he could. She struggled in his arms, in an unknown terror of him, and her senses reeled.

Then all at once, he let her go, and turned from her quickly, leaving her half fainting, so that she leaned against the wall and pressed her cheek to the rough hanging. She felt a storm of tears, that she could not understand, rising in her heart and eyes and throat. He had crossed the room, getting as far as he could from her, and stood there, turned to the wall, his arms bent against it and his face buried in his sleeve. He breathed hard, and spoke as if to himself in broken words.

"Worth it? My God! What are you not worth?"

There was such a ring of agony and struggling in his voice that Dolores forgot herself and stood up listening, suddenly filled with anxiety for him again. He was surely going mad. She would have gone to him again, forgetting her terror that was barely past, the woman's instinct to help the suffering man overruling everything else. It was for his sake that she stayed where she was, lest if she touched him he should lose his senses altogether.

"Oh, there is one place, where I am master and lord!" he was saying. "There is one thing to do—one thing—"

"What is the thing?" she asked very gently. "Why are you suffering so? Where is the place?"

He turned suddenly, as he would have turned in his saddle in battle at a trumpet call, straight and strong, with fixed eyes and set lips, that spoke deliberately.

"There is Granada," he said. "Do you understand now?"

"No," she answered timidly. "I do not understand. Granada? Why there? It is so far away—"

He laughed harshly.

"You do not understand? Yes, Granada is far away—far enough to be another kingdom—so far that John of Austria is master there—so far that with his army at his back he can be not only its master, but its King? Do you understand now? Do you see what I will do for your sake?"

He made one step towards her, and she was very white.

"I will take you, and go back to-morrow. Do you think the Moors are not men, because I beat them? I tell you that if I set up my standard in Granada and call them to me, they will follow me—if I lead them to the gate of Madrid. Yes—and so will more than half the Spanish army, if I will! But I do not want that—it is not the kingdom—what should I care for that? Could I not have taken it and held it? It is for you, dear love—for your sake only—that we may have a world of our own—a kingdom in which you are queen! Let there be war—why should I care? I will set the world ablaze and let it burn to its own ashes, but I will not let them take you from me, neither now, nor ever, while I am alive!"

He came quickly towards her now, and she could not draw back, for the wall was behind her. But she thrust out her hands against him to keep him off. The gesture stopped him, just when he would have taken her in his arms.

"No, no!" she cried vehemently. "You must not say such things, you must not think such thoughts! You are beside yourself, and you will drive me mad, too!"

"But it will be so easy—you shall see—"

She cut his words short.

"It must not be easy, it must not be possible, it must not be at all! Do you believe that I love you and that I would let you do such deeds? Oh, no! That would not be love at all—it would be hate, it would be treason to you, and worse treason than yours against your brother!"

The fierce light was sinking from his face. He had folded his arms and stood very still, listening to her.

"You!" she cried, with rising energy. "You, the brave soldier, the spotless man, the very soul of honour made flesh and blood! You, who have but just come back in triumph from fighting your

King's enemies—you against whom no living being has ever dared to breathe a slander or a slighting word. Oh, no, no, no, no! I could not bear that you should betray your faith and your country and yourself, and be called traitor for my sake! Not for ten lives of mine shall you ruin yours. And not because I might love you less if you had done that deed. God help me! I think I should love you if you committed any crime! The shame is the more to me—I know it. I am only a woman! But rather than let my love ruin you, make a traitor of you and lose you in this world and the next, my soul shall go first—life, soul, honour, everything! You shall not do it! You think that you love me more than I love you, but you do not. For to save you as you are, I love you so dearly that I will leave you—leave you to honour, leave you to your King, leave you to the undying glory of the life you have lived, and will live, in memory of my love!"

The splendid words rang from her lips like a voice from heaven, and her eyes were divinely lightened. For they looked up, and not at him, calling Heaven to witness that she would keep her promise. As her open hand unconsciously went out, he took it tenderly, and felt her fingers softly closing on his own, as if she would lift him to himself again, and to the dear light of her own thoughts. There was silence for a moment.

"You are better and wiser than I," he said, and his tone told her that the madness was past.

"And you know that I am right? You see that I must leave you, to save you from me?"

"Leave me—now?" he cried. "You only said that—you meant me to understand—you did not mean that you would leave me now?"

"I do mean it," she said, in a great effort. "It is all I can do, to show you how I love you. As long as I am in your life you will be in danger—you will never be safe from yourself—I see it all now! I stand between you and all the world would give you—I will not stand between you and honour!"

She was breaking down, fight as she would against the pain. He could say nothing, for he could not believe that she really was in earnest.

"I must!" she exclaimed suddenly. "It is all I can do for you—it is my life—take it!"

The tears broke from her eyes, but she held her head high, and let them fall unheeded.

"Take it!" she repeated. "It is all I have to give for yours and your honour. Good-by—oh, love, I love you so dearly! Once more, before I go—"

She almost, fell into his arms as she buried her face on his shoulder and clasped his throat as she was wont. He kissed her hair gently, and from time to time her whole frame shook with the sobs she was choking down.

"It kills me," she said in a broken voice. "I cannot—I thought I was so strong! Oh, I am the most miserable living woman in the world!"

She broke away from him wildly and threw herself upon a chair, turning from him to its cushion and hiding her face in her hands, choking, pressing the furious tears back upon her eyes, shaking from head to foot.

"You cannot go! You cannot!" he cried, falling on his knees beside her and trying to take her hands in his. "Dolores—look at me! I will do anything—promise anything—you will believe me! Listen, love—I give you my word—I swear before God—"

"No—swear nothing—" she said, between the sobs that broke her voice.

"But I will!" he insisted, drawing her hands down till she looked at him. "I swear upon my honour that I will never raise my hand against the King—that I will defend him, and fight for him, and be loyal to him, whatever he may do to me—and that even for you, I will never strike a blow in battle nor speak a word in peace that is not all honourable, through and through,—even as I have fought and spoken until now!"

As she listened to his words her weeping subsided, and her tearful eyes took light and life again. She drew him close, and kissed him on the forehead.

"I am so glad—so happy!" she cried softly. "I should never have had strength to really say good-by!"

CHAPTER X

Don John smoothed her golden hair. Never since he had known that he loved her, had she seemed so beautiful as then, and his thought tried to hold her as she was, that she might in memory be always the same. There was colour in her cheeks, a soft flush of happiness that destroyed all traces of her tears, so that they only left her grey eyes dark and tender under the long wet lashes.

"It was a cruel dream, dear love! It was not true!" Finding him again, her voice was low, and sweet with joy.

He smiled, too, and his own eyes were quiet and young, now that the tempest had passed away, almost out of recollection. It had raged but for a few moments, but in that time both he and she had lived and loved as it were through years, and their love had grown better and braver. She knew that his word was enough, and that he would die rather than break it; but though she had called herself weak, and had seemed to break down in despair, she would have left him for ever rather than believe that he was still in danger through her. She did not again ask herself whether her sudden resolution had been all for his sake, and had not formed itself because she dreaded to think of being bound to one who betrayed his country. She knew it and needed no further self-questioning to satisfy her. If such a man could have committed crimes, she would have hated them, not him, she would have pardoned him, not them, she would still have laid her hand in his before the whole world, though it should mean shame and infamy, because she loved him and would always love him, and could never have left him for her own sake, come all that might. She had said it was a shame to her that she would have loved him still; yet if it had been so, she would have gloried in being shamed for his sake, for even then her love might have brought him back from the depths of evil and made him again for her in truth what he had once seemed to the whole world. She could have done that, and if in the end she had saved him she would have counted the price of her name as very little to set against his salvation from himself. She would have given that and much more, for her love, as she would freely give all for him and even for his memory, if he were dead, and if by some unimaginable circumstances her ruin before the world could keep his name spotless, and his glory unsullied. For there is nothing that a true-hearted loving woman will not give and do for him she loves and believes and trusts; and though she will give the greatest thing last of all, she will give it in the end, if it can save him from infamy and destruction. For it is the woman's glory to give, as it is the man's to use strength in the hour of battle and gentleness in the day of peace, and to follow honour always.

"Forget it all," answered Don John presently. "Forget it, dear, and forgive me for it all."

"I can forget it, because it was only a dream," she said, "and I have nothing to forgive. Listen to me. If it were true—even if I believed that we had not been dreaming, you and I, could I have anything to forgive you? What?"

"The mere thought that I could betray a trust, turn against my sovereign and ruin my country," he answered bravely, and a blush of honest shame rose in his boyish cheeks.

"It was for me," said Dolores.

That should explain all, her heart said. But he was not satisfied, and being a man he began to insist.

"Not even for you should I have thought of it," he said. "And there is the thought to forgive, if nothing else."

"No—you are wrong, love. Because it was for me, it does not need my forgiveness. It is different— you do not understand yet. It is I who should have never forgiven myself on earth nor expected pardon hereafter, if I had let myself be the cause of such deeds, if I had let my love stand between you and honour. Do you see?"

"I see," he answered. "You are very brave and kind and good. I did not know that a woman could be like you."

"A woman could be anything—for you—dare anything, do anything, sacrifice anything! Did I not tell you so, long ago? You only half believed me, dear—perhaps you do not quite believe me now—"

"Indeed, indeed I do, with all my soul! I believe you as I love you, as I believe in your love—"

"Yes. Tell me that you do—and tell me that you love me! It is so good to hear, now that the bad dream is gone."

"Shall I tell you?" He smiled, playing with her hand. "How can I? There are so few words in which to say so much. But I will tell you this—I would give my word for you. Does that sound little? You should know, for you know at what price you would have saved my honour a while ago. I believe in you so truly that I would stake my word, and my honour, and my Christian oath upon your faith, and promise for you before God or man that you will always love me as you do to-day."

"You may pledge all three. I will, and I will give you all I have that is not God's—and if that is not enough, I will give my soul for yours, if I may, to suffer in your stead."

She spoke quietly enough, but there was a little quaver of true earnestness in her voice, that made each word a solemn promise.

"And besides that," she added, "you see how I trust you."

She smiled again as she looked at him, and knew how safe she was, far safer now than when she had first come with him to the door. Something told her that he had mastered himself—she would not have wished to think that she had ruled him? it was enough if she had shown him the way, and had helped him. He pressed her hand to his cheek and looked down thoughtfully, wishing that he could find such simple words that could say so much, but not trusting himself to speak. For though, in love, a man speaks first, he always finds the least to say of love when it has strongest hold of him; but a woman has words then, true and tender, that come from her heart unsought. Yet by and by, if love is not enduring, so that both tire of it, the man plays the better comedy, because he has the greater strength, and sometimes what he says has the old ring in it, because it is so well said, and the woman smiles and wonders that his love should have lasted longer than hers, and desiring the illusion, she finds old phrases again; yet there is no life in them, because when love is dead she thinks of herself, and instead, it was only of him she thought in the good days when her heart used to beat at the sound of his footfall, and the light grew dim and unsteady as she felt his kiss. But the love of these two was not born to tire; and because he was so young, and knew the world little, save at his sword's point, he was ashamed that he could not speak of love as well as she.

"Find words for me," he said, "and I will say them, for yours are better than mine."

"Say, 'I love you, dear,' very softly and gently—not roughly, as you sometimes do. I want to hear it gently now, that, and nothing else."

She turned a little, leaning towards him, her face near his, her eyes quiet and warm, and she took his hands and held them together before her as if he were her prisoner—and indeed she meant that he should not suddenly take her in his arms, as he often did.

"I love you, dear," he repeated, smiling, and pretending to be very docile.

"That is not quite the way," she said, with a girlish laugh. "Say it again—quite as softly, but more tenderly! You must be very much in earnest, you know, but you must not be in the least violent." She laughed again. "It is like teaching a young lion," she added. "He may eat you up at any moment, instead of obeying you. Tell me, you have a little lion that follows you like a dog when you are in your camp, have you not? You have not told me about him yet. How did you teach him?"

"I did not try to make him say 'I love you, dear,'" answered Don John, laughing in his turn.

As he spoke a distant sound caught his ear, and the smile vanished from his face, for though he heard only the far off rumbling of a coach in the great court, it recalled him to reality.

"We are playing with life and death," he said suddenly. "It is late, the King may be here at any moment, and we have decided nothing." He rose.

"Is it late?" asked Dolores, passing her hand over her eyes dreamily. "I had forgotten—it seems so short. Give me the key on my side of the door—we had decided that, you know. Go and sit down in your room, as we agreed. Shall you read my letter again, love? It may be half an hoar still before the King comes. When he is gone, we shall have all the night in which to decide, and the nights are very long now. Oh, I hate to lose one minute of you! What shall you say to the King?"

"I do not know what he may say to me," answered Don John. "Listen and you shall hear—I would rather know that you hear everything I say. It will be as if I were speaking before you, and of course I should tell you everything the King says. He will speak of you, I think."

"Indeed it would be hard not to listen," said Dolores. "I should have to stop my ears, for one cannot help hearing every word that is said in the next room. Do you know? I heard you ask for your white shoes! I hardly dared to breathe for fear the servants should find out that I was here."

"So much the better then. Sit in this chair near the door. But be careful to make no noise, for the King is very suspicious."

"I know. Do not be afraid; I will be as quiet as a mouse. Go, love, go! It is time—oh, how I hate to let you leave me! You will be careful? You will not be angry at what he says? You would be wiser if you knew I were not hearing everything; you will want to defend me if he says the least word you do not like, but let him say what he will! Anything is better than an open quarrel between you and the King! Promise me to be very moderate in what you say, and very patient. Remember that he is the King!"

"And my brother," said Don John, with some bitterness. "Do not fear. You know what I have promised you. I will bear anything he may say that concerns me as well as I can, but if he says anything slighting of you—"

"But he may—that is the danger. Promise me not to be angry—"

"How can I promise that, if he insults you?"

"No, I did not mean that exactly. Promise that you will not forget everything and raise your hand against him. You see I know you would."

"No, I will not raise my hand against him. That was in the promise I made you. And as for being angry, I will do my best to keep my temper."

"I know you will. Now you must go. Good-by, love! Good-by, for a little while."

"For such a little time shall we say good-by? I hate the word; it makes me think of the day when I left you last."

"How can I tell what may happen to you when you are out of my sight?" asked Dolores. "And what is 'good-by' but a blessing each prays for the other? That is all it means. It does not mean that we part for long love. Why, I would say it for an hour! Good-by, dear love, good-by!"

She put up her face to kiss him, and it was so full of trust and happiness that the word lost all the bitterness it has gathered through ages of partings, and seemed, what she said it was, a loving blessing. Yet she said it very tenderly, for it was hard to let him go even for less than an hour. He said it, too, to please her; but yet the syllables came mournfully, as if they meant a world more than hers, and the sound of them half frightened her, so that she was sorry she had asked him for the word.

"Not so " she cried, in quick alarm. "You are not keeping anything from me? You are only going to the next room to meet the King—are you sure?"

"That is all. You see, the word frightened you. It seems such a sad word to me—I will not say it again."

He kissed her gently, as if to soothe her fear, and then he opened the door and set the key in the lock on the inside. Then when he was outside, he lingered a moment, and their lips met once more without a word, and they nodded and smiled to one another a last time, and he closed the door and heard her lock it.

When she was alone, she turned away as if he were gone from her altogether instead of being in the next room, where she could hear him moving now and then, as he placed his chair near the light to read and arranged the candlesticks on the table. Then he went to the other door and opened it and opened the one beyond upon the terrace, and she knew that he was looking out to see if any one were there. But presently he came back and sat down, and she distinctly heard the rustle of the strong writing-paper as he unfolded a letter. It was hers. He was going to read it, as they had agreed.

So she sat down where she could look at the door, and she tried to force her eyes to see through it, to make him feel that she was watching him, that she came near him and stood beside him, and softly read the words for him, but without looking at them, because she knew them all by heart. But it was not the same as if she had seen him, and it was very hard to be shut off from his sight by an impenetrable piece of wood, to lose all the moments that might pass before the King chose to come. Another hour might pass. No one could even tell whether he would come at all after he had consulted with Antonio Perez. The skilful favourite desired a quarrel between his master and Don John with all his heart, but he was not ready for it yet. He must have possession of Dolores first and hide her safely; and when the quarrel came, Don John should believe that the King had stolen her and imprisoned her, and that she was treated ill; and for the woman he loved, Don John would tear down the walls of Madrid, if need be, and if at the last he found her dead, there would be no harm done, thought Perez, and Don John would hate his brother even to death, and all Spain would cry out in sympathy and horror. But all this Dolores could neither know nor even suspect. She only felt sure that the King and Perez were even now consulting together to hinder her marriage with Don John, and that Perez might persuade the King not to see his brother that night.

It was almost intolerable to think that she might wait there for hours, wasting the minutes for which she would have given drops of blood. Surely they both were overcautious. The door could be left open, so that they could talk, and at the first sound without, she could lock it again and sit down. That would be quite as safe.

She rose and was almost in the act of opening the door again when she stopped and hesitated. It was possible that at any moment the King might be at the door; for though she could hear every sound that came from the next room, the thick curtains that hid the window effectually shut out all sound from without. It struck her that she could go to the window, however, and look out. Yet a ray of light might betray her presence in the room to any one outside, and if she drew aside the curtain the light would shine out upon the terrace. She listened at Don John's door, and presently she heard him turn her letter in his hand, and all her heart went out to him, and she stood noiselessly kissing the panels and saying over again in her heart that she loved him more than any words could tell. If she could only see out of the window and assure herself that no one was coming yet, there would be time to go to him again, for one moment only, and say the words once more.

Then she sat down and told herself how foolish she was. She had been separated from him for many long and empty months, and now she had been with him and talked long with him twice in leas than three hours, and yet she could not bear that he should be out of her sight five minutes without wishing to risk everything to see him again. She tried to laugh at herself, repeating over and over again that she was very, very foolish, and that she should have a just contempt for any woman who could be as foolish as she. For some moments she sat still, staring at the wall.

In the thought of him that filled her heart and soul and mind, she saw that her own life had begun when he had first spoken to her, and she felt that it would end with the last good-by, because if he should die or cease to love her, there would be nothing more to live for. Her early girlhood seemed dim and far away, dull and lifeless, as if it had not been hers at all, and had no connection with the present. She saw herself in the past, as she could not see herself now, and the child she remembered seemed not herself but another—a fair-haired girl living in the gloomy old house in Valladolid, with her blind sister and an old maiden cousin of her father's, who had offered to bring up the two and to teach them, being a woman of some learning, and who fulfilled her promise in such a conscientious and austere way as made their lives something of a burden under her strict rule. But that was all forgotten now, and though she still lived in Valladolid she had probably changed but little in the few years since Dolores had seen her; she was part of the past, a relic of something that had hardly ever had a real existence, and which it was not at all necessary to remember. There was one great light in the girl's simple existence, it had come all at once, and it was with her still. There was nothing dim nor dark nor forgotten about the day when she had been presented at court by the Duchess Alvarez, and she had first seen Don John, and he had first seen her and had spoken to her, when he had talked with the Duchess herself. At the first glance—and it was her first sight of the great world—she had seen that of all the men in the great hall, there was no one at all like him. She had no sooner looked into his face and cast her eyes upon his slender figure, all in white then, as he was dressed to-night, than she began to compare him with the rest. She looked so quickly from one to another that any one might have thought her to be anxiously searching for a friend in the crowd. But she had none then, and she was but assuring herself once, and for all her life, that the man she was to love was immeasurably beyond all other men, though the others were the very flower of Spain's young chivalry.

Of course, as she told herself now, she had not loved him then, nor even when she heard his voice speaking to her the first time and was almost too happy to understand his words. But she had remembered them. He had asked her whether she lived in Madrid. She had told him that she lived in the Alcazar itself, since her father commanded the guards and had his quarters in the palace. And then Don John had looked at her very fixedly for a moment, and had seemed pleased, for he smiled and said that he hoped he might see her often, and that if it were in his power to be of use to her father, he would do what he could. She was sure that she had not loved him then, though she had dreamed of his winning face and voice and had thought of little else all the next day, and the day after that, with a sort of feverish longing to see him again, and had asked the Duchess Alvarez so many questions about him that the Duchess had smiled oddly, and had shaken her handsome young head a little, saying that it was better not to think too much about Don John of Austria. Surely, she had not loved him already, at first sight. But on the evening of the third day, towards sunset, when she had been walking with Inez on a deserted terrace where no one but the two sisters ever went, Don John had suddenly appeared, sauntering idly out with one of his gentlemen on his left, as if he expected nothing at all; and he had seemed very much surprised to see her, and had bowed low, and somehow very soon, blind Inez, who was little more than a child three years ago, was leading the gentleman about the terrace, to show him where the best roses grew, which she knew by their touch and smell, and Don John and Dolores were seated on an old stone bench, talking earnestly together. Even to herself she admitted that she had loved him from that evening, and whenever she thought of it she smelt the first scent of roses, and saw his face with the blaze of the sunset in his eyes, and heard his voice saying that he should come to the terrace again at that hour, in which matter he had kept his word as faithfully as he always did, and presumably without any especial effort. So she had known him as he really was, without the formalities of the court life, of which she was herself a somewhat insignificant part; and it was only when he said a few words to her before the other ladies that she took pains to say 'your Highness' to him once or twice, and he called her 'Doña Dolores,' and enquired in a friendly manner about her father's health. But on the terrace they managed to talk without any such formal mode of address, and used no names at all for each other, until one day—but she would not think of that now. If she let her memory run all its course, she could not sit there with the door closed between him and her, for something stronger than she would force her to go and open it, and make sure he was there. This method, indeed, would be a very certain one, leaving no doubt whatever, but at the present moment it would be foolish to resort to it, and, perhaps, it would be dangerous, too. The past was so beautiful and peaceful; she could think its history through many times up to that point, where thinking was sure to end suddenly in something which was too present for memory and too well remembered not to be present.

It came back to her so vividly that she left her seat again and went to the curtained window, as if to get as far as possible from the irresistible attraction. Standing there she looked back and saw the key in the lock. It was foolish, girlish, childish, at such a time, but she felt that as long as it was there she should want to turn it. With a sudden resolution and a smile that was for her own weakness, she went to the door again, listened for footsteps, and then quietly took the key from the lock. Instantly Don John was on the other side, calling to her softly.

"What is it?" he asked. "For Heaven's sake do not come in, for I think I hear him coming."

"No," she answered through the panel. "I was afraid I should turn the key, so I have taken it out." She paused. "I love you!" she said, so that he could hear, and she kissed the wood, where she thought his face must be, just above her own.

"I love you with all my heart!" he answered gently. "Hush, dear love, he is coming!"

They were like two children, playing at a game; but they were playing on the very verge of tragedy, playing at life with death at the door and the safety of a great nation hanging in the balance.

A moment later, Dolores heard Don John opening and shutting the other doors again, and then there were voices. She heard her father's name spoken in the King's unmistakable tones, at once harsh and muffled. Every word came to her from the other room, as if she were present.

"Mendoza," said Philip, "I have private matters to discuss with his Highness. I desire you to wait before the entrance, on the terrace, and to let no one pass in, as we do not wish to be disturbed."

Her father did not speak, but she knew how he was bending a little stiffly, before he went backwards through the open door. It closed behind him, and the two brothers were alone. Dolores' heart beat a little faster, and her face grew paler as she concentrated her attention upon making no noise. If they could hear her as she heard them, a mere rustling of her silk gown would be enough to betray her, and if then the King bade her father take her with him, all would be over, for Don John would certainly not use any violence to protect her.

"This is your bedchamber," said Philip's voice.

He was evidently examining the room, as Don John had anticipated that he would, for he was moving about. There was no mistaking his heavy steps for his brother's elastic tread.

"There is no one behind the curtain," said the King, by which it was clear that he was making search for a possible concealed listener. He was by no means above such precautions.

"And that door?" he said, with a question. "What is there?"

Dolores' heart almost stood still, as she held her breath, and heard the clumsy footfall coming nearer.

"It is locked," said Don John, with undisturbed calm. "I have not the key. I do not know where it is,—it is not here."

As Dolores had taken it from the lock, even the last statement was true to the letter, and in spite of her anxiety she smiled as she heard it, but the next moment she trembled, for the King was trying the door, and it shook under his hand, as if it must fly open.

"It is certainly locked," he said, in a discontented tone. "But I do not like locked doors, unless I know what is beyond them."

He crossed the room again and called out to Mendoza, who answered at once.

"Mendoza, come here with me. There is a door here, of which his Highness has not the key. Can you open it?"

"I will try, your Majesty," answered the General's hard voice.

A moment later the panels shook violently under the old man's weight, for he was stronger than one might have thought, being lean and tough rather than muscular. Dolores took the moment when the noise was loudest and ran a few steps towards the window. Then the sounds ceased suddenly, and she stood still.

"I cannot open it, your Majesty," said Mendoza, in a disconsolate tone.

"Then go and get the key," answered the King almost angrily.

CHAPTER XI

Inez remained hidden a quarter of an hour in the gallery over the throne room, before she ventured to open the door noiselessly and listen for any sound that might come from the passage. She was quite safe there, as long as she chose to remain, for the Princess had believed that she had fled far beyond and was altogether out of reach of any one whose dignity would not allow of running a race. It must be remembered that at the time she entered the gallery Mendoza had returned to his duty below, and that some time afterwards he had accompanied the King to Don John's apartments, and had then been sent in search of the key to the locked door.

The blind girl was of course wholly ignorant of his whereabouts, and believed him to be in or about the throne room. Her instinct told her that since Dolores had not gone to the court, as she had intended, with the Duchess Alvarez, she must have made some last attempt to see Don John alone. In her perfect innocence such an idea seemed natural enough to Inez, and it at first occurred to her that the two might have arranged to meet on the deserted terrace where they had spent so many hours in former times. She went there first, finding her way with some little difficulty from the corridor where the gallery was, for the region was not the one to which she was most accustomed, though there was hardly a corner of the upper story where she had never been. Reaching the terrace she went out and called softly, but there was no answer, nor could she hear any sound. The night was not cold now, but the breeze chilled her a little, and just then the melancholy cry of a screech owl pierced the air, and she shivered and went in again.

She would have gone to the Duchess Alvarez had she not been sure that the latter was below with the Queen, and even as it was, she would have taken refuge in the Duchess's apartments with the women, and she might have learned something of Dolores there. But her touch reminded her that she was dressed in her sister's clothes, and that many questions might be asked her which it would be hard to answer. And again, it grew quite clear to her that Dolores must be somewhere near Don John, perhaps waiting in some concealed corner until all should be quiet. It was more than probable that he would get her out of the palace secretly during the night and send her to his adoptive mother at Villagarcia. She had not believed the Princess's words in the least, but she had not forgotten them, and had argued rightly enough to their real meaning.

In the upper story all was still now. She and Dolores had known where Don John was to be lodged in the palace nearly a month before he had returned, and they had been there more than once, when no one was on the terrace, and Dolores had made her touch the door and the six windows, three on each side of it. She could get there without difficulty, provided that no one stopped her.

She went a little way in the right direction and then hesitated. There was more danger to Dolores than to herself if she should be recognized, and, after all, if Dolores was near Don John she was safer than she could be anywhere else. Inez could not help her very much in any way if she found her there, and it would be hard to find her if she had met Mendoza at first and if he had placed her in the keeping of a third person. She imagined what his astonishment would have been had he found the real Dolores in her court dress a few moments after Inez had been delivered over to the Princess disguised in Dolores' clothes, and she almost smiled. But then a great loneliness and a sense of helplessness came over her, and she turned back and went out upon the deserted terrace again and sat down upon the old stone seat, listening for the screech owl and the fluttering of the bats that flew aimlessly in and out, attracted by the light and then scared away by it again because the moon was at the full.

Inez had never before then wandered about the palace at night, and though darkness and daylight were one to her, there was something in the air that frightened her, and made her feel how really helpless she was in spite of her almost superhuman hearing and her wonderful sense of touch. It was very still—it was never so still by day. It seemed as if people must be lying in wait for her, holding their breath lest she should hear even that. She had never felt blind before; she had never so completely realized the difference between her life and the lives of others. By day, she could wander where she pleased on the upper story—it was cheerful, familiar; now and then some one passed and perhaps spoke to her kindly, as every one did who knew her; and then there was the warm sunlight at the windows, and the cool breath of the living day in the corridors. The sounds guided her, the sun warmed her, the air fanned her, the voices of the people made her feel that she was one of them. But now, the place was like an empty church, full of tombs and silent as the dead that lay there. She felt horribly lonely, and cold, and miserable, and she would have given anything to be in bed in her own room. She could not go there. Eudaldo would not understand her return, after being told that she was to stay with the Princess, and she would be obliged to give him some explanation. Then her voice would betray her, and there would be terrible trouble. If only she had kept her own cloak to cover Dolores' frock, she could have gone back and the servant would have thought it quite natural Indeed, by this time he would be expecting her. It would be almost better to go in after all, and tell him some story of her having mistaken her sister's skirt for her own, and beg him to say nothing. She could easily confuse him a little so that he would not really understand—and then in a few minutes she could be in her own room, safe and in bed, and far away from the dismal place where she was sitting and shivering as she listened to the owls.

She rose and began to walk towards her father's quarters. But suddenly she felt that it was cowardly to go back without accomplishing the least part of her purpose, and without even finding out whether Dolores was in safety after all. There was but one chance of finding her, and that lay in searching the neighbourhood of Don John's lodging. Without hesitating any longer, she began to find her way thither at once. She determined that if she were stopped, either by her father or the Princess, she would throw back her head and show her face at once. That would be the safest way in the end.

She reached Don John's windows unhindered at last. She had felt every corner, and had been into the empty sentry-box; and once or twice, after listening a long time, she had called Dolores in a very low tone. She listened by the first window, and by the second and third, and at the door, and then beyond, till she came to the last. There were voices there, and her heart beat quickly for a moment. It was impossible to distinguish the words that were spoken, through the closed window and the heavy curtains, but the mere tones told her that Don John and Dolores were there together. That was enough for her, and she could go back to her room; for it seemed quite natural to her that her sister should be in the keeping of the man she loved,—she was out of harm's way and beyond their father's power, and that was all that was necessary. She would go back to her room at once, and explain the matter of her dress to Eudaldo as best she might. After all, why should he care what she wore or where she had been, or whether in the Princess's apartments she had for some reason exchanged gowns with Dolores. Perhaps he would not even notice the dress at all.

She meant to go at once, but she stood quite still, her hands resting on the low sill of the window, while her forehead pressed against the cold round panes of glass. Something hurt her which she could not understand, as she tried to fancy the two beautiful young beings who were within,—for she knew what beauty they had, and Dolores had described Don John to her as a young god. His voice came to her like strains of very distant sweet music, that connect themselves to an unknown melody in the fancy of him who faintly hears. But Dolores was hearing every word he said, and it was all for her; and Dolores not only heard, but saw; and seeing and hearing, she was loved by the man who spoke to her, as dearly as she loved him.

Then utter loneliness fell upon the blind girl as she leaned against the window. She had expected nothing, she had asked nothing, even in her heart; and she had less than nothing, since never on earth, nor in heaven hereafter, could Don John say a loving word to her. And yet she felt that something had been taken from her and given to her sister,—something that was more to her than life, and dearer than the thought of sight to her blindness. She had taken what had not been given her, in innocent girlish thoughts that were only dreams, and could hurt no one. He had always spoken gently to her, and touched her hand kindly; and many a time, sitting alone in the sun, she had set those words to the well-remembered music of his voice, and she had let the memory of his light touch on her fingers thrill her strangely to the very quick. It had been but the reflection of a reflection in her darkness, wherein the shadow of a shadow seemed as bright as day. It had been all she had to make her feel that she was a part of the living, loving world she could never see. Somehow she had unconsciously fancied that with a little dreaming she could live happy in Dolores' happiness, as by a proxy, and she had never called it love, any more than she would have dared to hope for love in return. Yet it was that, and nothing else,—the love that is so hopeless and starving, and yet so innocent, that it can draw the illusion of an airy nourishment from that which to another nature would be the fountain of all jealousy and hatred.

But now, without reason and without warning, even that was taken from her, and in its place something burned that she did not know, save that it was a bad thing, and made even blackness blacker. She heard their voices still. They were happy together, while she was alone outside, her forehead resting against the chill glass, and her hands half numb upon the stone; and so it would always be hereafter. They would go, and take her life with them, and she should be left behind, alone for ever; and a great revolt against her fate rose quickly in her breast like a flame before the wind, and then, as if finding nothing to consume, sank down again into its own ashes, and left her more lonely than before. The voices had ceased now, or else the lovers were speaking very low, fearing, perhaps, that some one might be listening at the window. If Inez had heard their words at first, she would have stopped her ears or gone to a distance, for the child knew what that sort of honour meant, and had done as much before. But the unformed sound had been good to hear, and she missed it. Perhaps they were sitting close and, hand in hand, reading all the sweet unsaid things in one another's eyes. There must be silent voices in eyes that could see, she thought. She took little thought of the time, yet it seemed long to her since they had spoken. Perhaps they had gone to another room. She moved to the next window and listened there, but no sound came from within. Then she heard footfalls, and one was her father's. Two men were coming out by the corridor, and she had not time to reach the sentry-box. With her hands out before her, she went lightly away from the windows to the outer side of the broad terrace, and cowered down by the balustrade as she ran against it, not knowing whether she was in the moonlight or the shade. She had crossed like a shadow and was crouching there before Mendoza and the King came out. She knew by their steady tread, that ended at the door, that they had not noticed her; and as the door closed behind them, she ran back to the window again and listened, expecting to hear loud and angry words, for she could not doubt that the King and her father had discovered that Dolores was there, and had come to take her away. The Princess must have told Mendoza that Dolores had escaped. But she only heard men's voices speaking in an ordinary tone, and she understood that Dolores was concealed. Almost at once, and to her dismay, she heard her father's step in the hall, and now she could neither pass the door nor run across the terrace again. A moment later the King called him from within. Instantly she slipped across to the other side, and listened again. They were shaking a door,—they were in the very act of finding Dolores. Her heart hurt her. But then the noise stopped, as if they had given up the attempt, and presently she heard her father's step again. Thinking that he would remain in the hall until the King called him,—for she could not possibly guess what had happened,— she stood quite still.

The door opened without warning, and he was almost upon her before she knew it. To hesitate an instant was out of the question, and for the second time that night she fled, running madly to the corridor, which was not ten steps from where she had been standing, and as she entered it the light fell upon her from the swinging lamp, though she did not know it.

Old as he was, Mendoza sprang forward in pursuit when he saw her figure in the dimness, flying before him, but as she reached the light of the lamp he stopped himself, staggering one or two steps and then reeling against the wall. He had recognized Dolores' dress and hood, and there was not the slightest doubt in his mind but that it was herself. In that same dress he had seen her in the late afternoon, she had been wearing it when he had locked her into the sitting-room, and, still clad in it, she must have come out with the Princess. And now she was running before him from Don John's lodging. Doubtless she had been in another room and had slipped out while he was trying the door within.

He passed his hand over his eyes and breathed hard as he leaned against the wall, for her appearance there could only mean one thing, and that was ruin to her and disgrace to his name— the very end of all things in his life, in which all had been based upon his honour and every action had been a tribute to it.

He was too much stunned to ask himself how the lovers had met, if there had been any agreement between them, but the frightful conviction took hold of him that this was not the first time, that long ago, before Don John had led the army to Granada, Dolores had found her way to that same door and had spent long hours with her lover when no one knew. Else she could not have gone to him without agreement, at an instant's notice, on the very night of his return.

Despair took possession of the unhappy man from that moment. But that the King was with Don John, Mendoza would have gone back at that moment to kill his enemy and himself afterwards, if need be. He remembered his errand then. No doubt that was the very room where Dolores had been concealed, and she had escaped from it by some other way, of which her father did not know. He was too dazed to think connectedly, but he had the King's commands to execute at once. He straightened himself with a great effort, for the weight of his years had come upon him suddenly and bowed him like a burden. With the exertion of his will came the thirst for the satisfaction of blood, and he saw that the sooner he returned with the key, the sooner he should be near his enemy. But the pulses came and went in his throbbing temples, as when a man is almost spent in a struggle with death, and at first he walked uncertainly, as if he felt no ground under his feet.

By the time he had gone a hundred yards he had recovered a sort of mechanical self-possession, such as comes upon men at very desperate times, when they must not allow themselves to stop and think of what is before them. They were pictures, rather than thoughts, that formed themselves in his brain as he went along, for he saw all the past years again, from the day when his young wife had died, he being then already in middle age, until that afternoon. One by one the years came back, and the central figure in each was the fair-haired little child, growing steadily to be a woman, all coming nearer and nearer to the end he had seen but now, which was unutterable shame and disgrace, and beyond which there was nothing. He heard the baby voice again, and felt the little hands upon his brow, and saw the serious grey eyes close to his own; and then the girl, gravely lovely—and her far-off laugh that hardly ever rippled through the room when he was there; and then the stealing softness of grown maidenhood, winning the features one by one, and bringing back from death to life the face he had loved best, and the voice with long-forgotten tones that touched his soul's quick, and dimmed his sight with a mist, so that he grew hard and stern as he fought within him against the tenderness he loved and feared. All this he saw and heard and felt again, knowing that each picture must end but in one way, in the one sight he had seen and that had told his shame—a guilty woman stealing by night from her lover's door. Not only that, either, for there was the almost certain knowledge that she had deceived him for years, and that while he had been fighting so hard to save her from what seemed but a show of marriage, she had been already lost to him for ever and ruined beyond all hope of honesty.

They were not thoughts, but pictures of the false and of the true, that rose and glowed an instant and then sank like the inner darkness of his soul, leaving only that last most terrible one of all behind them, burned into his eyes till death should put out their light and bid him rest at last, if he could rest even in heaven with such a memory.

It was too much, and though he walked upright and gazed before him, he did not know his way, and his feet took him to his own door instead of on the King's errand. His hand was raised to knock before he understood, and it fell to his side in a helpless, hopeless way, when he saw where he was. Then he turned stiffly, as a man turns on parade, and gathered his strength and marched away with a measured tread. For the world and what it held he would not have entered his dwelling then, for he felt that his daughter was there before him, and that if he once saw her face he should not be able to hold his hand. He would not see her again on earth, lest he should take her life for what she had done.

He was more aware of outward things after that, though he almost commanded himself to do what he had to do, as he would have given orders to one of his soldiers. He went to the chief steward's office and demanded the key of the room in the King's name. But it was not forthcoming, and the fact that it could not be found strengthened his conviction that Don John had it in his keeping. Yet, for the sake of form, he insisted sternly, saying that the King was waiting for it even then. Servants were called and examined and threatened, but those who knew anything about it unanimously declared that it had been left in the door, while those who knew nothing supported their fellow-servants by the same unhesitating assertion, till Mendoza was convinced that he had done enough, and turned his back on them all and went out with a grey look of despair on his face.

He walked rapidly now, for he knew that he was going back to meet his enemy, and he was trying not to think what he should do when he should see Don John before him and at arm's length, but defended by the King's presence from any sudden violence. He knew that in his heart there was the wild resolve to tell the truth before his master and then to take the payment of blood with one thrust and destroy himself with the next, but though he was half mad with despair, he would not let the thought become a resolve. In his soldier's nature, high above everything else and dominating his austere conscience of right and wrong, as well as every other instinct of his heart, there was the respect of his sovereign and the loyalty to him at all costs, good or bad, which sent self out of sight where his duty to the King was concerned.

CHAPTER XII

When he had sent away Mendoza, the King remained standing and began to pace the floor, while Don John stood by the table watching him and waiting for him to speak. It was clear that he was still angry, for his anger, though sometimes suddenly roused, was very slow to reach its height, and slower still to subside; and when at last it had cooled, it generally left behind it an enduring hatred, such as could be satisfied only by the final destruction of the object that had caused it. That lasting hate was perhaps more dangerous than the sudden outburst had been, but in moments of furious passion Philip was undoubtedly a man to be feared.

He was evidently not inclined to speak until he had ascertained that no one was listening in the next room, but as he looked from time to time at Don John his still eyes seemed to grow almost yellow, and his lower lip moved uneasily. He knew, perhaps, that Mendoza could not at once find the servant in whose keeping the key of the door was supposed to be, and he grew impatient by quick degrees until his rising temper got the better of his caution. Don John instinctively drew himself up, as a man does who expects to be attacked. He was close to the table, and remained almost motionless during the discussion that followed, while Philip paced up and down, sometimes pausing before his brother for a moment, and then turning again to resume his walk. His voice was muffled always, and was hard to hear; now and then it became thick and indistinct with rage, and he cleared his throat roughly, as if he were angry with it, too. At first he maintained the outward forms of courtesy in words if not in tone, but long before his wrath had reached its final climax he forgot them altogether.

"I had hoped to speak with you in privacy, on matters of great importance. It has pleased your Highness to make that impossible by your extraordinary behaviour."

Don John raised his eyebrows a little incredulously, and answered with perfect calmness.

"I do not recollect doing anything which should seem extraordinary to your Majesty."

"You contradict me," retorted Philip. "That is extraordinary enough, I should think. I am not aware that it is usual for subjects to contradict the King. What have you to say in explanation?"

"Nothing. The facts explain themselves well enough."

"We are not in camp," said Philip. "Your Highness is not in command here, and I am not your subordinate. I desire you to remember whom you are addressing, for your words will be remembered."

"I never said anything which I wished another to forget," answered Don John proudly.

"Take care, then!" The King spoke sullenly, and turned away, for he was slow at retort until he was greatly roused.

Don John did not answer, for he had no wish to produce such a result, and moreover he was much more preoccupied by the serious question of Dolores' safety than by any other consideration. So far the King had said nothing which, but for some derogation from his dignity, might not have been said before any one, and Don John expected that he would maintain the same tone until Mendoza returned. It was hard to predict what might happen then. In all probability Dolores would escape by the window and endeavour to hide herself in the empty sentry-box until the interview was over. He could then bring her back in safety, but the discussion promised to be long and stormy, and meanwhile she would be in constant danger of discovery. But there was a worse possibility, not even quite beyond the bounds of the probable. In his present mood, Philip, if he lost his temper altogether, would perhaps be capable of placing Don John under arrest. He was all powerful, he hated his brother, and he was very angry. His last words had been a menace, or had sounded like one, and another word, when Mendoza returned, could put the threat into execution. Don John reflected, if such thought could be called reflection, upon the situation that must ensue, and upon the probable fate of the woman he loved. He wondered whether she were still in the room, for hearing that the door was to be opened, she might have thought it best to escape at once, while her father was absent from the terrace on his errand. If not, she could certainly go out by the window as soon as she heard him coming back. It was clearly of the greatest importance to prevent the King's anger from going any further. Antonio Perez had recognized the same truth from a very different point of view, and had spent nearly three-quarters of an hour in flattering his master with the consummate skill which he alone possessed. He believed that he had succeeded when the King had dismissed him, saying that he would not see Don John until the morning. Five minutes after Perez was gone, Philip was threading the corridors, completely disguised in a long black cloak, with the ever-loyal Mendoza at his heels. It was not the first time that he had deceived his deceivers.

He paced the room in silence after he had last spoken. As soon as Don John realized that his liberty might be endangered, he saw that he must say what he could in honour and justice to save himself from arrest, since nothing else could save Dolores.

"I greatly regret having done anything to anger your Majesty," he said, with quiet dignity. "I was placed in a very difficult position by unforeseen circumstances. If there had been time to reflect, I might have acted otherwise."

"Might have acted otherwise!" repeated Philip harshly. "I do not like those words. You might have acted otherwise than to defy your sovereign before the Queen! I trusted you might, indeed!"

He was silent again, his protruding lip working angrily, as if he had tasted something he disliked. Don John's half apology had not been received with much grace, but he saw no way open save to insist that it was genuine.

"It is certainly true that I have lived much in camps of late," he answered, "and that a camp is not a school of manners, any more than the habit of commanding others accustoms a man to courtly submission."

"Precisely. You have learned to forget that you have a superior in Spain, or in the world. You already begin to affect the manners and speech of a sovereign—you will soon claim the dignity of one, too, I have no doubt. The sooner we procure you a kingdom of your own, the better, for your Highness will before long become an element of discord in ours."

"Rather than that," answered Don John, "I will live in retirement for the rest of my life."

"We may require it of your Highness," replied Philip, standing still and facing his brother. "It may be necessary for our own safety that you should spend some time at least in very close retirement— very!" He almost laughed.

"I should prefer that to the possibility of causing any disturbance in your Majesty's kingdom."

Nothing could have been more gravely submissive than Don John's tone, but the King was apparently determined to rouse his anger.

"Your deeds belie your words," he retorted, beginning to walk again. "There is too much loyalty in what you say, and too much of a rebellious spirit in what you do. The two do not agree together. You mock me."

"God forbid that!" cried Don John. "I desire no praise for what I may have done, but such as my deeds have been they have produced peace and submission in your Majesty's kingdom, and not rebellion—"

"And is it because you have beaten a handful of ill-armed Moriscoes, in the short space of two years, that the people follow you in throngs wherever you go, shouting for you, singing your praises, bringing petitions to you by hundreds, as if you were King—as if you were more than that, a sort of god before whom every one must bow down? Am I so simple as to believe that what you have done with such leisure is enough to rouse all Spain, and to make the whole court break out into cries of wonder and applause as soon as you appear? If you publicly defy me and disobey me, do I not know that you believe yourself able to do so, and think your power equal to mine? And how could that all be brought about, save by a party that is for you, by your secret agents everywhere, high and low, forever praising you and telling men, and women, too, of your graces, and your generosities, and your victories, and saying that it is a pity so good and brave a prince should be but a leader of the King's armies, and then contrasting the King himself with you, the cruel King, the grasping King, the scheming King, the King who has every fault that is not found in Don John of Austria, the people's god! Is that peace and submission? Or is it the beginning of rebellion, and revolution, and civil war, which is to set Don John of Austria on the throne of Spain, and send King Philip to another world as soon as all is ready?"

Don John listened in amazement. It had never occurred to him any one could believe him capable of the least of the deeds Philip was attributing to him, and in spite of his resolution his anger began to rise. Then, suddenly, as if cold water had been dashed in his face, he remembered that an hour had not passed since he had held Dolores in his arms, swearing to do that of which he was now accused, and that her words only had held him back. It all seemed monstrous now. As she had said, it had been only a bad dream and he had wakened to himself again. Yet the thought of rebellion had more than crossed his mind, for in a moment it had taken possession of him and had seemed to change all his nature from good to bad. In his own eyes he was rebuked, and he did not answer at once.

"You have nothing to say!" exclaimed Philip scornfully. "Is there any reason why I should not try you for high treason?"

Don John started at the words, but his anger was gone, and he thought only of Dolores' safety in the near future.

"Your Majesty is far too just to accuse an innocent man who has served you faithfully," he answered.

Philip stopped and looked at him curiously and long, trying to detect some sign of anxiety if not of fear. He was accustomed to torture men with words well enough, before he used other means, and he himself had not believed what he had said. It had been only an experiment tried on a mere chance, and it had failed. At the root of his anger there was only jealousy and personal hatred of the brother who had every grace and charm which he himself had not.

"More kind than just, perhaps," he said, with a slight change of tone towards condescension. "I am willing to admit that I have no proofs against you, but the evidence of circumstances is not in your favour. Take care, for you are observed. You are too much before the world, too imposing a figure to escape observation."

"My actions will bear it. I only beg that your Majesty will take account of them rather than listen to such interpretation as may be put upon them by other men."

"Other men do nothing but praise you," said Philip bluntly. "Their opinion of you is not worth having! I thought I had explained that matter sufficiently. You are the idol of the people, and as if that were not enough, you are the darling of the court, besides being the women's favourite. That is too much for one man to be—take care, I say, take care! Be at more pains for my favour, and at less trouble for your popularity."

"So far as that goes," answered Don John, with some pride, "I think that if men praise me it is because I have served the King as well as I could, and with success. If your Majesty is not satisfied with what I have done, let me have more to do. I shall try to do even the impossible."

"That will please the ladies," retorted Philip, with a sneer. "You will be overwhelmed with correspondence—your gloves will not hold it all"

Don John did not answer, for it seemed wiser to let the King take this ground than return to his former position.

"You will have plenty of agreeable occupation in time of peace. But it is better that you should be married soon, before you become so entangled with the ladies of Madrid as to make your marriage impossible."

"Saving the last clause," said Don John boldly, "I am altogether of your Majesty's opinion. But I fear no entanglements here."

"No—you do not fear them. On the contrary, you live in them as if they were your element."

"No man can say that," answered Don John.

"You contradict me again. Pray, if you have no entanglements, how comes it that you have a lady's letter in your glove?"

"I cannot tell whether it was a lady's letter or a man's."

"Have you not read it?"

"Yes."

"And you refused to show it to me on the ground that it was a woman's secret?"

"I had not read it then. It was not signed, and it might well have been written by a man."

Don John watched the King's face. It was for from improbable, he thought, that the King had caused it to be written, or had written it himself, that he supposed his brother to have read it, and desired to regain possession of it as soon as possible. Philip seemed to hesitate whether to continue his cross-examination or not, and he looked at the door leading into the antechamber, suddenly wondering why Mendoza had not returned. Then he began to speak again, but he did not wish, angry though he was, to face alone a second refusal to deliver the document to him. His dignity would have suffered too much.

"The facts of the case are these," he said, as if he were recapitulating what had gone before in his mind. "It is my desire to marry you to the widowed Queen of Scots, as you know. You are doing all you can to oppose me, and you have determined to marry the dowerless daughter of a poor soldier. I am equally determined that you shall not disgrace yourself by such an alliance."

"Disgrace!" cried Don John loudly, almost before the word had passed the King's lips, and he made half a step forward. "You are braver than I thought you, if you dare use that word to me!"

Philip stepped back, growing livid, and his hand was on his rapier. Don John was unarmed, but his sword lay on the table within his reach. Seeing the King afraid, he stepped back.

"No," he said scornfully, "I was mistaken. You are a coward." He laughed as he glanced at Philip's hand, still on the hilt of his weapon and ready to draw it.

In the next room Dolores drew frightened breath, for the tones of the two men's voices had changed suddenly. Yet her heart had leapt for joy when she had heard Don John's cry of anger at the King's insulting word. But Don John was right, for Philip was a coward at heart, and though he inwardly resolved that his brother should be placed under arrest as soon as Mendoza returned, his present instinct was not to rouse him further. He was indeed in danger, between his anger and his fear, for at any moment he might speak some bitter word, accustomed as he was to the perpetual protection of his guards, but at the next his brother's hands might be on his throat, for he had the coward's true instinct to recognize the man who was quite fearless.

"You strangely forget yourself," he said, with an appearance of dignity. "You spring forward as if you were going to grapple with me, and then you are surprised that I should be ready to defend myself."

"I barely moved a step from where I stand," answered Don John, with profound contempt. "I am unarmed, too. There lies my sword, on the table. But since you are the King as well as my brother, I make all excuses to your Majesty for having been the cause of your fright."

Dolores understood what had happened, as Don John meant that she should. She knew also that her position was growing more and more desperate and untenable at every moment; yet she could not blame her lover for what he had said. Even to save her, she would not have had him cringe to the King and ask pardon for his hasty word and movement, still less could she have borne that he should not cry out in protest at a word that insulted her, though ever so lightly.

"I do not desire to insist upon our kinship," said Philip coldly. "If I chose to acknowledge it when you were a boy, it was out of respect for the memory of the Emperor. It was not in the expectation of being called brother by the son of a German burgher's daughter."

Don John did not wince, for the words, being literally true and without exaggeration, could hardly be treated as an insult, though they were meant for one, and hurt him, as all reference to his real mother always did.

"Yes," he said, still scornfully. "I am the son of a German burgher's daughter, neither better nor worse. But I am your brother, for all that, and though I shall not forget that you are King and I am subject, when we are before the world, yet here, we are man and man, you and I, brother and brother, and there is neither King nor prince. But I shall not hurt you, so you need fear nothing. I respect the brother far too little for that, and the sovereign too much."

There was a bad yellow light in Philip's face, and instead of walking towards Don John and away from him, as he had done hitherto, he began to pace up and down, crossing and recrossing before him, from the foot of the great canopied bed to one of the curtained windows, keeping his eyes upon his brother almost all the time.

"I warned you when I came here that your words should be remembered," he said. "And your actions shall not be forgotten, either. There are safe places, even in Madrid, where you can live in the retirement you desire so much, even in total solitude."

"If it pleases your Majesty to imprison Don John of Austria, you have the power. For my part, I shall make no resistance."

"Who shall, then?" asked the King angrily. "Do you expect that there will be a general rising of the people to liberate you, or that there will be a revolution within the palace, brought on by your party, which shall force me to set you free for reasons of state? We are not in Paris that you should expect the one, nor in Constantinople where the other might be possible. We are in Spain, and I am master, and my will shall be done, and no one shall cry out against it. I am too gentle with you, too kind! For the half of what you have said and done, Elizabeth of England would have had your life to-morrow— yes, I consent to give you a chance, the benefit of a doubt there is still in my thoughts about you, because justice shall not be offended and turned into an instrument of revenge. Yes—I am kind, I am clement. We shall see whether you can save yourself. You shall have the chance."

"What chance is that?" asked Don John, growing very quiet, for he saw the real danger near at hand again.

"You shall have an opportunity of proving that a subject is at liberty to insult his sovereign, and that the King is not free to speak his mind to a subject. Can you prove that?"

"I cannot."

"Then you can be convicted of high treason," answered Philip, his evil mouth curling. "There are several methods of interrogating the accused," he continued. "I daresay you have heard of them."

"Do you expect to frighten me by talking of torture?" asked Don John, with a smile at the implied suggestion.

"Witnesses are also examined," replied the King, his voice thickening again in anticipation of the effect he was going to produce upon the man who would not fear him. "With them, even more painful methods are often employed. Witnesses may be men or women, you know, my dear brother—" he pronounced the word with a sneer—"and among the many ladies of your acquaintance—"

"There are very few."

"It will be the easier to find the two or three, or perhaps the only one, whom it will be necessary to interrogate—in your presence, most probably, and by torture."

"I was right to call you a coward," said Don John, slowly turning pale till his face was almost as white as the white silks and satins of his doublet.

"Will you give me the letter you were reading when I came here?"

"No."

"Not to save yourself from the executioner's hands?"

"No."

"Not to save—" Philip paused, and a frightful stare of hatred fixed his eyes on his brother. "Will you give me that letter to save Dolores de Mendoza from being torn piecemeal?"

"Coward!"

By instinct Don John's hand went to the hilt of his sheathed sword this time, as he cried out in rage, and sprang forward. Even then he would have remembered the promise he had given and would not have raised his hand to strike. But the first movement was enough, and Philip drew his rapier in a flash of light, fearing for his life. Without waiting for an attack he made a furious pass at his brother's body. Don John's hand went out with the sheathed sword in a desperate attempt to parry the thrust, but the weapon was entangled in the belt that hung to it, and Philip's lunge had been strong and quick as lightning.

With a cry of anger Don John fell straight backwards, his feet seeming to slip from under him on the smooth marble pavement, and with his fall, as he threw out his hands to save himself, the sword flew high into the air, sheathed as it was, and landed far away. He lay at full length with one arm stretched out, and for a moment the hand twitched in quick spasms. Then it was quite still.

At his feet stood Philip, his rapier in his hand, and blood on its fine point. His eyes shone yellow in the candlelight, his jaw had dropped a little, and he bent forwards, looking intently at the still, white face.

He had longed for that moment ever since he had entered his brother's room, though even he himself had not guessed that he wanted his brother's life. There was not a sound in the room as he looked at what he had done, and two or three drops of blood fell one by one, very slowly, upon the marble. On the dazzling white of Don John's doublet there was a small red stain. As Philip watched it, he thought it grew wider and brighter.

Beyond the door, Dolores had fallen upon her knees, pressing her hands to her temples in an agony beyond thought or expression. Her fear had risen to terror while she listened to the last words that had been exchanged, and the King's threat had chilled her blood like ice, though she was brave. She had longed to cry out to Don John to give up her letter or the other, whichever the King wanted—she had almost tried to raise her voice, in spite of every other fear, when she had heard Don John's single word of scorn, and the quick footsteps, the drawing of the rapier from its sheath, the desperate scuffle that had not lasted five seconds, and then the dull fall which meant that one was hurt.

It could only be the King,—but that was terrible enough,—and yet, if the King had fallen, Don John would have come to the door the next instant. All was still in the room, but her terror made wild noises in her ears. The two men might have spoken now and she could not have heard them,—nor the opening of a door, nor any ordinary sound. It was no longer the fear of being heard, either, that made her silent. Her throat was parched and her tongue paralyzed. She remembered suddenly that Don John had been unarmed, and how he had pointed out to Philip that his sword lay on the table. It was the King who had drawn his own, then, and had killed his unarmed brother. She felt as if something heavy were striking her head as the thoughts made broken words, and flashes of light danced before her eyes. With her hands she tried to press feeling and reason and silence back into her brain that would not be quieted, but the certainty grew upon her that Don John was killed, and the tide of despair rose higher with every breath.

The sensation came upon her that she was dying, then and there, of a pain human nature could not endure, far beyond the torments Philip had threatened, and the thought was merciful, for she could not have lived an hour in such agony,—something would have broken before then. She was dying, there, on her knees before the door beyond which her lover lay suddenly dead. It would be easy to die. In a moment more she would be with him, for ever, and in peace. They would find her there, dead, and perhaps they would be merciful and bury her near him. But that would matter little, since she should be with him always now. In the first grief that struck her, and bruised her, and numbed her as with material blows, she had no tears, but there was a sort of choking fire in her throat, and her eyes burned her like hot iron.

She did not know how long she knelt, waiting for death. She was dying, and there was no time any more, nor any outward world, nor anything but her lover's dead body on the floor in the next room, and his soul waiting for hers, waiting beside her for her to die also, that they might go together. She was so sure now, that she was wondering dreamily why it took so long to die, seeing that death had taken him so quickly. Could one shaft be aimed so straight and could the next miss the mark? She shook all over, as a new dread seized her. She was not dying,—her life clung too closely to her suffering body, her heart was too young and strong to stand still in her breast for grief. She was to live, and bear that same pain a lifetime. She rocked herself gently on her knees, bowing her head almost to the floor.

She was roused by the sound of her father's voice, and the words he was speaking sent a fresh shock of horror through her unutterable grief, for they told her that Don John was dead, and then something else so strange that she could not understand it.

Philip had stood only a few moments, sword in hand, over his brother's body, staring down at his face, when the door opened. On the threshold stood old Mendoza, half-stunned by the sight he saw. Philip heard, stood up, and drew back as his eyes fell upon the old soldier. He knew that Mendoza, if no one else, knew the truth now, beyond any power of his to conceal it. His anger had subsided, and a sort of horror that could never be remorse, had come over him for what he had done. It must have been in his face, for Mendoza understood, and he came forward quickly and knelt down upon the floor to listen for the beating of the heart, and to try whether there was any breath to dim the brightness of his polished scabbard. Philip looked on in silence. Like many an old soldier Mendoza had some little skill, but he saw the bright spot on the white doublet, and the still face and the hands relaxed, and there was neither breath nor beating of the heart to give hope. He rose silently, and shook his head. Still looking down he saw the red drops that had fallen upon the pavement from Philip's rapier, and looking at that, saw that the point was dark. With a gesture of excuse he took the sword from the King's hand and wiped it quite dry and bright upon his own handkerchief, and gave it back to Philip, who sheathed it by his side, but never spoke.

Together the two looked at the body for a full minute and more, each silently debating what should be done with it. At last Mendoza raised his head, and there was a strange look in his old eyes and a sort of wan greatness came over his war-worn face. It was then that he spoke the words Dolores heard.

"I throw myself upon your Majesty's mercy! I have killed Don John of Austria in a private quarrel, and he was unarmed."

Philip understood well enough, and a faint smile of satisfaction flitted through the shadows of his face. It was out of the question that the world should ever know who had killed his brother, and he knew the man who offered to sacrifice himself by bearing the blame of the deed. Mendoza would die, on the scaffold if need be, and it would be enough for him to know that his death saved his King. No word would ever pass his lips. The man's loyalty would bear any proof; he could feel horror at the thought that Philip could have done such a deed, but the King's name must be saved at all costs, and the King's divine right must be sustained before the world. He felt no hesitation from the moment when he saw clearly how this must be done. To accuse some unknown murderer and let it be supposed that he had escaped would have been worse than useless; the court and half Spain knew of the King's jealousy of his brother, every one had seen that Philip had been very angry when the courtiers had shouted for Don John; already the story of the quarrel about the glove was being repeated from mouth to mouth in the throne room, where the nobles had reassembled after supper. As soon as it was known that Don John was dead, it would be believed by every one in the palace that the King had killed him or had caused him to be murdered. But if Mendoza took the blame upon himself, the court would believe him, for many knew of Dolores' love for Don John, and knew also how bitterly the old soldier was opposed to their marriage, on the ground that it would be no marriage at all, but his daughter's present ruin. There was no one else in the palace who could accuse himself of the murder and who would be believed to have done it without the King's orders, and Mendoza knew this, when he offered his life to shield Philip's honour. Philip knew it, too, and while he wondered at the old man's simple devotion, he accepted it without protest, as his vast selfishness would have permitted the destruction of all mankind, that it might be satisfied and filled.

He looked once more at the motionless body at his feet, and once more at the faithful old man. Then he bent his head with condescending gravity, as if he were signifying his pleasure to receive kindly, for the giver's sake, a gift of little value.

"So be it," he said slowly.

Mendoza bowed his head, too, as if in thanks, and then taking up the long dark cloak which the King had thrown off on entering, he put it upon Philip's shoulders, and went before him to the door. And Philip followed him without looking back, and both went out upon the terrace, leaving both doors ajar after them. They exchanged a few words more as they walked slowly in the direction of the corridor.

"It is necessary that your Majesty should return at once to the throne room, as if nothing had happened," said Mendoza. "Your Majesty should be talking unconcernedly with some ambassador or minister when the news is brought that his Highness is dead."

"And who shall bring the news?" asked Philip calmly, as if he were speaking to an indifferent person.

"I will, Sire," answered Mendoza firmly.

"They will tear you in pieces before I can save you," returned Philip, in a thoughtful tone.

"So much the better. I shall die for my King, and your Majesty will be spared the difficulty of pardoning a deed which will be unpardonable in the eyes of the whole world."

"That is true," said the King meditatively. "But I do not wish you to die, Mendoza," he added, as an afterthought. "You must escape to France or to England."

"I could not make my escape without your Majesty's help, and that would soon be known. It would then be believed that I had done the deed by your Majesty's orders, and no good end would have been gained."

"You may be right. You are a very brave man, Mendoza—the bravest I have ever known. I thank you. If it is possible to save you, you shall be saved."

"It will not be possible," replied the soldier, in a low and steady voice. "If your Majesty will return at once to the throne room, it may be soon over. Besides, it is growing late, and it must be done before the whole court."

They entered the corridor, and the King walked a few steps before Mendoza, covering his head with the hood of his cloak lest any one should recognize him, and gradually increasing his distance as the old man fell behind. Descending by a private staircase, Philip reëntered his own apartments by a small door that gave access to his study without obliging him to pass through the antechamber, and by which he often came and went unobserved. Alone in his innermost room, and divested of his hood and cloak, the King went to a Venetian mirror that stood upon a pier table between the windows, and examined his face attentively. Not a trace of excitement or emotion was visible in the features he saw, but his hair was a little disarranged, and he smoothed it carefully and adjusted it about his ears. From a silver box on the table he took a little scented lozenge and put it into his mouth. No reasonable being would have suspected from his appearance that he had been moved to furious anger and had done a murderous deed less than twenty minutes earlier. His still eyes were quite calm now, and the yellow gleam in them had given place to their naturally uncertain colour. With a smile of admiration for his own extraordinary powers, he turned and left the room. He was enjoying one of his rare moments of satisfaction, for the rival he had long hated and was beginning to dread was never to stand in his way again nor to rob him of the least of his attributes of sovereignty.

CHAPTER XIII

Dolores had not understood her father's words. All that was clear to her was that Don John was dead and that his murderers were gone. Had there been danger still for herself, she could not have felt it; but there was none now as she laid her hand upon the key to enter the bedchamber. At first the lock would not open, as it had been injured in some way by being so roughly shaken when Mendoza had tried it. But Dolores' desperate fingers wound themselves upon the key like little ropes of white silk, slender but very strong, and she wrenched at the thing furiously till it turned. The door flew open, and she stood motionless a moment on the threshold. Mendoza had said that Don John was dead, but she had not quite believed it.

He lay on his back as he had fallen, his feet towards her, his graceful limbs relaxed, one arm beside him, the other thrown back beyond his head, the colourless fingers just bent a little and showing the nervous beauty of the hand. The beautiful young face was white as marble, and the eyes were half open, very dark under the waxen lids. There was one little spot of scarlet on the white satin coat, near the left breast. Dolores saw it all in the bright light of the candles, and she neither moved nor closed her fixed eyes as she gazed. She felt that she was at the end of life; she stood still to see it all and to understand. But though she tried to think, it was as if she had no mind left, no capacity for grasping any new thought, and no power to connect those that had disturbed her brain with the present that stared her in the face. An earthquake might have torn the world open under her feet at that moment, swallowing up the old Alcazar with the living and the dead, and Dolores would have gone down to destruction as she stood, unconscious of her fate, her eyes fixed upon Don John's dead features, her own life already suspended and waiting to follow his. It seemed as if she might stand there till her horror should stop the beating of her own heart, unless something came to rouse her from the stupor she was in.

But gradually a change came over her face, her lids drooped and quivered, her face turned a little upward, and she grasped the doorpost with one hand, lest she should reel and fall. Then, knowing that she could stand no longer, instinct made a last effort upon her; its invisible power thrust her violently forward in a few swift steps, till her strength broke all at once, and she fell and lay almost upon the body of her lover, her face hidden upon his silent breast, one hand seeking his hand, the other pressing his cold forehead.

It was not probable that any one should find her there for a long time. The servants and gentlemen had been dismissed, and until it was known that Don John was dead, no one would come. Even if she could have thought at all, she would not have cared who saw her lying there; but thought was altogether gone now, and there was nothing left but the ancient instinct of the primeval woman mourning her dead mate alone, with long-drawn, hopeless weeping and blinding tears.

They came, too, when she had lain upon his breast a little while and when understanding had wholly ceased and given way to nature. Then her body shook and her breast heaved strongly, almost throwing her upon her side as she lay, and sounds that were hardly human came from her lips; for the first dissolving of a woman's despair into tears is most like the death agony of those who die young in their strength, when the limbs are wrung at the joints and the light breaks in the upturned eyes, when the bosom heaves and would take in the whole world at one breath, when the voice makes sounds of fear that are beyond words and worse to hear than any words could be.

Her weeping was wild at first, measureless and violent, broken by sharp cries that hurt her heart like jagged knives, then strangled to a choking silence again and again, as the merciless consciousness that could have killed, if it had prevailed, almost had her by the throat, but was forced back again with cruel pain by the young life that would not die, though living was agony and death would have been as welcome as air.

Then her loud grief subsided to a lower key, and her voice grew by degrees monotonous and despairing as the turning tide on a quicksand, before bad weather,—not diminished, but deeper drawn within itself; and the low moan came regularly with each breath, while the tears flowed steadily. The first wild tempest had swept by, and the more enduring storm followed in its track.

So she lay a long time weeping; and then strong hands were upon her, lifting her up and dragging her away, without warning and without word. She did not understand, and she fancied herself in the arms of some supernatural being of monstrous strength that was tearing her from what was left of life and love. She struggled senselessly, but she could find no foothold as she was swept through the open door. She gasped for breath, as one does in bad dreams, and bodily fear almost reached her heart through its sevenfold armour of such grief as makes fear ridiculous and turns mortal danger to an empty show. The time had seemed an age since she had fallen upon dead Don John—it had measured but a short few minutes; it seemed as if she were being dragged the whole length of the dim palace as the strong hands bore her along, yet she was only carried from the room to the terrace; and when her eyes could see, she knew that she was in the open air on a stone seat in the moonlight, the cool night breeze fanning her face, while a gentle hand supported her head,—the same hand that had been so masterfully strong a moment earlier. A face she knew and did not dread, though it was unlike other faces, was just at the same height with her own, though the man was standing beside her and she was seated; and the moonlight made very soft shadows in the ill-drawn features of the dwarf, so that his thin and twisted lips were kind and his deep-set eyes were overflowing with human sympathy. When he understood that she saw him and was not fainting, he gently drew away his hand and let her head rest against the stone parapet.

She was dazed still, and the tears veiled her sight. He stood before her, as if guarding her, ready in case she should move and try to leave him. His long arms hung by his sides, but not quite motionless, so that he could have caught her instantly had she attempted to spring past him; and he was wise and guessed rightly what she would do. Her eyes brightened suddenly, and she half rose before he held her again.

"No, no!" she said desperately. "I must go to him—let me go—let me go back!"

But his hands were on her shoulders in an instant, and she was in a vise, forced back to her seat.

"How dare you touch me!" she cried, in the furious anger of a woman beside herself with grief. "How dare you lay hands on me!" she repeated in a rising key, but struggling in vain against his greater strength.

"You would have died, if I had left you there," answered the jester. "And besides, the people will come soon, and they would have found you there, lying on his body, and your good name would have gone forever."

"My name! What does a name matter? Or anything? Oh, let me go! No one must touch him—no hands that do not love him must come near him—let me get up—let me go in again!"

She tried to force the dwarf from her—she would have struck him, crushed him, thrown him from the terrace, if she could. She was strong, too, in her grief; but his vast arms were like iron bars, growing from his misshapen body. His face was very grave and kind, and his eyes more tender than they had ever been in his life.

"No," he said gently. "You must not go. By and by you shall see him again, but not now. Do not try, for I am much stronger than you, and I will not let you go back into the room."

Then her strength relaxed, and she turned to the stone parapet, burying her face in her crossed arms, and her tears came again. For this the jester was glad, knowing that tears quench the first white heat of such sorrows as can burn out the soul and drive the brain raving mad, when life can bear the torture. He stood still before her, watching her and guarding her, but he felt that the worst was past, and that before very long he could lead her away to a place of greater safety. He had indeed taken her as far as he could from Don John's door, and out of sight of it, where the long terrace turned to the westward, and where it was not likely that any one should pass at that hour. It had been the impulse of the moment, and he himself had not recovered from the shock of finding Don John's body lifeless on the floor. He had known nothing of what had happened, but lurking in a corner to see the King pass on his way back from his brother's quarters, he had made sure that Don John was alone, and had gone to his apartment to find out, if he could, how matters had fared, and whether he himself were in further danger or not. He meant to escape from the palace, or to take his own life, rather than be put to the torture, if the King suspected him of being involved in a conspiracy. He was not a common coward, but he feared bodily pain as only such sensitive organizations can, and the vision of the rack and the boot had been before him since he had seen Philip's face at supper. Don John was kind, and would have warned him if he were in danger, and so all might have been well, and by flight or death he might have escaped being torn limb from limb. So he had gone boldly in, and had found the door ajar and had entered the bedchamber, and when he had seen what was there, he would have fled at once, for his own safety, not only because Don John's murder was sure to produce terrible trouble, and many enquiries and trials, in the course of which he was almost sure to be lost, but also for the more immediate reason that if he were seen near the body when it was discovered, he should certainly be put to the question ordinary and extraordinary for his evidence.

But he was not a common coward, and in spite of his own pardonable terror, he thought first of the innocent girl whose name and fame would be gone if she were found lying upon her murdered lover's body, and so far as he could, he saved her before he thought of saving himself, though with infinite difficulty and against her will.

Half paralyzed by her immeasurable grief, she lay against the parapet, and the great sobs came evenly, as if they were counted, shaking her from her head to her waist, and just leaving her a breathing space between each one and the next. The jester felt that he could do nothing. So long as she had seemed unconscious, he had tried to help her a little by supporting her head with his hand and arm, as tenderly as if she had been his own child. So long as she did not know what he was doing, she was only a human being in distress, and a woman, and deep down in the jester's nature there was a marvellous depth of pity for all things that suffered—the deeper and truer because his own sufferings in the world were great. But it was quite different now that she knew where she was and recognized him. She was no longer a woman now, but a high-born lady, one of the Queen's maids of honour, a being infinitely far removed above his sphere, and whose hand he was not worthy to touch. He would have dared to be much more familiar with the King himself than with this young girl whom fate had placed in his keeping for a moment. In the moonlight he watched her, and as he gazed upon her graceful figure and small head and slender, bending arms, it seemed to him that she had come down from an altar to suffer in life, and that it had been almost sacrilege to lay his hands upon her shoulders and keep her from doing her own will. He almost wondered how he had found courage to be so rough and commanding. He was gentle of heart, though it was his trade to make sharp speeches, and there were wonderful delicacies of thought and feeling far down in his suffering cripple's nature.

"Come," he said softly, when he had waited a long time, and when he thought she was growing more quiet. "You must let me take you away, Doña Maria Dolores, for we cannot stay here."

"Take me back to him," she answered. "Let me go back to him!"

"No—to your father—I cannot take you to him. You will be safe there."

Dolores sprang to her feet before the dwarf could prevent her.

"To my father? oh, no, no, no! Never, as long as I live! I will go anywhere, but not to him! Take your hands from me—do not touch me! I am not strong, but I shall kill you if you try to take me to my father!"

Her small hands grasped the dwarfs wrists and wrung them with desperate energy, and she tried to push him away, so that she might pass him. But he resisted her quietly, planting himself in a position of resistance on his short bowed legs, and opposing the whole strength of his great arms to her girlish violence. Her hands relaxed suddenly in despair.

"Not to my father!" she pleaded, in a broken voice. "Oh, please, please—not to my father!"

The jester did not fully understand, but he yielded, for he could not carry her to Mendoza's apartments by force.

"But what can I do to put you in a place of safety?" he asked, in growing distress. "You cannot stay here."

While he was speaking a light figure glided out from the shadows, with outstretched hands, and a low voice called Dolores' name, trembling with terror and emotion. Dolores broke from the dwarf and clasped her sister in her arms.

"Is it true?" moaned Inez. "Is it true? Is he dead?" And her voice broke.

CHAPTER XIV

The courtiers had assembled again in the great throne room after supper, and the stately dancing, for which the court of Spain was even then famous throughout Europe, had begun. The orchestra was placed under the great arch of the central window on a small raised platform draped with velvets and brocades that hung from a railing, high enough to conceal the musicians as they sat, though some of the instruments and the moving bows of the violins could be seen above it.

The masked dancing, if it were dancing at all, which had been general in the days of the Emperor Maximilian, and which had not yet gone out of fashion altogether at the imperial court of Vienna, had long been relegated to the past in Spain, and the beautiful "pavane" dances, of which awkward travesties survive in our day, had been introduced instead. As now, the older ladies of the court withdrew to the sides of the hall, leaving the polished floor free for those who danced, and sets formed themselves in the order of their rank from the foot of the throne dais to the lower end. As now, too, the older and graver men congregated together in outer rooms; and there gaming-tables were set out, and the nobles lost vast sums at games now long forgotten, by the express authorization of the pious Philip, who saw that everything which could injure the fortunes of the grandees must consolidate his own, by depriving them of some of that immense wealth which was an ever-ready element of revolution. He did everything in his power to promote the ruin of the most powerful grandees in the kingdom by encouraging gaming and all imaginable forms of extravagance, and he looked with suspicion and displeasure upon those more prudent men who guarded their riches carefully, as their fathers had done before them. But these were few, for it was a part of a noble's dignity to lose enormous sums of money without the slightest outward sign of emotion or annoyance.

It had been announced that the King and Queen would not return after supper, and the magnificent gravity of the most formal court in the world was a little relaxed when this was known. Between the strains of music, the voices of the courtiers rose in unbroken conversation, and now and then there was a ripple of fresh young laughter that echoed sweetly under the high Moorish vault, and died away just as it rose again from below.

Yet the dancing was a matter of state, and solemn enough, though it was very graceful. Magnificent young nobles in scarlet, in pale green, in straw colour, in tender shades of blue, all satin and silk and velvet and embroidery, led lovely women slowly forward with long and gliding steps that kept perfect time to the music, and turned and went back, and wound mazy figures with the rest, under the waxen light of the waxen torches, and returned to their places with deep curtsies on the one side, and sweeping obeisance on the other. The dresses of the women were richer by far with gold and silver, and pearls and other jewels, than those of the men, but were generally darker in tone, for that was the fashion then. Their skirts were straight and barely touched the floor, being made for a time when dancing was a part of court life, and when every one within certain limits of age was expected to dance well. There was no exaggeration of the ruffle then, nor had the awkward hoop skirt been introduced in Spain. Those were the earlier days of Queen Elizabeth's reign, before Queen Mary was imprisoned; it was the time, indeed, when the rough Bothwell had lately carried her off and married her, after a fashion, with so little ceremony that Philip paid no attention to the marriage at all, and deliberately proposed to make her Don John's wife. The matter was freely talked of on that night by the noble ladies of elder years who gossiped while they watched the dancing.

That was indeed such a court as had not been seen before, nor was ever seen again, whether one count beauty first, or riches and magnificence, or the marvel of splendid ceremony and the faultless grace of studied manners, or even the cool recklessness of great lords and ladies who could lose a fortune at play, as if they were throwing a handful of coin to a beggar in the street.

The Princess of Eboli stood a little apart from the rest, having just returned to the ball-room, and her eyes searched for Dolores in the crowd, though she scarcely expected to see her there. It would have been almost impossible for the girl to put on a court dress in so short a time, though since her father had allowed her to leave her room, she could have gone back to dress if she had chosen. The Princess had rarely been at a loss in her evil life, and had seldom been baffled in anything she had undertaken, since that memorable occasion on which her husband, soon after her marriage, had forcibly shut her up in a convent for several months, in the vain hope of cooling her indomitable temper. But now she was nervous and uncertain of herself. Not only had Dolores escaped her, but Don John had disappeared also, and the Princess had not the least doubt but that the two were somewhere together, and she was very far from being sure that they had not already left the palace. Antonio Perez had informed her that the King had promised not to see Don John that night, and for once she was foolish enough to believe the King's word. Perez came up to her as she was debating what she should do. She told him her thoughts, laughing gaily from time to time, as if she were telling him some very witty story, for she did not wish those who watched them to guess that the conversation was serious. Perez laughed, too, and answered in low tones, with many gestures meant to deceive the court.

"The King did not take my advice," he said. "I had scarcely left him, when he went to Don John's apartments."

"How do you know that?" asked the Princess, with some anxiety.

"He found the door of an inner room locked, and he sent Mendoza to find the key. Fortunately for the old man's feelings it could not be found! He would have had an unpleasant surprise."

"Why?"

"Because his daughter was in the room that was locked," laughed Perez.

"When? How? How long ago was that?"

"Half an hour—not more."

"That is impossible. Half an hour ago Dolores de Mendoza was with me."

"Then there was another lady in the room." Perez laughed again. "Better two than one," he added.

"You are wrong," said the Princess, and her face darkened. "Don John has not so much as deigned to look at any other woman these two years."

"You should know that best," returned the Secretary, with a little malice in his smile.

It was well known in the court that two or three years earlier, during the horrible intrigue that ended in the death of Don Carlos, the Princess of Eboli had done her best to bring Don John of Austria to her feet and had failed notoriously, because he was already in love with Dolores. She was angry now, and the rich colour came into her handsome dark face.

"Don Antonio Perez," she said, "take care! I have made you. I can also unmake you."

Perez assumed an air of simple and innocent surprise, as if he were quite sure that he had said nothing to annoy her, still less to wound her deeply. He believed that she really loved him and that he could play with her as if his own intelligence far surpassed hers. In the first matter he was right, but he was very much mistaken in the second.

"I do not understand," he said. "If I have done anything to offend you, pray forgive my ignorance, and believe in the unchanging devotion of your most faithful slave."

His dark eyes became very expressive as he bowed a little, with a graceful gesture of deprecation. The Princess laughed lightly, but there was still a spark of annoyance in her look.

"Why does Don John not come?" she asked impatiently. "We should have danced together. Something must have happened—can you not find out?"

Others were asking the same question in surprise, for it had been expected that Don John would enter immediately after the supper. His name was heard from end to end of the hall, in every conversation, wherever two or three persons were talking together. It was in the air, like his popularity, everywhere and in everything, and the expectation of his coming produced a sort of tension that was felt by every one. The men grew more witty, the younger women's eyes brightened, though they constantly glanced towards the door of the state apartments by which Don John should enter, and as the men's conversation became more brilliant the women paid less attention to it, for there was hardly one of them who did not hope that Don John might notice her before the evening was over,—there was not one who did not fancy herself a little in love with him, as there was hardly a man there who would not have drawn his sword for him and fought for him with all his heart. Many, though they dared not say so, secretly wished that some evil might befall Philip, and that he might soon die childless, since he had destroyed his only son and only heir, and that Don John might be King in his stead. The Princess of Eboli and Perez knew well enough that their plan would be popular, if they could ever bring it to maturity.

The music swelled and softened, and rose again in those swaying strains that inspire an irresistible bodily longing for rhythmical motion, and which have infinite power to call up all manner of thoughts, passionate, gentle, hopeful, regretful, by turns. In the middle of the hall, more than a hundred dancers moved, swayed, and glided in time with the sound, changed places, and touched hands in the measure, tripped forward and back and sideways, and met and parted again without pause, the colours of their dresses mingling to rich unknown hues in the soft candlelight, as the figure brought many together, and separating into a hundred elements again, when the next steps scattered them again; the jewels in the women's hair, the clasps of diamonds and precious stones at throat, and shoulder, and waist, all moved with an intricate motion, in orbits that crossed and recrossed in the tinted sea of silk, and flashed all at once, as the returning burden of the music brought the dancers to stand and turn at the same beat of the measure. Yet it was all unlike the square dancing of these days, which is either no dancing at all, but a disorderly walk, or else is so stiffly regular and awkward that it makes one think of a squad of recruits exercising on the drill ground. There was not a motion, then, that lacked grace, or ease, or a certain purpose of beauty, nor any, perhaps, that was not a phrase in the allegory of love, from which all dancing is, and was, and always must be, drawn. Swift, slow, by turns, now languorous, now passionate, now full of delicious regret, singing love's triumph, breathing love's fire, sighing in love's despair, the dance and its music were one, so was sight intermingled with sound, and motion a part of both. And at each pause, lips parted and glance sought glance in the light, while hearts found words in the music that answered the language of love. Men laugh at dancing and love it, and women, too, and no one can tell where its charm is, but few have not felt it, or longed to feel it, and its beginnings are very far away in primeval humanity, beyond the reach of theory, unless instinct may explain all simply, as it well may. For light and grace and sweet sound are things of beauty which last for ever, and love is the source of the future and the explanation of the past; and that which can bring into itself both love and melody, and grace and light, must needs be a spell to charm men and women.

There was more than that in the air on that night, for Don John's return had set free that most intoxicating essence of victory, which turns to a mad fire in the veins of a rejoicing people, making the least man of them feel himself a soldier, and a conqueror, and a sharer in undying fame. They had loved him from a child, they had seen him outgrow them in beauty, and skill, and courage, and they had loved him still the more for being the better man; and now he had done a great deed, and had fulfilled and overfilled their greatest expectations, and in an instant he leapt from the favourite's place in their hearts to the hero's height on the altar of their wonder, to be the young god of a nation that loved him. Not a man, on that night, but would have sworn that Don John was braver than Alexander, wiser than Charlemagne, greater than Cæsar himself; not a man but would have drawn his sword to prove it on the body of any who should dare to contradict him,—not a mother was there, who did not pray that her sons might be but ever so little like him, no girl of Spain but dreamt she heard his soft voice speaking low in her ear. Not often in the world's story has a man so young cone such great things as he had done and was to do before his short life was ended; never, perhaps, was any man so honoured by his own people, so trusted, and so loved.

They could talk only of him, wondering more and more that he stayed away from them on such a night, yet sure that he would come, and join the dancing, for as he fought with a skill beyond that of other swordsmen, so he danced with the most surpassing grace. They longed to see him, to look into his face to hear his voice, perhaps to touch his hand; for he was free of manner and gentle to all, and if he came he would go from one to another, and remember each with royal memory, and find kind words for every one. They wanted him among them, they felt a sort of tense desire to see him again, and even to shout for him again, as the vulgar herd did in the streets,—as they themselves had done but an hour ago when he had stood out beside the throne. And still the dancers danced through the endless measures, laughing and talking at each pause, and repeating his name till it was impossible not to hear it, wherever one might be in the hall, and there was no one, old or young, who did not speak it at least once in every five minutes. There was a sort of intoxication in its very sound, and the more they heard it, the more they wished to hear it, coupled with every word of praise that the language possessed. From admiration they rose to enthusiasm, from enthusiasm to a generous patriotic passion in which Spain was the world and Don John was Spain, and all the rest of everything was but a dull and lifeless blank which could have no possible interest for natural people.

Young men, darkly flushed from dancing, swore that whenever Don John should be next sent with an army, they would go, too, and win his battles and share in his immortal glory; and grand, grey men who wore the Golden Fleece, men who had seen great battles in the Emperor's day, stood together and talked of him, and praised God that Spain had another hero of the Austrian house, to strike terror to the heart of France, to humble England at last, and to grasp what little of the world was not already gathered in the hollow of Spain's vast hand.

Antonio Perez and the Princess of Eboli parted and went among the courtiers, listening to all that was to be heard and feeding the fire of enthusiasm, and met again to exchange glances of satisfaction, for they were well pleased with the direction matters were taking, and the talk grew more free from minute to minute, till many, carried away by a force they could not understand and did not seek to question, were openly talking of the succession to the throne, of Philip's apparent ill health, and of the chance that they might before long be doing service to his Majesty King John.

The music ceased again, and the couples dispersed about the hall, to collect again in groups. There was a momentary lull in the talk, too, as often happens when a dance is just over, and at that moment the great door beside the throne was opened, with a noise that attracted the attention of all; and all believed that Don John was returning, while all eyes were fixed upon the entrance to catch the first glimpse of him, and every one pronounced his name at once in short, glad tones of satisfaction.

"Don John is coming! It is Don John of Austria! Don John is there!"

It was a most a universal cry of welcome. An instant later a dead silence followed as a chamberlain's clear voice announced the royal presence, and King Philip advanced upon the platform of the throne. For several seconds not a sound broke the stillness, and he came slowly forward followed by half a dozen nobles in immediate attendance upon him. But though he must have heard his brother's name in the general chorus of voices as soon as the door had been thrown open, he seemed by no means disconcerted; on the contrary, he smiled almost affably, and his eyes were less fixed than usual, as he looked about him with something like an air of satisfaction. As soon as it was clear that he meant to descend the steps to the floor of the hall, the chief courtiers came forward, Ruy Gomez de Silva, Prince of Eboli, Alvarez de Toledo, the terrible Duke of Alva, the Dukes of

Medina Sidonia and of Infantado, Don Antonio Perez the chief Secretary, the Ambassadors of Queen Elizabeth of England and of France, and a dozen others, bowing so low that the plumes of their hats literally touched the floor beside them.

"Why is there no dancing?" asked Philip, addressing Ruy Gomez, with a smile.

The Minister explained that one of the dances was but just over.

"Let there be more at once," answered the King. "Let there be dancing and music without end to-night. We have good reason to keep the day with rejoicing, since the war is over, and Don John of Austria has come back in triumph."

The command was obeyed instantly, as Ruy Gomez made a sign to the leader of the musicians, who was watching him intently in expectation of the order. The King smiled again as the long strain broke the silence and the conversation began again all through the hall, though in a far more subdued tone than before, and with much more caution. Philip turned to the English Ambassador.

"It is a pity," he said, "that my sister of England cannot be here with us on such a night as this. We saw no such sights in London in my day, my lord."

"There have been changes since then, Sire," answered the Ambassador. "The Queen is very much inclined to magnificence and to great entertainments, and does not hesitate to dance herself, being of a very vital and pleasant temper. Nevertheless, your Majesty's court is by far the most splendid in the world."

"There you are right, my lord!" exclaimed the King. "And for that matter, we have beauty also, such as is found nowhere else."

The Princess of Eboli was close by, waiting for him to speak to her, and his eyes fixed themselves upon her face with a sort of cold and snakelike admiration, to which she was well accustomed, but which even now made her nervous. The Ambassador was not slow to take up the cue of flattery, for Englishmen still knew how to flatter in Elizabeth's day.

"The inheritance of universal conquest," he said, bowing and smiling to the Princess. "Even the victories of Don John of Austria must yield to that."

The Princess laughed carelessly. Had Perez spoken the words, she would have frowned, but the King's eyes were watching her.

"His Highness has fled from the field without striking a blow," she said. "We have not seen him this evening." As she spoke she met the King's gaze with a look of enquiry.

"Don John will be here presently, no doubt," he said, as if answering a question. "Has he not been here at all since supper?"

"No, Sire; though every one expected him to come at once."

"That is strange," said Philip, with perfect self-possession. "He is fond of dancing, too—no one can dance better than he. Have you ever known a man so roundly gifted as my brother, my lord?"

"A most admirable prince," answered the Ambassador, gravely and without enthusiasm, for he feared that the King was about to speak of his brother's possible marriage with Queen Mary of Scots.

"And a most affectionate and gentle nature," said Philip, musing. "I remember from the time when he was a boy that every one loved him and praised him, and yet he is not spoiled. He is always the same. He is my brother—how often have I wished for such a son! Well, he may yet be King. Who should, if not he, when I am gone?"

"Your Majesty need not anticipate such a frightful calamity!" cried the Princess fervently, though she was at that moment weighing the comparative advantage of several mortal diseases by which, in appearance at least, his exit from the world might be accelerated.

"Life is very uncertain, Princess," observed the King. "My lord," he turned to the English Ambassador again, "do you consider melons indigestible in England? I have lately heard much against them."

"A melon is a poor thing, of a watery constitution, your Majesty," replied the Ambassador glibly. "There can be but little sustenance in a hollow piece of water that is sucked from a marsh and enclosed in a green rind. To tell the truth, I hear it ill spoken of by our physicians, but I cannot well speak of the matter, for I never ate one in my life, and please God I never will!"

"Why not!" enquired the King, who took an extraordinary interest in the subject. "You fear them, then! Yet you seem to be exceedingly strong and healthy."

"Sire, I have sometimes drunk a little water for my stomach's sake, but I will not eat it."

The King smiled pleasantly.

"How wise the English are!" he said. "We may yet learn much of them."

Philip turned away from the Ambassador and watched the dance in silence. The courtiers now stood in a wide half circle to the right and left of him as he faced the hall, and the dancers passed backwards and forwards across the open space. His slow eyes followed one figure without seeing the rest. In the set nearest to him a beautiful girl was dancing with one of Don John's officers. She was of the rarest type of Andalusian beauty, tall, pliant, and slenderly strong, with raven's-wing hair and splendidly languorous eyes, her creamy cheek as smooth as velvet, and a mouth like a small ripe fruit. As she moved she bent from the waist as easily and naturally as a child, and every movement followed a new curve of beauty from her white throat to the small arched foot that darted into sight as she stepped forward now and then, to disappear instantly under the shadow of the gold-embroidered skirt. As she glanced towards the King, her shadowy lids half hid her eyes and the long black lashes almost brushed her cheek. Philip could not look away from her.

But suddenly there was a stir among the courtiers, and a shadow came between the King and the vision he was watching. He started a little, annoyed by the interruption and at being rudely reminded of what had happened half an hour earlier, for the shadow was cast by Mendoza, tall and grim in his armour, his face as grey as his grey beard, and his eyes hard and fixed. Without bending, like a soldier on parade, he stood there, waiting by force of habit until Philip should speak to him. The King's brows bent together, and he almost unconsciously raised one hand to signify that the music should cease. It stopped in the midst of a bar, leaving the dancers at a standstill in their measure, and all the moving sea of light and colour and gleaming jewels was arrested instantly in its motion, while every look was turned towards the King. The change from sound to silence, from motion to immobility, was so sudden that every one was startled, as if some frightful accident had happened, or as if an earthquake had shaken the Alcazar to its deep foundation.

Mendoza's harsh voice spoke out alone in accents that were heard to the end of the hall.

"Don John of Austria is dead! I, Mendoza, have killed him unarmed."

It was long before a sound was heard, before any man or woman in the hall had breath to utter a word. Philip's voice was heard first.

"The man is mad," he said, with undisturbed coolness. "See to him, Perez."

"No, no!" cried Mendoza. "I am not mad. I have killed Don John. You shall find him in his room as he fell, with the wound in his breast."

One moment more the silence lasted, while Philip's stony face never moved. A single woman's shriek rang out first, long, ear-piercing, agonized, and then, without warning, a cry went up such as the old hall had never heard before. It was a bad cry to hear, for it clamoured for blood to be shed for blood, and though it was not for him, Philip turned livid and shrank back a step. But Mendoza stood like a rock, waiting to be taken.

In another moment furious confusion filled the hall. From every side at once rose women's cries, and the deep shouts of angry men, and high, clear yells of rage and hate. The men pushed past the ladies of the court to the front, and some came singly, but a serried rank moved up from behind, pushing the others before them.

"Kill him! Kill him at the King's feet! Kill him where he stands!"

And suddenly something made blue flashes of light high over the heads of all; a rapier was out and wheeled in quick circles from a pliant wrist. An officer of Mendoza's guard had drawn it, and a dozen more were in the air in an instant, and then daggers by scores, keen, short, and strong, held high at arm's length, each shaking with the fury of the hand that held it.

"Sangre! Sangre!"

Some one had screamed out the wild cry of the Spanish soldiers—'Blood! Blood!'—and the young men took it up in a mad yell, as they pushed forwards furiously, while the few who stood in front tried to keep a space open round the King and Mendoza.

The old man never winced, and disdained to turn his head, though he heard the cry of death behind him, and the quick, soft sound of daggers drawn from leathern sheaths, and the pressing of men who would be upon him in another moment to tear him limb from limb with their knives.

Tall old Ruy Gomez had stepped forwards to stem the tide of death, and beside him the English Ambassador, quietly determined to see fair play or to be hurt himself in preventing murder.

"Back!" thundered Ruy Gomez, in a voice that was heard. "Back, I say! Are you gentlemen of Spain, or are you executioners yourselves that you would take this man's blood? Stand back!"

"Sangre! Sangre!" echoed the hall.

"Then take mine first!" shouted the brave old Prince, spreading his short cloak out behind him with his hands to cover Mendoza more completely.

But still the crowd of splendid young nobles surged up to him, and back a little, out of sheer respect for his station and his old age, and forwards again, dagger in hand, with blazing eyes.

"Sangre! Sangre! Sangre!" they cried, blind with fury.

But meanwhile, the guards filed in, for the prudent Perez had hastened to throw wide the doors and summon them. Weapons in hand and ready, they formed a square round the King and Mendoza and Ruy Gomez, and at the sight of their steel caps and breastplates and long-tasselled halberds, the yells of the courtiers subsided a little and turned to deep curses and execrations and oaths of vengeance. A high voice pierced the low roar, keen and cutting as a knife, but no one knew whose it was, and Philip almost reeled as he heard the words.

"Remember Don Carlos! Don John of Austria is gone to join Don Carlos and Queen Isabel!"

Again a deadly silence fell upon the multitude, and the King leaned on Perez' arm. Some woman's hate had bared the truth in a flash, and there were hundreds of hands in the hall that were ready to take his life instead of Mendoza's; and he knew it, and was afraid.

CHAPTER XV

The agonized cry that had been first heard in the hall had come from Inez's lips. When she had fled from her father, she had regained her hiding-place in the gallery above the throne room. She would not go to her own room, for she felt that rest was out of the question while Dolores was in such danger; and yet there would have been no object in going to Don John's door again, to risk being caught by her father or met by the King himself. She had therefore determined to let an hour pass before attempting another move. So she slipped into the gallery again, and sat upon the little wooden bench that had been made for the Moorish women in old times; and she listened to the music and the sound of the dancers' feet far below, and to the hum of voices, in which she often distinguished the name of Don John. She had heard all,—the cries when it was thought that he was coming, the chamberlain's voice announcing the King, and then the change of key in the sounds that had followed. Lastly, she had heard plainly every syllable of her father's speech, so that when she realized what it meant, she had shrieked aloud, and had fled from the gallery to find her sister if she could, to find Don John's body most certainly where it lay on the marble floor, with the death wound at the breast. Her instinct—she could not have reasoned then—told her that her father must have found the lovers together, and that in sudden rage he had stabbed Don John, defenceless.

Dolores' tears answered her sister's question well enough when the two girls were clasped in one another's arms at last. There was not a doubt left in the mind of either. Inez spoke first. She said that she had hidden in the gallery.

"Our father must have come in some time after the King," she said, in broken sentences, and almost choking. "Suddenly the music stopped. I could hear every word. He said that he had done it,—that he had murdered Don John,—and then I ran here, for I was afraid he had killed you, too."

"Would God he had!" cried Dolores. "Would to Heaven that I were dead beside the man I love!"

"And I!" moaned Inez pitifully, and she began to sob wildly, as Dolores had sobbed at first.

But Dolores was silent now, as if she had shed all her tears at once, and had none left. She held her sister in her arms, and soothed her almost unconsciously, as if she had been a little child. But her own thoughts were taking shape quickly, for she was strong; and after the first paroxysm of her grief, she saw the immediate future as clearly as the present. When she spoke again she had the mastery of her voice, and it was clear and low.

"You say that our father confessed before the whole court that he had murdered Don John?" she said, with a question. "What happened then? Did the King speak? Was our father arrested? Can you remember?"

"I only heard loud cries," sobbed Inez. "I came to you—as quickly as I could—I was afraid."

"We shall never see our father again—unless we see him on the morning when he is to die."

"Dolores! They will not kill him, too?" In sudden and greater fear than before, Inez ceased sobbing.

"He will die on the scaffold," answered Dolores, in the same clear tone, as if she were speaking in a dream, or of things that did not come near her. "There is no pardon possible. He will die to-morrow or the next day."

The present truth stood out in all its frightful distinctness. Whoever had done the murder—since Mendoza had confessed it, he would be made to die for it,—of that she was sure. She could not have guessed what had really happened; and though the evidence of the sounds she had heard through the door would have gone to show that Philip had done the deed himself, yet there had been no doubt about Mendoza's words, spoken to the King alone over Don John's dead body, and repeated before the great assembly in the ball-room. If she guessed at an explanation, it was that her father, entering the bedchamber during the quarrel, and supposing from what he saw that Don John was about to attack the King, had drawn and killed the Prince without hesitation. The only thing quite clear was that Mendoza was to suffer, and seemed strangely determined to suffer, for what he had or had not done. The dark shadow of the scaffold rose before Dolores' eyes.

It had seemed impossible that she could be made to bear more than she had borne that night, when she had fallen upon Don John's body to weep her heart out for her dead love. But she saw that there was more to bear, and dimly she guessed that there might be something for her to do. There was Inez first, and she must be cared for and placed in safety, for she was beside herself with grief. It was only on that afternoon by the window that Dolores had guessed the blind girl's secret, which Inez herself hardly suspected even now, though she was half mad with grief and utterly broken-hearted.

Dolores felt almost helpless, but she understood that she and her sister were henceforth to be more really alone in what remained of life than if they had been orphans from their earliest childhood. The vision of the convent, that had been unbearable but an hour since, held all her hope of peace and safety now, unless her father could be saved from his fate by some miracle of heaven. But that was impossible. He had given himself up as if he were determined to die. He had been out of his mind, beside himself, stark mad, in his fear that Don John might bring harm upon his daughter. That was why he had killed him—there could be no other reason, unless he had guessed that she was in the locked room, and had judged her then and at once, and forever. The thought had not crossed her mind till then, and it was a new torture now, so that she shrank under it as under a bodily blow; and her grasp tightened violently upon her sister's arm, rousing the half-fainting girl again to the full consciousness of pain.

It was no wonder that Mendoza should have done such a deed, since he had believed her ruined and lost to honour beyond salvation. That explained all. He had guessed that she had been long with Don John, who had locked her hastily into the inner room to hide her from the King. Had the King been Don John, had she loved Philip as she loved his brother, her father would have killed his sovereign as unhesitatingly, and would have suffered any death without flinching. She believed that, and there was enough of his nature in herself to understand it.

She was as innocent as the blind girl who lay in her arms, but suddenly it flashed upon her that no one would believe it, since her own father would not, and that her maiden honour and good name were gone for ever, gone with her dead lover, who alone could have cleared her before the world. She cared little for the court now, but she cared tenfold more earnestly for her father's thought of her, and she knew him and the terrible tenacity of his conviction when he believed himself to be right. He had proved that by what he had done. Since she understood all, she no longer doubted that he had killed Don John with the fullest intention, to avenge her, and almost knowing that she was within hearing, as indeed she had been. He had taken a royal life in atonement for her honour, but he was to give his own, and was to die a shameful death on the scaffold, within a few hours, or, at the latest, within a few days, for her sake.

Then she remembered how on that afternoon she had seen tears in his eyes, and had heard the tremor in his voice when he had said that she was everything to him, that she had been all his life since her mother had died—he had proved that, too; and though he had killed the man she loved, she shrank from herself again as she thought what he must have suffered in her dishonour. For it was nothing else. There was neither man nor woman nor girl in Spain who would believe her innocent against such evidence. The world might have believed Don John, if he had lived, because the world had loved him and trusted him, and could never have heard falsehood in his voice; but it would not believe her though she were dying, and though she should swear upon the most sacred and true things. The world would turn from her with an unbelieving laugh, and she was to be left alone in her dishonour, and people would judge that she was not even a fit companion for her blind sister in their solitude. The King would send her to Las Huelgas, or to some other distant convent of a severe order, that she might wear out her useless life in grief and silence and penance as quickly as possible. She bowed her head. It was too hard to bear.

Inez was more quiet now, and the two sat side by side in mournful silence, leaning against the parapet. They had forgotten the dwarf, and he had disappeared, waiting, perhaps, in the shadow at a distance, in case he might be of use to them. But if he was within hearing, they did not see him. At last Inez spoke, almost in a whisper, as if she were in the presence of the dead.

"Were you there, dear?" she asked. "Did you see?"

"I was in the next room," Dolores answered. "I could not see, but I heard. I heard him fall," she added almost inaudibly, and choking.

Inez shuddered and pressed nearer to her sister, leaning against her, but she did not begin to sob again. She was thinking.

"Can we not help our father, at least?" she asked presently. "Is there nothing we can say, or do? We ought to help him if we can, Dolores—though he did it."

"I would save him with my life, if I could. God knows, I would! He was mad when he struck the blow. He did it for my sake, because he thought Don John had ruined my good name. And we should have been married the day after to-morrow! God of heaven, have mercy!"

Her grief took hold of her again, like a material power, shaking her from head to foot, and bowing her down upon herself and wringing her hands together, so that Inez, calmer than she, touched her gently and tried to comfort her without any words, for there were none to say, since nothing mattered now, and life was over at its very beginning. Little by little the sharp agony subsided to dull pain once more, and Dolores sat upright. But Inez was thinking still, and even in her sorrow and fright she was gathering all her innocent ingenuity to her aid.

"Is there no way?" she asked, speaking more to herself than to her sister. "Could we not say that we were there, that it was not our father but some one else? Perhaps some one would believe us. If we told the judges that we were quite, quite sure that he did not do it, do you not think—but then," she checked herself—"then it could only have been the King."

"Only the King himself," echoed Dolores, half unconsciously, and in a dreamy tone.

"That would be terrible," said Inez. "But we could say that the King was not there, you know—that it was some one else, some one we did not know—"

Dolores rose abruptly from the seat and laid her hand upon the parapet steadily, as if an unnatural strength had suddenly grown up in her. Inez went on speaking, confusing herself in the details she was trying to put together to make a plan, and losing the thread of her idea as she attempted to build up falsehoods, for she was truthful as their father was. But Dolores did not hear her.

"You can do nothing, child," she said at last, in a firm tone. "But I may. You have made me think of something that I may do—it is just possible—it may help a little. Let me think."

Inez waited in silence for her to go on, and Dolores stood as motionless as a statue, contemplating in thought the step she meant to take if it offered the slightest hope of saving her father. The thought was worthy of her, but the sacrifice was great even then. She had not believed that the world still held anything with which she would not willingly part, but there was one thing yet. It might be taken from her, though her father had slain Don John of Austria to save it, and was to die for it himself. She could give it before she could be robbed of it, perhaps, and it might buy his life. She could still forfeit her good name of her own free will, and call herself what she was not. In words she could give her honour to the dead man, and the dead could not rise up and deny her nor refuse the gift. And it seemed to her that when the people should hear her, they would believe her, seeing that it was her shame, a shame such as no maiden who had honour left would bear before the world. But it was hard to do. For honour was her last and only possession now that all was taken from her.

It was not the so-called honour of society, either, based on long-forgotten traditions, and depending on convention for its being—not the sort of honour within which a man may ruin an honest woman and suffer no retribution, but which decrees that he must take his own life if he cannot pay a debt of play made on his promise to a friend, which allows him to lie like a cheat, but ordains that he must give or require satisfaction of blood for the imaginary insult of a hasty word—the honour which is to chivalry what black superstition is to the true Christian faith, which compares with real courage and truth and honesty, as an ape compares with a man. It was not that, and Dolores knew it, as every maiden knows it; for the honour of woman is the fact on which the whole world turns, and has turned and will turn to the end of things; but what is called the honour of society has been a fiction these many centuries, and though it came first of a high parentage, of honest thought wedded to brave deed, and though there are honourable men yet, these are for the most part the few who talk least loudly about honour's code, and the belief they hold has come to be a secret and a persecuted faith, at which the common gentleman thinks fit to laugh lest some one should presume to measure him by it and should find him wanting.

Dolores did not mean to hesitate, after she had decided what to do. But she could not avoid the struggle, and it was long and hard, though she saw the end plainly before her and did not waver. Inez did not understand and kept silence while it lasted.

It was only a word to say, but it was the word which would be repeated against her as long as she lived, and which nothing she could ever say or do afterwards could take back when it had once been spoken—it would leave the mark that a lifetime could not efface. But she meant to speak it. She could not see what her father would see, that he would rather die, justly or unjustly, than let his daughter be dishonoured before the world. That was a part of a man's code, perhaps, but it should not hinder her from saving her father's life, or trying to, at whatever cost. What she was fighting against was something much harder to understand in herself. What could it matter now, that the world should think her fallen from her maiden estate? The world was nothing to her, surely. It held nothing, it meant nothing, it was nothing. Her world had been her lover, and he lay dead in his room. In heaven, he knew that she was innocent, as he was himself, and he would see that she was going to accuse herself that she might save her father. In heaven, he had forgiven his murderer, and he would understand. As for the world and what it said, she knew that she must leave it instantly, and go from the confession she was about to make to the convent where she was to die, and whence her spotless soul would soon be wafted away to join her true lover beyond the earth. There was no reason why she should find it hard to do, and yet it was harder than anything she had ever dreamed of doing. But she was fighting the deepest and strongest instinct of woman's nature, and the fight went hard.

She fancied the scene, the court, the grey-haired nobles, the fair and honourable women, the brave young soldiers, the thoughtless courtiers, the whole throng she was about to face, for she meant to speak before them all, and to her own shame. She was as white as marble, but when she thought of what was coming the blood sprang to her face and tingled in her forehead, and she felt her eyes fall and her proud head bend, as the storm of humiliation descended upon her. She could hear beforehand the sounds that would follow her words, the sharp, short laugh of jealous women who hated her, the murmur of surprise among the men. Then the sea of faces would seem to rise and fall before her in waves, the lights would dance, her cheeks would burn like flames, and she would grow dizzy. That would be the end. Afterwards she could go out alone. Perhaps the women would shrink from her, no man would be brave enough to lead her kindly from the room. Yet all that she would bear, for the mere hope of saving her father. The worst, by far the worst and hardest to endure, would be something within herself, for which she had neither words nor true understanding, but which was more real than anything she could define, for it was in the very core of her heart and in the secret of her soul, a sort of despairing shame of herself and a desolate longing for something she could never recover.

She closed her tired eyes and pressed her hand heavily upon the stone coping of the parapet. It was the supreme effort, and when she looked down at Inez again she knew that she should live to the end of the ordeal without wavering.

"I am going down to the throne room," she said, very quietly and gently. "You had better go to our apartment, dear, and wait for me there. I am going to try and save our father's life—do not ask me how. It will not take long to say what I have to say, and then I will come to you."

Inez had risen now, and was standing beside her, laying a hand upon her arm.

"Let me come, too," she said. "I can help you, I am sure I can help you."

"No," answered Dolores, with authority. "You cannot help me, dearest, and it would hurt you, and you must not come."

"Then I will stay here," said Inez sorrowfully. "I shall be nearer to him," she added under her breath.

"Stay here—yes. I will come back to you, and then—then we will go in together, and say a prayer— his soul can hear us still—we will go and say good-by to him—together."

Her voice was almost firm, and Inez could not see the agony in her white face. Then Dolores clasped her in her arms and kissed her forehead and her blind eyes very lovingly, and pressed her head to her own shoulders and patted it and smoothed the girl's dark hair.

"I will come back," she said, "and, Inez—you know the truth, my darling. Whatever evil they may say of me after to-night, remember that I have said it of myself for our father's sake, and that it is not true."

"No one will believe it," answered Inez. "They will not believe anything bad of you."

"Then our father must die."

Dolores kissed her once more and made her sit down, then turned and went away. She walked quickly along the corridors and descended the second staircase, to enter the throne room by the side door reserved for the officers of the household and the maids of honour. She walked swiftly, her head erect, one hand holding the folds of her cloak pressed to her bosom, and the other, nervously clenched, and hanging down, as if she were expecting to strike a blow.

She reached the door, and for a moment her heart stopped beating, and her eyes closed. She heard many loud voices within, and she knew that most of the court must still be assembled. It was better that all the world should hear her—even the King, if he were still there. She pushed the door open and went in by the familiar way, letting the dark cloak that covered her court dress fall to the ground as she passed the threshold. Half a dozen young nobles, grouped near the entrance, made way for her to pass.

When they recognized her, their voices dropped suddenly, and they stared after her in astonishment that she should appear at such a time. She was doubtless in ignorance of what had happened, they thought. As for the throng in the hall, there was no restraint upon their talk now, and words were spoken freely which would have been high treason half an hour earlier. There was the noise, the tension, the ceaseless talking, the excited air, that belong to great palace revolutions.

The press was closer near the steps of the throne, where the King and Mendoza had stood, for after they had left the hall, surrounded and protected by the guards, the courtiers had crowded upon one another, and those near the further door and outside it in the outer apartments had pressed in till there was scarcely standing room on the floor of the hall. Dolores found it hard to advance. Some made way for her with low exclamations of surprise, but others, not looking to see who she was, offered a passive resistance to her movements.

"Will you kindly let me pass?" she asked at last, in a gentle tone, "I am Dolores de Mendoza."

At the name the group that barred her passage started and made way, and going through she came upon the Prince of Eboli, not far from the steps of the throne. The English Ambassador, who meant to stay as long as there was anything for him to observe, was still by the Prince's side. Dolores addressed the latter without hesitation.

"Don Ruy Gomez," she said, "I ask your help. My father is innocent, and I can prove it. But the court must hear me—every one must hear the truth. Will you help me? Can you make them listen?"

Ruy Gomez looked down at Dolores' pale and determined features in courteous astonishment.

"I am at your service," he answered. "But what are you going to say? The court is in a dangerous mood to-night."

"I must speak to all," said Dolores. "I am not afraid. What I have to say cannot be said twice—not even if I had the strength. I can save my father—"

"Why not go to the King at once?" argued the Prince, who feared trouble.

"For the love of God, help me to do as I wish!" Dolores grasped his arm, and spoke with an effort. "Let me tell them all, how I know that my father is not guilty of the murder. After that take me to the King if you will."

She spoke very earnestly, and he no longer opposed her. He knew the temper of the court well enough, and was sure that whatever proved Mendoza innocent would be welcome just then, and though he was far too loyal to wish the suspicion of the deed to be fixed upon the King, he was too just not to desire Mendoza to be exculpated if he were innocent.

"Come with me," he said briefly, and he took Dolores by the hand, and led her up the first three steps of the platform, so that she could see over the heads of all present.

It was no time to think of court ceremonies or customs, for there was danger in the air. Ruy Gomez did not stop to make any long ceremony. Drawing himself up to his commanding height, he held up his white gloves at arm's length to attract the attention of the courtiers, and in a few moments there was silence. They seemed an hour of torture to Dolores. Ruy Gomez raised his voice.

"Grandees! The daughter of Don Diego de Mendoza stands here at my side to prove to you that he is innocent of Don John of Austria's death!"

The words had hardly left his lips when a shout went up, like a ringing cheer. But again he raised his hand.

"Hear Doña Maria Dolores de Mendoza!" he cried.

Then he stepped a little away from Dolores, and looked towards her. She was dead white, and her lips trembled. There was an almost glassy look in her eyes, and still she pressed one hand to her bosom, and the other hung by her side, the fingers twitching nervously against the folds of her skirt. A few seconds passed before she could speak.

"Grandees of Spain!" she began, and at the first words she found strength in her voice so that it reached the ends of the hall, clear and vibrating. The silence was intense, as she proceeded.

"My father has accused himself of a fearful crime. He is innocent. He would no more have raised his hand against Don John of Austria than against the King's own person. I cannot tell why he wishes to sacrifice his life by taking upon himself the guilt. But this I know. He did not do the deed. You ask me how I know that, how I can prove it? I was there, I, Dolores de Mendoza, his daughter, was there unseen in my lover's chamber when he was murdered. While he was alive I gave him all, my heart, my soul, my maiden honour; and I was there to-night, and had been with him long. But now that he is dead, I will pay for my father's life with my dishonour. He must not die, for he is innocent. Grandees of Spain, as you are men of honour, he must not die, for he is one of you, and this foul deed was not his."

She ceased, her lids drooped till her eyes were half closed and she swayed a little as she stood. Roy Gomez made one long stride and held her, for he thought she was fainting. But she bit her lips, and forced her eyes to open and face the crowd again.

"That is all," she said in a low voice, but distinctly, "It is done. I am a ruined woman. Help me to go out."

The old Prince gently led her down the steps. The silence had lasted long after she had spoken, but people were beginning to talk again in lower tones. It was as she had foreseen it. She heard a scornful woman's laugh, and as she passed along, she saw how the older ladies shrank from her and how the young ones eyed her with a look of hard curiosity, as if she were some wild creature, dangerous to approach, though worth seeing from a distance.

But the men pressed close to her as she passed, and she heard them tell each other that she was a brave woman who could dare to save her father by such means, and there were quick applauding words as she passed, and one said audibly that he could die for a girl who had such a true heart, and another answered that he would marry her if she could forget Don John. And they did not speak without respect, but in earnest, and out of the fulness of their admiration.

At last she was at the door, and she paused to speak before going out.

"Have I saved his life?" she asked, looking up to the old Prince's kind face. "Will they believe me?"

"They believe you," he answered. "But your father's life is in the King's hands. You should go to his Majesty without wasting time. Shall I go with you? He will see you, I think, if I ask it."

"Why should I tell the King?" asked Dolores. "He was there—he saw it all—he knows the truth."

She hardly realized what she was saying.

CHAPTER XVI

Ruy Gomez was as loyal, in his way, as Mendoza himself, but his loyalty was of a very different sort, for it was tempered by a diplomatic spirit which made it more serviceable on ordinary occasions, and its object was altogether a principle rather than a person. Mendoza could not conceive of monarchy, in its abstract, without a concrete individuality represented by King Philip; but Ruy Gomez could not imagine the world without the Spanish monarchy, though he was well able to gauge his sovereign's weaknesses and to deplore his crimes. He himself was somewhat easily deceived, as good men often are, and it was he who had given the King his new secretary, Antonio Perez; yet from the moment when Mendoza had announced Don John's death, he had been convinced that the deed had either been done by Philip himself or by his orders, and that Mendoza had bravely sacrificed himself to shield his master. What Dolores had said only confirmed his previous opinion, so far as her father's innocence was at stake. As for her own confession, he believed it, and in spite of himself he could not help admiring the girl's heroic courage. Dolores might have been in reality ten times worse than she had chosen to represent herself; she would still have been a model of all virtue compared with his own wife, though he did not know half of the Princess's doings, and was certainly ignorant of her relations with the King.

He was not at all surprised when Dolores told him at the door that Philip knew the truth about the supposed murder, but he saw how dangerous it might be for Dolores to say as much to others of the court. She wished to go away alone, as she had come, but he insisted on going with her.

"You must see his Majesty," he said authoritatively. "I will try to arrange it at once. And I entreat you to be discreet, my dear, for your father's sake, if not for any other reason. You have said too much already. It was not wise of you, though it showed amazing courage. You are your father's own daughter in that—he is one of the bravest men I ever knew in my life."

"It is easy to be brave when one is dead already!" said Dolores, in low tones.

"Courage, my dear, courage!" answered the old Prince, in a fatherly tone, as they went along. "You are not as brave as you think, since you talk of death. Your life is not over yet."

"There is little left of it. I wish it were ended already."

She could hardly speak, for an inevitable and overwhelming reaction had followed on the great effort she had made. She put out her hand and caught her companion's arm for support. He led her quickly to the small entrance of the King's apartments, by which it was his privilege to pass in. They reached a small waiting-room where there were a few chairs and a marble table, on which two big wax candles were burning. Dolores sank into a seat, and leaned back, closing her eyes, while Ruy Gomez went into the antechamber beyond and exchanged a few words with the chamberlain on duty. He came back almost immediately.

"Your father is alone with the King," he said. "We must wait."

Dolores scarcely heard what he said, and did not change her position nor open her eyes. The old man looked at her, sighed, and sat down near a brazier of wood coals, over which he slowly warmed his transparent hands, from time to time turning his rings slowly on his fingers, as if to warm them, too. Outside, the chamberlain in attendance walked slowly up and down, again and again passing the open door, through which he glanced at Dolores' face. The antechamber was little more than a short, broad corridor, and led to the King's study. This corridor had other doors, however, and it was through it that the King's private rooms communicated with the hall of the royal apartments.

As Ruy Gomez had learned, Mendoza was with Philip, but not alone. The old officer was standing on one side of the room, erect and grave, and King Philip sat opposite him, in a huge chair, his still eyes staring at the fire that blazed in the vast chimney, and sent sudden flashes of yellow through the calm atmosphere of light shed by a score of tall candles. At a table on one side sat Antonio Perez, the Secretary. He was provided with writing-materials and appeared to be taking down the conversation as it proceeded. Philip asked a question from time to time, which Mendoza answered in a strange voice unlike his own, and between the questions there were long intervals of silence.

"You say that you had long entertained feelings of resentment against his Highness," said the King, "You admit that, do you?"

"I beg your Majesty's pardon. I did not say resentment. I said that I had long looked upon his Highness's passion for my daughter with great anxiety."

"Is that what he said, Perez?" asked Philip, speaking to the Secretary without looking at him. "Read that."

"He said: I have long resented his Highness's admiration for my daughter," answered Perez, reading from his notes.

"You see," said the King. "You resented it. That is resentment. I was right. Be careful, Mendoza, for your words may be used against you to-morrow. Say precisely what you mean, and nothing but what you mean."

Mendoza inclined his head rather proudly, for he detested Antonio Perez, and it appeared to him that the King was playing a sort of comedy for the Secretary's benefit. It seemed an unworthy interlude in what was really a solemn tragedy.

"Why did you resent his Highness's courtship of your daughter?" enquired Philip presently, continuing his cross-examination.

"Because I never believed that there could be a real marriage," answered Mendoza boldly. "I believed that my child must become the toy and plaything of Don John of Austria, or else that if his Highness married her, the marriage would soon be declared void, in order that he might marry a more important personage."

"Set that down," said the King to Perez, in a sharp tone. "Set that down exactly. It is important." He waited till the Secretary's pen stopped before he went on. His next question came suddenly.

"How could a marriage consecrated by our holy religion ever be declared null and void?"

"Easily enough, if your Majesty wished it," answered Mendoza unguardedly, for his temper was slowly heating.

"Write down that answer, Perez. In other words, Mendoza, you think that I have no respect for the sacrament of marriage, which I would at any time cause to be revoked to suit my political purposes. Is that what you think?"

"I did not say that, Sire. I said that even if Don John married my daughter—"

"I know quite well what you said," interrupted the King suavely. "Perez has got every word of it on paper."

The Secretary's bad black eyes looked up from his writing, and he slowly nodded as he looked at Mendoza. He understood the situation perfectly, though the soldier was far too honourable to suspect the truth.

"I have confessed publicly that I killed Don John defenceless," he said, in rough tones. "Is not that enough?"

"Oh, no!" Philip almost smiled, "That is not enough. We must also know why you committed such an abominable crime. You do not seem to understand that in taking your evidence here myself, I am sparing you the indignity of an examination before a tribunal, and under torture—in all probability. You ought to be very grateful, my dear Mendoza."

"I thank your Majesty," said the brave old soldier coldly.

"That is right. So we know that your hatred of his Highness was of long standing, and you had probably determined some time ago that you would murder him on his return." The King paused a moment and then continued. "Do you deny that on this very afternoon you swore that if Don John attempted to see your daughter, you would kill him at once?"

Mendoza was taken by surprise, and his haggard eyes opened wide as he stared at Philip.

"You said that, did you not?" asked the King, insisting upon the point. "On your honour, did you say it?"

"Yes, I said that," answered Mendoza at last. "But how did your Majesty know that I did?"

The King's enormous under lip thrust itself forward, and two ugly lines of amusement were drawn in his colourless cheeks. His jaw moved slowly, as if he were biting something of which he found the taste agreeable.

"I know everything," he said slowly. "I am well served in my own house. Perez, be careful. Write down everything. We also know, I think, that your daughter met his Highness this evening. You no doubt found that out as others did. The girl is imprudent. Do you confess to knowing that the two had met this evening?"

Mendoza ground his teeth as if he were suffering bodily torture. His brows contracted, and as Perez looked up, he faced him with such a look of hatred and anger that the Secretary could hot meet his eyes. The King was a sacred and semi-divine personage, privileged to ask any question he chose and theoretically incapable of doing wrong, but it was unbearable that this sleek black fox should have the right to hear Diego de Mendoza confess his daughter's dishonour. Antonio Perez was not an adventurer of low birth, as many have gratuitously supposed, for his father had held an honourable post at court before him; but he was very far from being the equal of one who, though poor and far removed from the head of his own family, bore one of the most noble names in Spain.

"Let your Majesty dismiss Don Antonio Perez," said Mendoza boldly. "I will then tell your Majesty all I know."

Perez smiled as he bent over his notes, for he knew what the answer would be to such a demand. It came sharply.

"It is not the privilege of a man convicted of murder to choose his hearers. Answer my questions or be silent. Do you confess that you knew of your daughter's meeting with Don John this evening?"

Mendoza's lips set themselves tightly under his grey beard, and he uttered no sound. He interpreted the King's words literally.

"Well, what have you to say?"

"Nothing, Sire, since I have your Majesty's permission to be silent."

"It does not matter," said Philip indifferently. "Note that he refuses to answer the question, Perez. Note that this is equivalent to confessing the fact, since he would otherwise deny it. His silence is & reason, however, for allowing the case to go to the tribunal to be examined in the usual way—the usual way," he repeated, looking hard at Mendoza and emphasizing the words strongly.

"Since I do not deny the deed, I entreat your Majesty to let me suffer for it quickly. I am ready to die, God knows. Let it be to-morrow morning or to-night. Your Majesty need only sign the warrant for my execution, which Don Antonio Perez has, no doubt, already prepared."

"Not at all, not at all," answered the King, with horrible coolness. "I mean that you shall have a fair and open trial and every possible opportunity of justifying yourself. There must be nothing secret about this. So horrible a crime must be treated in the most public manner. Though it is very painful to me to refer to such a matter, you must remember that after it had pleased Heaven, in its infinite justice, to bereave me of my unfortunate son, Don Carlos, the heir to the throne, there were not wanting ill-disposed and wicked persons who actually said that I had caused his life to be shortened by various inhuman cruelties. No, no! we cannot have too much publicity. Consider how terrible a thing it would be if any one should dare to suppose that my own brother had been murdered with my consent! You should love your country too much not to fear such a result; for though you have murdered my brother in cold blood, I am too just to forget that you have proved your patriotism through a long and hitherto honourable career. It is my duty to see that the causes of your atrocious action are perfectly clear to my subjects, so that no doubt may exist even in the most prejudiced minds. Do you understand? I repeat that if I have condescended to examine you alone, I have done so only out of a merciful desire to spare an old soldier the suffering and mortification of an examination by the tribunal that is to judge you. Understand that."

"I understand that and much more besides," answered Mendoza, in low and savage tones.

"It is not necessary that you should understand or think that you understand anything more than what I say," returned the King coldly. "At what time did you go to his Highness's apartments this evening?"

"Your Majesty knows."

"I know nothing of it," said the King, with the utmost calm. "You were on duty after supper. You escorted me to my apartments afterwards. I had already sent for Perez, who came at once, and we remained here, busy with affairs, until I returned to the throne room, five minutes before you came and confessed the murder; did we not, Perez?"

"Most certainly, Sire," answered the Secretary gravely. "Your Majesty must have been at work with me an hour, at least, before returning to the throne room."

"And your Majesty did not go with me by the private staircase to Don John of Austria's apartment?" asked Mendoza, thunderstruck by the enormous falsehood.

"With you?" cried the King, in admirably feigned astonishment. "What madness is this? Do not write that down, Perez. I really believe the man is beside himself!"

Mendoza groaned aloud, for he saw that he had been frightfully deceived. In his magnificent generosity, he had assumed the guilt of the crime, being ready and willing to die for it quickly to save the King from blame and to put an end to his own miserable existence. But he had expected death quickly, mercifully, within a few hours. Had he suspected what Philip had meant to do,—that he was to be publicly tried for a murder he had not committed, and held up to public hatred and ignominy for days and perhaps weeks together, while a slow tribunal dragged out its endless procedure,— neither his loyalty nor his desire for death could have had power to bring his pride to such a sacrifice. And now he saw that he was caught in a vise, and that no accusation he could bring against the King could save him, even if he were willing to resort to such a measure and so take back his word. There was no witness for him but himself. Don John was dead, and the infamous Perez was ready to swear that Philip had not left the room in which they had been closeted together. There was not a living being to prove that Mendoza had not gone alone to Don John's apartments with the deliberate intention of killing him. He had, indeed, been to the chief steward's office in search of a key, saying that the King desired to have it and was waiting; but it would be said that he had used the King's authority to try and get the key for himself because he knew that his daughter was hidden in the locked room. He had foolishly fancied that the King would send for him and see him alone before he died, that his sovereign would thank him for the service that was costing his life, would embrace him and send him to his death for the good of Spain and the divine right of monarchy. Truly, he had been most bitterly deceived.

"You said," continued Philip mercilessly, "that you killed his Highness when he was unarmed. Is that true?"

"His Highness was unarmed," said Mendoza, almost through his closed teeth, for he was suffering beyond words.

"Unarmed," repeated the King, nodding to Perez, who wrote rapidly. "You might have given him a chance for his life. It would have been more soldier-like. Had you any words before you drew upon him? Was there any quarrel?"

"None. We did not speak to each other." Mendoza tried to make Philip meet his eyes, but the King would not look at him.

"There was no altercation," said the King, looking at Perez. "That proves that the murder was premeditated. Put it down—it is very important. You could hardly have stabbed him in the back, I suppose. He must have turned when he heard you enter. Where was the wound?"

"The wound that killed his Highness will be found near the heart."

"Cruel!" Philip looked down at his own hands, and he shook his head very sadly. "Cruel, most cruel," he repeated in a low tone.

"I admit that it was a very cruel deed," said Mendoza, looking at him fixedly. "In that, your Majesty is right."

"Did you see your daughter before or after you had committed the murder?" asked the King calmly.

"I have not seen my daughter since the murder was committed."

"But you saw her before? Be careful, Perez. Write down every word. You say that you saw your daughter before you did it."

"I did not say that," answered Mendoza firmly.

"It makes very little difference," said the King, "If you had seen her with his Highness, the murder would have seemed less cold-blooded, that is all. There would then have been something like a natural provocation for it."

There was a low sound, as of some one scratching at the door. That was the usual way of asking admittance to the King's room on very urgent matters. Perez rose instantly, the King nodded to him, and he went to the door. On opening, someone handed him a folded paper on a gold salver. He brought it to Philip, dropped on one knee very ceremoniously, and presented it. Philip took the note and opened it, and Perez returned to his seat at once.

The King unfolded the small sheet carefully. The room was so full of light that he could read it when he sat, without moving. His eyes followed the lines quickly to the end, and returned to the beginning, and he read the missive again more carefully. Not the slightest change of expression was visible in his face, as he folded the paper neatly again in the exact shape in which he had received it. Then he remained silent a few moments. Perez held his pen ready to write, moving it mechanically now and then as if he were writing in the air, and staring at the fire, absorbed in his own thoughts, though his ear was on the alert.

"You refuse to admit that you found your daughter and Don John together, then?" The King spoke with an interrogation.

"I did not find them together," answered Mendoza. "I have said so." He was becoming exasperated under the protracted cross-examination.

"You have not said so. My memory is very good, but if it should fail we have everything written down. I believe you merely refused to answer when I asked if you knew of their meeting—which meant that you did know of it. Is that it, Perez?"

"Exactly so, Sire." The Secretary had already found the place among his notes.

"Do you persistently refuse to admit that you had positive evidence of your daughter's guilt before the murder?"

"I will not admit that, Sire, for it would not be true."

"Your daughter has given her evidence since," said the King, holding up the folded note, and fixing his eyes at last on his victim's face. If it were possible, Mendoza turned more ashy pale than before, and he started perceptibly at the King's words.

"I shall never believe that!" he cried in a voice which nevertheless betrayed his terror for his child.

"A few moments before this note was written," said Philip calmly, "your daughter entered the throne room, and addressed the court, standing upon the steps of the throne—a very improper proceeding and one which Ruy Gomez should not have allowed. Your daughter Dolores—is that the girl's name? Yes. Your daughter Dolores, amidst the most profound silence, confessed that she—it is so monstrous that I can hardly bring myself to say it—that she had yielded to the importunities of his late Highness, that she was with him in his room a long time this evening, and that, in fact, she was actually in his bedchamber when he was murdered."

"It is a lie!" cried Mendoza vehemently. "It is an abominable lie—she was not in the room!"

"She has said that she was," answered Philip. "You can hardly suppose a girl capable of inventing such damning evidence against herself, even for the sake of saving her own father. She added that his Highness was not killed by you. But that is puerile. She evidently saw you do it, and has boldly confessed that she was in the room—hidden somewhere, perhaps, since you absolutely refuse to admit that you saw her there. It is quite clear that you found the two together and that you killed his Highness before your daughter's eyes. Why not admit that, Mendoza? It makes you seem a little less cold-blooded. The provocation was great—"

"She was not there," protested Mendoza, interrupting the King, for he hardly knew what he was doing.

"She was there, since she confesses to have been in the room. I do not tolerate interruption when I am speaking. She was there, and her evidence will be considered. Even if you did not see her, how can you be sure that your daughter was not there? Did you search the room? Did you look behind the curtains?"

"I did not." The stern old man seemed to shrink bodily under the frightful humiliation to which he was subjected.

"Very well, then you cannot swear that she was not in the room. But you did not see her there. Then I am sorry to say that there can have been no extenuating circumstances. You entered his Highness's bedchamber, you did not even speak to him, you drew your sword and you killed him. All this shows that you went there fully determined to commit the crime. But with regard to its motive, this strange confession of your daughter's makes that quite clear. She had been extremely imprudent with Don John, you were aware of the fact, and you revenged yourself in the most brutal way. Such vengeance never can produce any but the most fatal results. You yourself must die, in the first place, a degrading and painful death on the scaffold, and you die leaving behind you a ruined girl, who must bury herself in a convent and never be seen by her worldly equals again. And besides that, you have deprived your King of a beloved brother, and Spain of her most brilliant general. Could anything be worse?"

"Yes. There are worse things than that, your Majesty, and worse things have been done. It would have been a thousand times worse if I had done the deed and cast the blame of it on a man so devoted to me that he would bear the guilt in my stead, and a hundred thousand times worse if I had then held up that man to the execration of mankind, and tortured him with every distortion of evidence which great falsehoods can put upon a little truth. That would indeed have been far worse than anything I have done. God may find forgiveness for murderers, but there is only hell for traitors, and the hell of hells is the place of men who betray their friends."

"His mind is unsettled, I fear," said the King, speaking to Perez. "These are signs of madness."

"Indeed I fear so, Sire," answered the smooth Secretary, shaking his head solemnly. "He does not know what he says."

"I am not mad, and I know what I am saying, for I am a man under the hand of death." Mendoza's eyes glared at the King savagely as he spoke, and then at Perez, but neither could look at him, for neither dared to meet his gaze. "As for this confession my daughter has made, I do not believe in it. But if she has said these things, you might have let me die without the bitterness of knowing them, since that was in your power. And God knows that I have staked my life freely for your Majesty and for Spain these many years, and would again if I had it to lose instead of having thrown it away. And God knows, too, that for what I have done, be it good or bad, I will bear whatsoever your Majesty shall choose to say to me alone in the way of reproach. But as I am a dying man I will not forgive that scribbler there for having seen a Spanish gentleman's honour torn to rags, and an old soldier's last humiliation, and I pray Heaven with my dying breath, that he may some day be tormented as he has seen me tormented, and worse, till he shall cry out for mercy—as I will not!"

The cruelly injured man's prayer was answered eight years from that day, and even now Perez turned slowly pale as he heard the words, for they were spoken with all the vehemence of a dying man's curse. But Philip was unmoved. He was probably not making Mendoza suffer merely for the pleasure of watching his pain, though others' suffering seems always to have caused him a sort of morbid satisfaction. What he desired most was to establish a logical reason for which Mendoza might have committed the crime, lest in the absence of sound evidence he himself should be suspected of having instigated it. He had no intention whatever of allowing Mendoza to be subjected to torture during the trial that was to ensue. On the contrary, he intended to prepare all the evidence for the judges and to prevent Mendoza from saying anything in self-defence. To that end it was necessary that the facts elicited should be clearly connected from first cause to final effect, and by the skill of Antonio Perez in writing down only the words which contributed to that end, the King's purpose was now accomplished. He heard every word of Mendoza's imprecation and thought it proper to rebuke him for speaking so freely.

"You forget yourself, sir," he said coldly. "Don Antonio Perez is my private Secretary, and you must respect him. While you belonged to the court his position was higher and more important than your own; now that you stand convicted of an outrageous murder in cold blood, you need not forget that he is an innocent man. I have done, Mendoza. You will not see me again, for you will be kept in confinement until your trial, which can only have one issue. Come here."

He sat upright in his chair and held out his hand, while Mendoza approached with unsteady steps, and knelt upon one knee, as was the custom.

"I am not unforgiving," said the King. "Forgiveness is a very beautiful Christian virtue, which we are taught to exercise from our earliest childhood. You have cut off my dearly loved brother in the flower of his youth, but you shall not die believing that I bear you any malice. So far as I am able, I freely forgive you for what you have done, and in token I give you my hand, that you may have that comfort at the last."

With incredible calmness Philip took Mendoza's hand as he spoke, held it for a moment in his, and pressed it almost warmly at the last words. The old man's loyalty to his sovereign had been a devotion almost amounting to real adoration, and bitterly as he had suffered throughout the terrible interview, he well-nigh forgot every suffering as he felt the pressure of the royal fingers. In an instant he had told himself that it had all been but a play, necessary to deceive Perez, and to clear the King from suspicion before the world, and that in this sense the unbearable agony he had borne had served his sovereign. He forgot all for a moment, and bending his iron-grey head, he kissed the thin and yellow hand fervently, and looked up to Philip's cold face and felt that there were tears of gratitude in his own eyes, of gratitude at being allowed to leave the world he hated with the certainty that his death was to serve his sovereign idol.

"I shall be faithful to your Majesty until the end," he said simply, as the King withdrew his fingers, and he rose to his feet.

The King nodded slowly, and his stony look watched Mendoza with a sort of fixed curiosity. Even he had not known that such men lived.

"Call the guards to the door, Perez," he said coldly. "Tell the officer to take Don Diego Mendoza to the west tower for to-night, and to treat him with every consideration."

Perez obeyed. A detachment of halberdiers with an officer were stationed in the short, broad corridor that led to the room where Dolores was waiting. Perez gave the lieutenant his orders.

Mendoza walked backwards to the door from the King's presence, making three low bows as he went. At the door he turned, taking no notice of the Secretary, marched out with head erect, and gave himself up to the soldiers.

CHAPTER XVII

The halberdiers closed round their old chief, but did not press upon him. Three went before him, three behind, and one walked on each side, and the lieutenant led the little detachment. The men were too much accustomed to seeing courtiers in the extremes of favour and disfavour to be much surprised at the arrest of Mendoza, and they felt no great sympathy for him. He had always been too rigidly exacting for their taste, and they longed for a younger commander who should devote more time to his own pleasure and less to inspecting uniforms and finding fault with details. Yet Mendoza had been a very just man, and he possessed the eminently military bearing and temper which always impose themselves on soldiers. At the present moment, too, they were more inclined to pity him than to treat him roughly, for if they did not guess what had really taken place, they were quite sure that Don John of Austria had been murdered by the King's orders, like Don Carlos and Queen Isabel and a fair number of other unfortunate persons; and if the King had chosen Mendoza to do the deed, the soldiers thought that he was probably not meant to suffer for it in the end, and that before long he would be restored to his command. It would, therefore, be the better for them, later, if they showed him a certain deference in his misfortune. Besides, they had heard Antonio Perez tell their officer that Mendoza was to be treated with every consideration.

They marched in time, with heavy tread and the swinging gait to right and left that is natural to a soldier who carries for a weapon a long halberd with a very heavy head. Mendoza was as tall as any of them, and kept their step, holding his head high. He was bareheaded, but was otherwise still in the complete uniform he wore when on duty on state occasions.

The corridor, which seemed short on account of its breadth and in comparison with the great size of the halls in the palace, was some thirty paces long and lighted by a number of chandeliers that hung from the painted vault. The party reached the door of the waiting room and halted a moment, while one of the King's footmen opened the doors wide. Don Ruy Gomez and Dolores were waiting within. The servant passed rapidly through to open the doors beyond. Ruy Gomez stood up and drew his chair aside, somewhat surprised at the entrance of the soldiers, who rarely passed that way. Dolores opened her eyes at the sound of marching, but in the uncertain light of the candles she did not at first see Mendoza, half hidden as he was by the men who guarded him. She paid little attention, for she was accustomed to seeing such detachments of halberdiers marching through the corridors when the sentries were relieved, and as she had never been in the King's apartments she was not surprised by the sudden appearance of the soldiers, as her companion was. But as the latter made way for them he lifted his hat, which as a Grandee he wore even in the King's presence, and he bent his head courteously as Mendoza went by. He hoped that Dolores would not see her father, but his own recognition of the prisoner had attracted her attention. She sprang to her feet with a cry. Mendoza turned his head and saw her before she could reach him, for she was moving forward. He stood still, and the soldiers halted instinctively and parted before her, for they all knew their commander's daughter.

"Father!" she cried, and she tried to take his hand.

But he pushed her away and turned his face resolutely towards the door before him.

"Close up! Forward—march!" he said, in his harsh tone of command.

The men obeyed, gently forcing Dolores aside. They made two steps forward, but Ruy Gomez stopped them by a gesture, standing in their way and raising one hand, while he laid the other on the young lieutenant's shoulder. Ruy Gomez was one of the greatest personages in Spain; he was the majorduomo of the palace, and had almost unlimited authority. But the officer had his orders directly from the King and felt bound to carry them out to the letter.

"His Majesty has directed me to convey Don Diego de Mendoza to the west tower without delay," he said. "I beg your Excellency to let us proceed."

Ruy Gomez still held him by the shoulder with a gentle pressure.

"That I will not," he said firmly; "and if you are blamed for being slow in the execution of your duty, say that Ruy Gomez de Silva hindered you, and fear nothing. It is not right that father and daughter should part as these two are parting."

"I have nothing to say to my daughter," said Mendoza harshly; but the words seemed to hurt him.

"Don Diego," answered Ruy Gomez, "the deed of which you have accused yourself is as much worse than anything your child has done as hatred is worse than love. By the right of mere humanity I take upon myself to say that you shall be left here a while with your daughter, that you may take leave of one another." He turned to the officer. "Withdraw your men, sir," he said. "Wait at the door. You have my word for the security of your prisoner, and my authority for what you do. I will call you when it is time."

He spoke in a tone that admitted of no refusal, and he was obeyed. The officers and the men filed out, and Ruy Gomez closed the door after them. He himself recrossed the room and went out by the other way into the broad corridor. He meant to wait there. His orders had been carried out so quickly that Mendoza found himself alone with Dolores, almost as by a surprise. In his desperate mood he resented what Ruy Gomez had done, as an interference in his family affairs, and he bent his bushy brows together as he stood facing Dolores, with folded arms. Four hours had not passed since they had last spoken together alone in his own dwelling; there was a lifetime of tragedy between that moment and this.

Dolores had not spoken since he had pushed her away. She stood beside a chair, resting one hand upon it, dead white, with the dark shadow of pain under her eyes, her lips almost colourless, but firm, and evenly closed. There were lines of suffering in her young face that looked as if they never could be effaced. It seemed to her that the worst conflict of all was raging in her heart as she watched her father's face, waiting for the sound of his voice; and as for him, he would rather have gone back to the King's presence to be tormented under the eyes of Antonio Perez than stand there, forced to see her and speak to her. In his eyes, in the light of what he had been told, she was a ruined and shameless woman, who had deceived him day in, day out, for more than two years. And to her, so far as she could understand, he was the condemned murderer of the man she had so innocently and truly loved. But yet, she had a doubt, and for that possibility, she had cast her good name to the winds in the hope of saving his life. At one moment, in a vision of dread, she saw his armed hand striking at her lover—at the next she felt that he could never have struck the blow, and that there was an unsolved mystery behind it all. Never were two innocent human beings so utterly deceived, each about the other.

"Father," she said, at last, in a trembling tone, "can you not speak to me, if I can find heart to hear you?"

"What can we two say to each other?" he asked sternly. "Why did you stop me? I am ready to die for killing the man who ruined you. I am glad. Why should I say anything to you, and what words can you have for me? I hope your end may come quickly, with such peace as you can find from your shame at the last. That is what I wish for you, and it is a good wish, for you have made death on the scaffold look easy to me, so that I long for it. Do you understand?"

"Condemned to death!" she cried out, almost incoherently, before he had finished speaking. "But they cannot condemn you—I have told them that I was there—that it was not you—they must believe me—O God of mercy!"

"They believe you—yes. They believe that I found you together and killed him. I shall be tried by judges, but I am condemned beforehand, and I must die." He spoke calmly enough. "Your mad confession before the court only made my conviction more certain," he said. "It gave the reason for the deed—and it burned away the last doubt I had. If they are slow in trying me, you will have been before the executioner, for he will find me dead—by your hand. You might have spared me that— and spared yourself. You still had the remnant of a good name, and your lover being dead, you might have worn the rag of your honour still. You have chosen to throw it away, and let me know my full disgrace before I die a disgraceful death. And yet you wish to speak to me. Do you expect my blessing?"

Dolores had lost the power of speech. Passing her hand now and then across her forehead, as though trying to brush away a material veil, she stood half paralyzed, staring wildly at him while he spoke. But when she saw him turn away from her towards the door, as if he would go out and leave her there, her strength was loosed from the spell, and she sprang before him and caught his wrists with her hands.

"I am as innocent as when my mother bore me," she said, and her low voice rang with the truth. "I told the lie to save your life. Do you believe me now?"

He gazed at her with haggard eyes for many moments before he spoke.

"How can it be true?" he asked, but his voice shook in his throat. "You were there—I saw you leave his room—"

"No, that you never saw!" she cried, well knowing how impossible it was, since she had been locked in till after he had gone away.

"I saw your dress—not this one—what you wore this afternoon."

"Not this one? I put on this court dress before I got out of the room in which you had locked me up. Inez helped me—I pretended that I was she, and wore her cloak, and slipped away, and I have not been back again. You did not see me."

Mendoza passed his hand over his eyes and drew back from her. If what she said were true, the strongest link was gone from the chain of facts by which he had argued so much sorrow and shame. Forgetting himself and his own near fate, he looked at the court dress she wore, and a mere glance convinced him that it was not the one he had seen.

"But—" he was suddenly confused—"but why did you need to disguise yourself? I left the Princess of Eboli with you, and I gave her permission to take you away to stay with her. You needed no disguise."

"I never saw her. She must have found Inez in the room. I was gone long before that."

"Gone—where?" Mendoza was fast losing the thread of it all—in his confusion of ideas he grasped the clue of his chief sorrow, which was far beyond any thought for himself. "But if you are innocent—pray God you may be, as you say—how is it possible—oh, no! I cannot believe it—I cannot! No woman could do that—no innocent girl could stand out before a multitude of men and women, and say what you said—"

"I hoped to save your life. I had the strength. I did it."

Her clear grey eyes looked into his, and his doubt began to break away before the truth.

"Make me believe it!" he cried, his voice breaking. "Oh, God! Make me believe it before I die!"

"It is true," she cried, in a low, strong voice that carried belief to his breast in spite of such reasoning as still had some power over him. "It is true, and you shall believe it; and if you will not, the man you have killed, the man I loved and trusted, the dead man who knows the whole truth as I know it, will come back from the dead to prove it true—for I swear it upon his soul in heaven, and upon yours and mine that will not be long on earth—as I will swear it in the hour of your death and mine, since we must die!"

He could not take his eyes from hers that held him, and suddenly in the pure depths he seemed to see her soul facing him without fear, and he knew that what she said was true, and his tortured heart leapt up at the good certainty.

"I believe you, my child," he said at last, and then his grey lids half closed over his eyes and he bent down to her, and put his arm round her.

But she shuddered at the touch of his right hand, and though she knew that he was a condemned man, and that she might never see him again, she could not bear to receive his parting kiss upon her forehead.

"Oh, father, why did you kill him?" she asked, turning her head away and moving to escape from his hold.

But Mendoza did not answer. His arm dropped by his side, and his face grew white and stony. She was asking him to give up the King's secret, to keep which he was giving his life. He felt that it would be treason to tell even her. And besides, she would not keep the secret—what woman could, what daughter would? It must go out of the world with him, if it was to be safe. He glanced at her and saw her face ravaged by an hour's grief. Yet she would not mourn Don John the less if she knew whose hand had done the deed. It could make but a little difference to her, though to himself that difference would be great, if she knew that he died innocent.

And then began a struggle fierce and grim, that tore his soul and wounded his heart as no death agony could have hurt him. Since he had judged her unjustly, since it had all been a hideous dream, since she was still the child that had been all in all to him throughout her life, since all was changed, he did not wish to die, he bore the dead man no hatred, it was no soothing satisfaction to his outraged heart to know him dead of a sword wound in the breast, far away in the room where they had left him, there was no fierce regret that he had not driven the thrust himself. The man was as innocent as the innocent girl, and he himself, as innocent as both, was to be led out to die to shield the King—no more. His life was to be taken for that only, and he no longer set its value at naught nor wished it over. He was the mere scapegoat, to suffer for his master's crime, since crime it was and nothing better. And since he was willing to bear the punishment, or since there was now no escape from it, had he not at least the human right to proclaim his innocence to the only being he really loved? It would be monstrous to deny it. What could she do, after all, even if she knew the truth? Nothing. No one would dare to believe her if she accused the King. She would be shut up in a convent as a mad woman, but in any case, she would certainly disappear to end her life in some religious house as soon as he was dead. Poor girl—she had loved Don John with all her heart—what could the world hold for her, even if the disgrace of her father's death were not to shut her out of the world altogether, as it inevitably must. She would not live long, but she would live in the profoundest sorrow. It would be an alleviation, almost the greatest possible, to know that her father's hand was not stained by such a deed.

The temptation to speak out was overwhelming, and he knew that the time was short. At any moment Ruy Gomez might open the door, and bid him part from her, and there would be small chance for him of seeing her again. He stood uncertain, with bent head and folded arms, and she watched him, trying to bring herself to touch his hand again and bear his kiss.

His loyalty to the King, that was like a sort of madness, stood between him and the words he longed to say. It was the habit of his long soldier's life, unbending as the corslet he wore and enclosing his soul as the steel encased his body, proof against every cruelty, every unkindness, every insult. It was better to die a traitor's death for the King's secret than to live for his own honour. So it had always seemed to him, since he had been a boy and had learned to fight under the great Emperor. But now he knew that he wavered as he had never done in the most desperate charge, when life was but a missile to be flung in the enemy's face, and found or not, when the fray was over. There was no intoxication of fury now, there was no far ring of glory in the air, there was no victory to be won. The hard and hideous fact stared him in the face, that he was to die like a malefactor by the hangman's hand, and that the sovereign who had graciously deigned to accept the sacrifice had tortured him for nearly half an hour without mercy in the presence of an inferior, in order to get a few facts on paper which might help his own royal credit. And as if that were not enough, his own daughter was to live after him, believing that he had cruelly murdered the man she most dearly loved. It was more than humanity could bear.

His brow unbent, his arms unfolded themselves, and he held them out to Dolores with a smile almost gentle.

"There is no blood on these hands, my little girl," he said tenderly. "I did not do it, child. Let me hold you in my arms once, and kiss you before I go. We are both innocent—we can bless one another before we part for ever."

The pure, grey eyes opened wide in amazement. Dolores could hardly believe her ears, as she made a step towards him, and then stopped, shrinking, and then made one step more. Her lips moved and wondering words came to him, so low that he could hardly understand, save that she questioned him.

"You did not do it!" she breathed. "You did not kill him after all? But then—who—why?"

Still she hesitated, though she came slowly nearer, and a faint light warmed her sorrowful face.

"You must try to guess who and why," he said, in a tone as low as her own. "I must not tell you that."

"I cannot guess," she answered; but she was close to him now, and she had taken one of his hands softly in both her own, while she gazed into his eyes. "How can I understand unless you tell me? Is it so great a secret that you must die for it, and never tell it? Oh, father, father! Are you sure—quite sure?"

"He was dead already when I came into the room," Mendoza answered. "I did not even see him hurt."

"But then—yes—then"—her voice sank to a whisper—"then it was the King!"

He saw the words on her lips rather than heard them, and she saw in his face that she was right. She dropped his hand and threw her arms round his neck, pressing her bosom to his breastplate; and suddenly her love for him awoke, and she began to know how she might have loved him if she had known him through all the years that were gone.

"It cannot be that he will let you die!" she cried softly. "You shall not die!" she cried again, with sudden strength, and her light frame shook his as if she would wrench him back from inevitable fate.

"My little girl," he answered, most tenderly clasping her to him, and most thoughtfully, lest his armour should hurt her, "I can die happy now, for I have found all of you again."

"You shall not die! You shall not die!" she cried. "I will not let you go—they must take me, too—"

"No power can save me now, my darling," he answered. "But it does not matter, since you know. It will be easy now."

She could only hold him with her small hands, and say over and over again that she would not let him go.

"Ah! why have you never loved me before in all these years?" he cried. "It was my fault—all my fault."

"I love you now with all my heart," she answered, "and I will save you, even from the King; and you and I and Inez will go far away, and you two shall comfort me and love me till I go to him."

Mendoza shook his head sadly, looking over her shoulder as he held her, for he knew that there was no hope now. Had he known, or half guessed, but an hour or two ago, he would have turned on his heel from the door of Don John's chamber, and he would have left the King to bear the blame or shift it as he could.

"It is too late, Dolores. God bless you, my dear, dear child! It will soon be over—two days at most, for the people will cry out for the blood of Don John's murderer; and when they see mine they will be satisfied. It is too late now. Good-by, my little girl, good-by! The blessing of all heaven be on your dear head!"

Dolores nestled against him, as she had never done before, with the feeling that she had found something that had been wanting in her life, at the very moment when the world, with all it held for her, was slipping over the edge of eternity.

"I will not leave you," she cried again. "They shall take me to your prison, and I will stay with you and take care of you, and never leave you; and at last I shall save your life, and then—"

The door of the corridor opened, and she saw Ruy Gomez standing in the entrance, as if he were waiting His face was calm and grave as usual, but she saw a profound pity in his eyes.

"No, no!" she cried to him, "not yet—one moment more!"

But Mendoza turned his head at her words, looking over his shoulder, and he saw the Prince also.

"I am ready," he said briefly, and he tried to take Dolores' hands from his neck. "It is time," he said to her. "Be brave, my darling! We have found each other at last. It will not be long before we are together for ever."

He kissed her tenderly once more, and loosed her hold, putting her two hands together and kissing them also.

"I will not say good-by," she said. "It is not good-by—it shall not be. I shall be with you soon."

His eyes lingered upon hers for a moment, and then he broke away, setting his teeth lest he should choke and break down. He opened the door and presented himself to the halberdiers. Dolores heard his familiar voice give the words of command.

"Close up! Forward, march!"

The heavy tramp she knew so well began at once, and echoed along the outer entries, growing slowly less distinct till it was only a distant and rumbling echo, and then died away altogether. Her hand was still on the open door, and Ruy Gomez was standing beside her. He gently drew her away, and closed the door again. She let him lead her to a chair, and sat down where she had sat before. But this time she did not lean back exhausted, with half-closed eyes,—she rested her elbow on her knee and her chin in her hand, and she tried to think connectedly to a conclusion. She remembered all the details of the past hours one by one, and she felt that the determination to save her father had given her strength to live.

"Don Ruy Gomez," she said at last, looking up to the tall old nobleman, who stood by the brazier warming his hands again, "can I see the King alone?"

"That is more than I can promise," answered the Prince. "I have asked an audience for you, and the chamberlain will bring word presently whether his Majesty is willing to see you. But if you are admitted, I cannot tell whether Perez will be there or not. He generally is. His presence need make no difference to you. He is an excellent young man, full of heart. I have great confidence in him,—so much so that I recommended him to his Majesty as Secretary. I am sure that he will do all he can to be of use to you."

Dolores looked up incredulously, and with a certain wonder at the Prince's extreme simplicity. Yet he had been married ten years to the clever woman who ruled him and Perez and King Philip, and made each one believe that she was devoted to him only, body and soul. Of the three, Perez alone may have guessed the truth, but though it was degrading enough, he would not let it stand in the way of his advancement; and in the end it was he who escaped, leaving her to perish, the victim of the King's implacable anger, Dolores could not help shaking her head in answer to the Prince of Eboli's speech.

"People are very unjust to Perez," he said. "But the King trusts him. If he is there, try to conciliate him, for he has much influence with his Majesty."

Dolores said nothing, and resuming her attitude, returned to her sad meditations, and to the study of some immediate plan. But she could think of no way. Her only fixed intention was to see the King himself. Ruy Gomez could do no more to help her than he had done already, and that indeed was not little, since it was to his kindly impulse that she owed her meeting with her father.

"And if Perez is not inclined to help Don Diego," said the Prince, after a long pause which had not interrupted the slow progression of, his kindly thought, "I will request my wife to speak to him. I have often noticed that the Princess can make Perez do almost anything she wishes. Women are far cleverer than men, my dear—they have ways we do not understand. Yes, I will interest my wife in the affair. It would be a sad thing if your father—"

The old man stopped short, and Dolores wondered vaguely what he had been going to say. Ruy Gomez was a very strange compound of almost childlike and most honourable simplicity, and of the experienced wisdom with regard to the truth of matters in which he was not concerned, which sometimes belongs to very honourable and simple men.

"You do not believe that my father is guilty," said Dolores, boldly asserting what she suspected.

"My dear child," answered Ruy Gomez, twisting his rings on his fingers as he spread his hands above the coals in the brazier, "I have lived in this court for fifty years, and I have learned in that time that where great matters are at stake those who do not know the whole truth are often greatly deceived by appearances. I know nothing of the real matter now, but it would not surprise me if a great change took place before to-morrow night. A man who has committed a crime so horrible as the one your father confessed before us all rarely finds it expedient to make such a confession, and a young girl, my dear, who has really been a little too imprudently in love with a royal Prince, would be a great deal too wise to make a dramatic statement of her fault to the assembled Grandees of Spain."

He looked across at Dolores and smiled gently. But she only shook her head gravely in answer, though she wondered at what he said, and wondered, too, whether there might not be a great many persons in the court who thought as he did. She was silent, too, because it hurt her to talk when she could not draw breath without remembering that what she had lived for was lying dead in that dim room on the upper story.

The door opened, and a chamberlain entered the room.

"His Majesty is pleased to receive Doña Dolores de Mendoza, in private audience," he said.

Ruy Gomez rose and led Dolores out into the corridor.

CHAPTER XVIII

Dolores had prepared no speech with which to appeal to the King, and she had not counted upon her own feelings towards him when she found herself in the room where Mendoza had been questioned, and heard the door closed behind her by the chamberlain who had announced her coming. She stood still a moment, dazzled by the brilliant lights after having been so long in the dimmer waiting room. She had never before been in the King's study, and she had fancied it very different from what it really was when she had tried to picture to herself the coming interview. She had supposed the room small, sombre, littered with books and papers, and cold; it was, on the contrary, so spacious as to be almost a hall, it was brightly illuminated and warmed by the big wood fire. Magnificent tapestries covered the walls with glowing colour, and upon one of these, in barbaric bad taste, was hung a single great picture by Titian, Philip's favourite master. Dolores blushed as she recognized in the face of the insolent Venus the features of the Princess of Eboli. From his accustomed chair, the King could see this painting. Everywhere in the room there were rich objects that caught and reflected the light, things of gold and silver, of jade and lapis lazuli, in a sort of tasteless profusion that detracted from the beauty of each, and made Dolores feel that she had been suddenly transported out of her own element into another that was hard to breathe and in which it was bad to live. It oppressed her, and though her courage was undiminished, the air of the place seemed to stifle her thought and speech.

As she entered she saw the King in profile, seated in his great chair at some distance from the fire, but looking at it steadily. He did not notice her presence at first. Antonio Perez sat at the table, busily writing, and he only glanced at Dolores sideways when he heard the door close after her. She sank almost to the ground as she made the first court curtsey before advancing, and she came forward into the light. As her skirt swept the ground a second time, Philip looked slowly round, and his dull stare followed her as she came round in a quarter of a wide circle and curtsied a third time immediately in front of him.

She was very beautiful, as she stood waiting for him to speak, and meeting his gaze fearlessly with a look of cold contempt in her white face such as no living person had ever dared to turn to him, while the light of anger burned in her deep grey eyes. But for the presence of the Secretary, she would have spoken first, regardless of court ceremony. Philip looked at her attentively, mentally comparing her with his young Queen's placidly dull personality and with the Princess of Eboli's fast disappearing and somewhat coarse beauty. For the Princess had changed much since Titian had painted his very flattering picture, and though she was only thirty years of age, she was already the mother of many children. Philip stared steadily at the beautiful girl who stood waiting before him, and he wondered why she had never seemed so lovely to him before. There was a half morbid, half bitter savour in what he felt, too,—he had just condemned the beauty's father to death, and she must therefore hate him with all her heart. It pleased him to think of that; she was beautiful and he stared at her long.

"Be seated, Doña Dolores," he said at last, in a muffled voice that was not harsh. "I am glad that you have come, for I have much to say to you."

Without lifting his wrist from the arm of the chair on which it rested, the King moved his hand, and his long forefinger pointed to a low cushioned stool that was placed near him. Dolores came forward unwillingly and sat down. Perez watched the two thoughtfully, and forgot his writing. He did not remember that any one excepting the Princess of Eboli had been allowed to be seated in the King's study. The Queen never came there. Perez' work exempted him in private, of course, from much of the tedious ceremonial upon which Philip insisted. Dolores sat upon the edge of the stool, very erect, with her hands folded on her knees.

"Doña Dolores is pale," observed the King. "Bring a cordial, Perez, or a glass of Oporto wine."

"I thank your Majesty," said the young girl quickly. "I need nothing."

"I will be your physician," answered Philip, very suavely. "I shall insist upon your taking the medicine I prescribe."

He did not turn his eyes from her as Perez brought a gold salver and offered Dolores the glass. It was impossible to refuse, so she lifted it to her lips and sipped a little.

"I thank your Majesty," she said again. "I thank you, sir," she said gravely to Perez as she set down the glass, but she did not raise her eyes to his face as she spoke any more than she would have done if he had been a footman.

"I have much to say to you, and some questions to ask of you," the King began, speaking very slowly, but with extreme suavity.

He paused, and coughed a little, but Dolores said nothing. Then he began to look at her again, and while he spoke he steadily examined every detail of her appearance till his inscrutable gaze had travelled from her headdress to the points of her velvet slippers, and finally remained fixed upon her mouth in a way that disturbed her even more than the speech he made. Perez had resumed his seat.

"In my life," he began, speaking of himself quite without formality, "I have suffered more than most men, in being bereaved of the persons to whom I have been most sincerely attached. The most fortunate and successful sovereign in the world has been and is the most unhappy man in his kingdom. One after another, those I have loved have been taken from me, until I am almost alone in the world that is so largely mine. I suppose you cannot understand that, my dear, for my sorrows began before you were born. But they have reached their crown and culmination to-day in the death of my dear brother."

He paused, watching her mouth, and he saw that she was making a superhuman effort to control herself, pressing the beautiful lips together, though they moved gainfully in spite of her, and visibly lost colour.

"Perez," he said after a moment, "you may go and take some rest. I will send for you when I need you."

The Secretary rose, bowed low, and left the room by a small masked door in a corner. The King waited till he saw it close before he spoke again. His tone changed a little then and his words came quickly, as if he felt here constraint.

"I feel," he said, "that we are united by a common calamity, my dear. I intend to take you under my most particular care and protection from this very hour. Yes, I know!" he held up his hand o deprecate any interruption, for Dolores seemed about to speak. "I know why you come to me, you wish to intercede for your father. That is natural, and you are right to come to me yourself, for I would rather hear your voice than that of another speaking for you, and I would rather grant any mercy in my power to you directly than to some personage of the court who would be seeking his own interest as much as yours."

"I ask justice, not mercy, Sire," said Dolores, in a firm, low voice, and the fire lightened in her eyes.

"Your father shall have both," answered Philip, "for they are compatible."

"He needs no mercy," returned the young girl, "for he has done no harm. Your Majesty knows that as well as I."

"If I knew that, my dear, your father would not be under arrest. I cannot guess what you know or do not know—"

"I know the truth." She spoke so confidently that the King's expression changed a little.

"I wish I did," he answered, with as much suavity as ever. "But tell me what you think you know about this matter. You may help me to sift it, and then I shall be the better able to help you, if such a thing be possible. What do you know?"

Dolores leaned forward toward him from her seat, almost rising as she lowered her voice to a whisper, her eyes fixed on his face.

"I was close behind the door your Majesty wished to open," she said. "I heard every word; I heard your sword drawn and I heard Don John fall—and then it was some time before I heard my father's voice, taking the blame upon himself, lest it should be said that the King had murdered his own brother in his room, unarmed. Is that the truth, or not?"

While she was speaking, a greenish hue overspread Philip's face, ghastly in the candlelight. He sat upright in his chair, his hands straining on its arms and pushing, as if he would have got farther back if he could. He had foreseen everything except that Dolores had been in the next room, for his secret spies had informed him through Perez that her father had kept her a prisoner during the early part of the evening and until after supper.

"When you were both gone," Dolores continued, holding him under her terrible eyes, "I came in, and I found him dead, with the wound in his left breast, and he was unarmed, murdered without a chance for his life. There is blood upon my dress where it touched his—the blood of the man I loved, shed by you. Ah, he was right to call you coward, and he died for me, because you said things of me that no loving man would bear. He was right to call you coward—it was well said—it was the last word he spoke, and I shall not forget it. He had borne everything you heaped upon himself, your insults, your scorn of his mother, but he would not let you cast a slur upon my name, and if you had not killed him out of sheer cowardice, he would have struck you in the face. He was a man! And then my father took the blame to save you from the monstrous accusation, and that all might believe him guilty he told the lie that saved you before them all. Do I know the truth? Is one word of that not true?"

She had quite risen now and stood before him like an accusing angel. And he, who was seldom taken unawares, and was very hard to hurt, leaned back and suffered, slowly turning his head from side to side against the back of the high carved chair.

"Confess that it is true!" she cried, in concentrated tones. "Can you not even find courage for that? You are not the King now, you are your brother's murderer, and the murderer of the man I loved, whose wife I should have been to-morrow. Look at me, and confess that I have told the truth. I am a Spanish woman, and I would not see my country branded before the world with the shame of your royal murders, and if you will confess and save my father, I will keep your secret for my country's sake. But if not—then you must either kill me here, as you slew him, or by the God that made you and the mother that bore you, I will tell all Spain what you are, and the men who loved Don John of Austria shall rise and take your blood for his blood, though it be blood royal, and you shall die, as you killed, like the coward you are!"

The King's eyes were closed, and still his great pale head moved slowly from side to side; for he was suffering, and the torture of mind he had made Mendoza bear was avenged already. But he was silent.

"Will you not speak?" asked the young girl, with blazing eyes. "Then find some weapon and kill me here before I go, for I shall not wait till you find many words."

She was silent, and she stood upright in the act to go. He made no sound, and she moved towards the door, stood still, then moved again and then again, pausing for his answer at each step. He heard her, but could not bring himself to speak the words she demanded of him. She began to walk quickly. Her hand was almost on the door when he raised himself by the arms of his chair, and cried out to her in a frightened voice:—

"No, no! Stay here—you must not go—what do you want me to say?"

She advanced a step again, and once more stood still and met his scared eyes as he turned his face towards her.

"Say, 'You have spoken the truth,'" she answered, dictating to him as if she were the sovereign and he a guilty subject.

She waited a moment and then moved as if she would go out.

"Stay—yes—it is true—I did it—for God's mercy do not betray me!"

He almost screamed the words out to her, half rising, his body bent, his face livid in his extreme fear. She came slowly back towards him, keeping her eyes upon him as if he were some dangerous wild animal that she controlled by her look alone.

"That is not all," she said. "That was for me, that I might hear the words from your own lips. There is something more."

"What more do you want of me?" asked Philip, in thick tones, leaning back exhausted in his chair.

"My father's freedom and safety," answered Dolores. "I must have an order for his instant release. He can hardly have reached his prison yet. Send for him. Let him come here at once, as a free man."

"That is impossible," replied Philip. "He has confessed the deed before the whole court—he cannot possibly be set at liberty without a trial. You forget what you are asking—indeed you forget yourself altogether too much."

He was gathering his dignity again, by force of habit, as his terror subsided, but Dolores was too strong for him.

"I am not asking anything of your Majesty; I am dictating terms to my lover's murderer," she said proudly.

"This is past bearing, girl!" cried Philip hoarsely. "You are out of your mind—I shall call servants to take you away to a place of safety. We shall see what you will do then. You shall not impose your insolence upon me any longer."

Dolores reflected that it was probably in his power to carry out the threat, and to have her carried off by the private door through which Perez had gone out. She saw in a flash how great her danger was, for she was the only witness against him, and if he could put her out of the way in a place of silence, he could send her father to trial and execution without risk to himself, as he had certainly intended to do. On the other hand, she had been able to terrify him to submission a few moments earlier. In the instant working of her woman's mind, she recollected how his fright had increased as she had approached the door by which she had entered. His only chance of accomplishing her disappearance lay in having her taken away by some secret passage, where no open scandal could be possible.

Before she answered his last angry speech, she had almost reached the main entrance again.

"Call whom you will," she said contemptuously. "You cannot save yourself. Don Ruy Gomez is on the other side of that door, and there are chamberlains and guards there, too. I shall have told them all the truth before your men can lay hands on me. If you will not write the order to release my father, I shall go out at once. In ten minutes there will be a revolution in the palace, and to-morrow all Spain will be on fire to avenge your brother. Spain has not forgotten Don Carlos yet! There are those alive who saw you give Queen Isabel the draught that killed her—with your own hand. Are you mad enough to think that no one knows those things, that your spies, who spy on others, do not spy on you, that you alone, of all mankind, can commit every crime with impunity?"

"Take care, girl! Take care!"

"Beware—Don Philip of Austria, King of Spain and half the world, lest a girl's voice be heard above yours, and a girl's hand loosen the foundation of your throne, lest all mankind rise up to-morrow and take your life for the lives you have destroyed! Outside this door here, there are men who guess the truth already, who hate you as they hate Satan, and who loved your brother as every living being loved him—except you. One moment more—order my father to be set free, or I will open and speak. One moment! You will not? It is too late—you are lost!"

Her hand went out to open, but Philip was already on his feet, and with quick, clumsy steps he reached the writing-table, seized the pen Perez had thrown down, and began to scrawl words rapidly in his great angular handwriting. He threw sand upon it to dry the ink, and then poured the grains back into the silver sandbox, glanced at the paper and held it out to Dolores without a word. His other hand slipped along the table to a silver bell, used for calling his private attendants, but the girl saw the movement and instinctively suspected his treachery. He meant her to come to the table, when he would ring the bell and then catch her and hold her by main force till help came. Her faculties were furiously awake under the strain she bore, and outran his slow cunning.

"If you ring that bell, I will open," she said imperiously. "I must have the paper here, where I am safe, and I must read it myself before I shall be satisfied."

"You are a terrible woman," said the King, but she did not like his smile as he came towards her, holding out the document.

She took it from his hand, keeping her eyes on his, for something told her that he would try to seize her and draw her from the door while she was reading it. For some seconds they faced each other in silence, and she knew by his determined attitude that she was right, and that it would not be safe to look down. She wondered why he did not catch her in his arms as she stood, and then she realized that her free hand was on the latch of the door, and that he knew it. She slowly turned the handle, and drew the door to her, and she saw his face fall. She moved to one side so that she could have sprung out if he had tried violence, and then at last she allowed her eyes to glance at the paper. It was in order and would be obeyed; she saw that, at a glance, for it said that Don Diego de Mendoza was to be set at liberty instantly and unconditionally.

"I humbly thank your Majesty, and take my leave," she said, throwing the door wide open and curtseying low.

A chamberlain who had seen the door move on its hinges stepped in to shut it, for it opened inward. The King beckoned him in, and closed it, but before it was quite shut, he heard Dolores' voice.

"Don Ruy Gomez," she was saying, "this is an order to set my father at liberty unconditionally and at once. I do not know to whom it should be given. Will you take it for me and see to it?"

"I will go to the west tower myself," he said, beginning to walk with her. "Such good news is even better when a friend brings it."

"Thank you. Tell him from me that he is safe, for his Majesty has told me that he knows the whole truth. Will you do that? You have been very kind to me to-night, Prince—let me thank you with all my heart now, for we may not meet again. You will not see me at court after this, and I trust my father will take us back to Valladolid and live with us."

"That would be wise," answered Ruy Gomez. "As for any help I have given you, it has been little enough and freely given. I will not keep your father waiting for his liberty. Good-night, Doña Dolores."

CHAPTER XIX

All that had happened from the time when Don John had fallen in his room to the moment when Dolores left her sister on the terrace had occupied little more than half an hour, during which the King had descended to the hall, Mendoza had claimed the guilt of Don John's murder, and the two had gone out under the protection of the guards. As soon as Dolores was out of hearing, Inez rose and crept along the terrace to Don John's door. In the confusion that had ensued upon the announcement of his death no one had thought of going to him; every one took it for granted that some one else had done what was necessary, and that his apartments were filled with physicians and servants. It was not the first time in history that a royal personage had thus been left alone an hour, either dead or dying, because no one was immediately responsible, and such things have happened since.

Inez stole along the terrace and found the outer door open, as the dwarf had left it when he had carried Dolores out in his arms. She remembered that the voices she had heard earlier had come from rooms on the left of the door, and she felt her way to the entrance of the bedchamber, and then went in without hesitation. Bending very low, so that her hands touched the floor from time to time, she crept along, feeling for the body she expected to find. Suddenly she started and stood upright in an instant. She had heard a deep sigh in the room, not far off.

She listened intently, but even her ears could detect no sound after that. She was a little frightened, not with any supernatural fear, for the blind, who live in the dark for ever, are generally singularly exempt from such terrors, but because she had thought herself alone with the dead man, and did not wish to be discovered.

"Who is here?" she asked quickly, but there was no answer out of the dead stillness.

She stood quite still a few seconds and then crept forward again, bending down and feeling before her along the floor. A moment later her hand touched velvet, and she knew that she had found what she sought. With a low moan she fell upon her knees and felt for the cold hand that lay stretched out upon the marble pavement beyond the thick carpet. Her hand followed the arm, reached the shoulder and then the face. Her fingers fluttered lightly upon the features, while her own heart almost stood still She felt no horror of death, though she had never been near a dead person before; and those who were fond of her had allowed her to feel their features with her gentle hands, and she knew beauty through her touch, by its shape. Though her heart was breaking, she had felt that once, before it was too late, she must know the face she had long loved in dreams. Her longing satisfied, her grief broke out again, and she let herself fall her length upon the floor beside Don John, one arm across his chest, her head resting against the motionless shoulder, her face almost hidden against the gathered velvet and silk of his doublet. Once or twice she sobbed convulsively, and then she lay quite still, trying with all her might to die there, on his arm, before any one came to disturb her. It seemed very simple, just to stop living and stay with him for ever.

Again she heard a sound of deep-drawn breath—but it was close to her now, and her own arm moved with it on his chest—the dead man had moved, he had sighed. She started up wildly, with a sharp cry, half of paralyzing fear, and half of mad delight in a hope altogether impossible. Then, he drew his breath again, and it issued from his lips with a low groan. He was not quite dead yet, he might speak to her still, he could hear her voice, perhaps, before he really died. She could never have found courage to kiss him, even then she could have blushed scarlet at the thought, but she bent down to his face, very close to it, till her cheek almost touched his as she spoke in a very trembling, low voice.

"Not yet—not yet—come back for one moment, only for one little moment! Oh, let it be God's miracle for me!"

She hardly knew what she said, but the miracle was there, for she heard his breath come again and again, and as she stared into her everlasting night, strange flashes, like light, shot through her brain, her bosom trembled, and her hands stiffened in the spasm of a delirious joy.

"Come back!" she cried again. "Come back!" Her hands shook as they felt his body move.

His voice came again, not in a word yet, but yet not in a groan of pain. His eyes, that had been half open and staring, closed with a look of rest, and colour rose slowly in his cheeks. Then he felt her breath, and his strength returned for an instant, his arms contracted and clasped her to him violently.

"Dolores!" he cried, and in a moment his lips rained kisses on her face, while his eyes were still closed.

Then he sank back again exhausted, and her arm kept his head from striking the marble floor. The girl's cheek flushed a deep red, as she tried to speak, and her words came broken and indistinct.

"I am not Dolores," she managed to say. "I am Inez—"

But he did not hear, for he was swooning again, and the painful blush sank down again, as she realized that he was once more unconscious. She wondered whether the room were dark or whether there were lights, or whether he had not opened his eyes when he had kissed her. His head was very heavy on her arm. With her other hand she drew off the hood she wore and rolled it together, and lifting him a little she made a pillow of it so that he rested easily. He had not recognized her, and she believed he was dying, he had kissed her, and all eternity could not take from her the memory of that moment. In the wild confusion of her thoughts she was almost content that he should die now, for she had felt what she had never dared to feel in sweetest dreams, and it had been true, and no one could steal it away now, nor should any one ever know it, not even Dolores herself. The jealous thought was there, in the whirlwind of her brain, with all the rest, sudden, fierce, and strong, as if Don John had been hers in life, and as if the sister she loved so dearly had tried to win him from her. He was hers in death, and should be hers for ever, and no one should ever know. It did not matter that he had taken her for another, his kisses were her own. Once only had a man's lips, not her father's, touched her cheek, and they had been the lips of the fairest, and best, and bravest man in the world, her idol and her earthly god. He might die now, and she would follow him, and in the world beyond God would make it right somehow, and he, and she, and her sister would all be but one loving soul for ever and ever. There was no reasoning in all that—it was but the flash of wild thoughts that all seemed certainties.

But Don John of Austria was neither dead nor dying. His brother's sword had pierced his doublet and run through the outer flesh beneath his left arm, as he stood sideways with his right thrust forward. The wound was a mere scratch, as soldiers count wounds, and though the young blood had followed quickly, it had now ceased to flow. It was the fall that had hurt him, not the stab. The carpet had slipped from under his feet, and he had fallen backwards to his full length, as a man falls on ice, and his head had struck the marble floor so violently that he had lain half an hour almost in a swoon, like a dead man at first, with neither breath nor beating of the heart to give a sign of life, till after Dolores had left him; and then he had sighed back to consciousness by very slow degrees, because no one was there to help him, to raise his head a few inches from the floor, to dash a little cold water into his face.

He stirred uneasily now, and moved his hands again, and his eyes opened wide. Inez felt the slight motion and heard his regular breathing, and an instinct told her that he was conscious, and not in a dream as he had been when he had kissed her.

"I am Inez," she said, almost mechanically, and not knowing why she had feared that he should take her for her sister. "I found your Highness here—they all think that you are dead."

"Dead?" There was surprise in his voice, and his eyes looked at her and about the room as he spoke, though he did not yet lift his head from the hood on which it lay. "Dead?" he repeated, dazed still. "No—I must have fallen. My head hurts me."

He uttered a sharp sound as he moved again, more of annoyance than of suffering, as strong men do who unexpectedly find themselves hurt or helpless, or both. Then, as his eyes fell upon the open door of the inner room, he forgot his pain instantly and raised himself upon his hand with startled eyes.

"Where is Dolores?" he cried, in utmost anxiety. "Where have they taken her? Did she get out by the window?"

"She is safe," answered Inez, hardly knowing what she said, for he turned pale instantly and had barely heard her answer, when he reeled as he half sat and almost fell against her.

She held him as well as she could, but the position was strained and she was not very strong. Half mad now, between fear lest he should die in her arms and the instinctive belief that he was to live, she wished with all her heart that some one would come and help her, or send for a physician. He might die for lack of some simple aid she did not know how to give him. But he had only been dizzy with the unconscious effort he had made, and presently he rested on his own hand again.

"Thank God Dolores is safe!" he said, in a weak voice. "Can you help me to get to a chair, my dear child? I must have been badly stunned. I wonder how long I have been here. I remember—"

He paused and passed one hand over his eyes. The first instinct of strong persons who have been unconscious is to think aloud, and to try and recall every detail of the accident that left them unconscious.

"I remember—the King was here—we talked and we quarrelled—oh!"

The short exclamation ended his speech, as complete recollection returned, and he knew that the secret must be kept, for his brother's sake. He laid one head on the slight girl's shoulder to steady himself, and with his other he helped himself to kneel on one knee.

"I am very dizzy," he said. "Try and help me to a chair, Inez."

She rose swiftly, holding his hand, and then putting one arm round him under his own. He struggled to his feet and leaned his weight upon her, and breathed hard. The effort hurt him where the flesh was torn.

"I am wounded, too," he said quietly, as he glanced at the blood on his vest. "But it is nothing serious, I think."

With the instinct of the soldier hurt in the chest, he brushed his lips with the small lace ruffle of his sleeve, and looked at it, expecting to see the bright red stains that might mean death. There was nothing.

"It is only a scratch," he said, with an accent of indifference. "Help me to the chair, my dear."

"Where?" she asked. "I do not know the room."

"One forgets that you are blind," he answered, with a smile, and leaning heavily upon her, he led her by his weight, till he could touch the chair in which he had sat reading Dolores' letter when the King had entered an hour earlier.

He sat down with a sigh of relief, and stretched first one leg and then the other, and leaned back with half-closed eyes.

"Where is Dolores?" he asked at last. "Why did she go away?"

"The jester took her away, I think," answered Inez. "I found them together on the terrace. She was trying to come back to you, but he prevented her. They thought you were dead."

"That was wise of him." He spoke faintly still, and when he opened his eyes, the room swam with him. "And then?"

"Then I told her what had happened at court; I had heard everything from the gallery. And Dolores went down alone. I could not understand what she was going to do, but she is trying to save our father."

"Your father!" Don John looked at her in surprise, forgetting his hurt, but it was as if some one had struck his head again, and he closed his eyes. "What has happened?" he asked faintly. "Try and tell me. I do not understand."

"My father thought he had killed you," answered Inez, in surprise. "He came into the great hall when the King was there, and he cried out in a loud voice that he had killed you, unarmed."

"Your father?" He forgot his suffering altogether now. "Your father was not even in the room when—when I fell! And did the King say nothing? Tell me quickly!"

"There was a great uproar, and I ran away to find Dolores. I do not know what happened afterwards."

Don John turned painfully in his chair and lifted his hand to the back of his head. But he said nothing at first, for he was beginning to understand, and he would not betray the secret of his accident even to Inez.

"I knew he could not have done it! I thought he was mad—he most have been! But I also thought your Highness was dead."

"Dear child!" Don John's voice was very kind. "You brought me to life. Your father was not here. It was some one else who hurt me. Do you think you could find Dolores or send some one to tell her—to tell every one that I am alive? Say that I had a bad fall and was stunned for a while. Never mind the scratch—it is nothing—do not speak of it. If you could find Adonis, he could go."

He groaned now, for the pain of speaking was almost intolerable. Inez put out her hand towards him.

"Does it hurt very much?" she asked, with a sort of pathetic, childlike sympathy.

"Yes, my head hurts, but I shall not faint. There is something to drink by the bed, I think—on this side. If you could only find it. I cannot walk there yet, I am so giddy."

"Some one is coming!" exclaimed Inez, instead of answering him. "I hear some one on the terrace. Hark!" she listened with bent head. "It is Adonis. I know his step. There he is!"

Almost as she spoke the last words the dwarf was in the doorway. He stood still, transfixed with astonishment.

"Mercy of heaven!" he exclaimed devoutly. "His Highness is alive after all!"

"Yes," said Inez, in a glad tone. "The Prince was only stunned by the fall. Go and tell Dolores—go out and tell every one—bring every one here to me!"

"No!" cried Don John. "Try and bring Doña Dolores alone, and let no one else know. The rest can wait."

"But your Highness needs a physician," protested the dwarf, not yet recovered from his astonishment. "Your Highness is wounded, and must therefore be bled at once. I will call the Doctor Galdos—"

"I tell you it is nothing," interrupted Don John. "Do as I order you, and bring Doña Dolores. Give me that drink there, first—from the little table. In a quarter of an hour I shall be quite well again. I have been as badly stunned before when my horse has fallen with me at a barrier."

The jester swung quickly to the table, in his awkward, bow-legged gait, and brought the beaker that stood there. Don John drank eagerly, for his lips were parched with pain.

"Go!" he said imperatively. "And come back quickly."

"I will go," said Adonis. "But I may not come back quickly, for I believe that Doña Dolores is with his Majesty at this moment, or with her father, unless the three are together. Since it has pleased your Highness not to remain dead, it would have been much simpler not to die at all, for your Highness's premature death has caused trouble which your Highness's premature resurrection may not quickly set right."

"The sooner you bring Doña Dolores, the sooner the tremble will be over," said Don John. "Go at once, and do your best."

Adonis rolled away, shaking his head and almost touching the floor with his hands as he walked.

"So the Last Trumpet is not merely another of those priests' tales!" he muttered. "I shall meet Don Carlos on the terrace, and the Emperor in the corridor, no doubt! They might give a man time to confess his sins. It was unnecessary that the end of the world should come so suddenly!"

The last words of his jest were spoken to himself, for he was already outside when he uttered them, and he had no intention of wasting time in bearing the good news to Dolores. The difficulty was to find her. He had been a witness of the scene in the hall from the balcony, and he guessed that when she left the hall with Ruy Gomez she would go either to her father or the King. It would not be an easy matter to see her, and it was by no means beyond the bounds of possibility that he might be altogether hindered from doing so, unless he at once announced to every one he met the astounding fact that Don John was alive after all. He was strongly tempted to do that, without waiting for it seemed by far the most sensible thing to do in the disturbed state of the court; but it was his business to serve and amuse many masters, and his office, if not his life, depended upon obeying each in turn and finding the right jest for each. He placed the King highest, of course, among those he had to please, and before he had gone far in the corridor he slackened his pace to give himself time to think over the situation. Either the King had meant to kill Don John himself, or he had ordered Mendoza to do so. That much was clear to any one who had known the secret of Don Carlos' death, and the dwarf had been one of the last who had talked with the unfortunate Prince before that dark tragedy. And on this present night he had seen everything, and knew more of the thoughts of each of the actors in the drama than any one else, so that he had no doubt as to his conclusions. If, then, the King had wished to get rid of Don John, he would be very much displeased to learn that the latter was alive after all. It would not be good to be the bearer of that news, and it was more than likely that Philip would let Mendoza go to the scaffold for the attempt, as he long afterwards condemned Antonio Perez to death for the murder of Escobedo, Don John's secretary, though he himself had ordered Perez to do that deed; as he had already allowed the ecclesiastic Doctor Cazalla to be burned alive, though innocent, rather than displease the judges who had condemned him. The dwarf well knew that there was no crime, however monstrous, of which Philip was not capable, and of the righteous necessity of which he could not persuade himself if he chose. Nothing could possibly be more dangerous than to stand between him and the perpetration of any evil he considered politically necessary, except perhaps to hinder him in the pursuit of his gloomy and secret pleasures. Adonis decided at once that he would not be the means of enlightening the King on the present occasion. He most go to some one else. The second person in command of his life, and whom he dreaded most after Philip himself, was the Princess of Eboli.

He knew her secret, too, as he had formerly known how she had forged the letters that brought about the deaths of Don Carlos and of Queen Isabel; for the Princess ruled him by fear, and knew that she could trust him as long as he stood in terror of her. He knew, therefore, that she had not only forgiven Don John for not yielding to her charm in former days, but that she now hoped that he might ascend the throne in Philip's stead, by fair means or foul, and that the news of his death must have been a destructive blow to her hopes. He made up his mind to tell her first that he was alive, unless he could get speech with Dolores alone, which seemed improbable. Having decided this, he hastened his walk again.

Before he reached the lower story of the palace he composed his face to an expression of solemnity, not to say mourning, for he remembered that as no one knew the truth but himself, he must not go about with too gay a look. In the great vestibule of the hall he found a throng of courtiers, talking excitedly in low tones, but neither Dolores nor Ruy Gomez was there. He sidled up to a tall officer of the guards who was standing alone, looking on.

"Could you inform me, sir," he asked, "what became of Doña Dolores de Mendoza when she left the hall with the Prince of Eboli?"

The officer looked down at the dwarf, with whom he had never spoken before, but who, in his way, was considered to be a personage of importance by the less exalted members of the royal household. Indeed, Adonis was by no means given to making acquaintance at haphazard with all those who wished to know him in the hope that he might say a good word for them when the King was in a pleasant humour.

"I do not know, Master Adonis," answered the magnificent lieutenant, very politely. "But if you wish it, I will enquire."

"You are most kind and courteous, sir," answered the dwarf ceremoniously. "I have a message for the lady."

The officer turned away and went towards the King's apartments, leaving the jester in the corner. Adonis knew that he might wait some time before his informant returned, and he shrank into the shadow to avoid attracting attention. That was easy enough, so long as the crowd was moving and did not diminish, but before long he heard some one speaking within the hall, as if addressing a number of persons at once, and the others began to leave the vestibule in order to hear what was passing. Though the light did not fall upon him directly, the dwarf, in his scarlet dress, became a conspicuous object. Yet he did not dare to go away, for fear of missing the officer when the latter should return. His anxiety to escape observation was not without cause, since he really wished to give Don John's message to Dolores before any one else knew the truth. In a few moments he saw the Princess of Eboli coming towards him, leaning on the arm of the Duke of Medina Sidonia. She came from the hall as if she had been listening to the person who was still speaking near the door, and her handsome face wore a look of profound dejection and disappointment. She had evidently seen the dwarf, for she walked directly towards him, and at half a dozen paces she stopped and dismissed her companion, who bowed low, kissed the tips of her fingers, and withdrew.

Adonis drew down the corners of his mouth, bent his head still lower, and tried to look as unhappy as possible, in imitation of the Princess's expression. She stood still before him, and spoke briefly in imperious tones.

"What is the meaning of all this?" she asked. "Tell me the truth at once. It will be the better for you."

"Madam," answered Adonis, with all the assurance he could muster, "I think your Excellency knows the truth much better than I."

The Princess bent her black brows and her eyes began to gleam angrily. Titian would not have recognized in her stern face the smiling features of his portrait of her—of the insolently beautiful Venus painted by order of King Philip when the Princess was in the height of his favour.

"My friend," she said, in a mocking tone, "I know nothing, and you know everything. At the present moment your disappearance from the court will not attract even the smallest attention compared with the things that are happening. If you do not tell me what you know, you will not be here to-morrow, and I will see that you are burned alive for a sorcerer next week. Do you understand? Now tell me who killed Don John of Austria, and why. Be quick, I have no time to lose."

Adonis made up his mind very suddenly that it would be better to disobey Don John than the angry woman who was speaking to him.

"Nobody killed him," he answered bluntly.

The Princess was naturally violent, especially with her inferiors, and when she was angry she easily lost all dignity. She seized the dwarf by the arm and shook him.

"No jesting!" she cried. "He did not kill himself—who did it?"

"Nobody," repeated Adonis doggedly, and quite without fear, for he knew how glad she would be to know the truth. "His Highness is not dead at all—"

"You little hound!" The Princess shook him furiously again and threatened to strike him with her other hand.

He only laughed.

"Before heaven, Madam," he said, "the Prince is alive and recovered, and is sitting in his chair. I have just been talking with him. Will you go with me to his Highness's apartment? If he is not there, and safe, burn me for a heretic to-morrow."

The Princess's hands dropped by her sides in sheer amazement, for she saw that the jester was in earnest.

"He had a scratch in the scuffle," he continued, "but it was the fall that killed him, his resurrection followed soon afterwards—and I trust that his ascension may be no further distant than your Excellency desires."

He laughed at his blasphemous jest, and the Princess laughed too, a little wildly, for she could hardly control her joy.

"And who wounded him?" she asked suddenly. "You know everything, you must know that also."

"Madam," said the dwarf, fixing his eyes on hers, "we both know the name of the person who wounded Don John, very well indeed, I regret that I should not be able to recall it at this moment. His Highness has forgotten it too, I am sure."

The Princess's expression did not change, but she returned his gaze steadily during several seconds, and then nodded slowly to show that she understood. Then she looked away and was silent for a moment.

"I am sorry I was rough with you, Adonis," she said at last, thoughtfully. "It was hard to believe you at first, and if the Prince had been dead, as we all believed, your jesting would have been abominable. There,"—she unclasped a diamond brooch from her bodice—"take that, Adonis—you can turn it into money."

The Princess's financial troubles were notorious, and she hardly ever possessed any ready gold.

"I shall keep it as the most precious of my possessions," answered the dwarf readily.

"No," she said quickly. "Sell it. The King—I mean—some one may see it if you keep it."

"It shall be sold to-morrow, then," replied the jester, bending his head to hide his smile, for he understood what she meant.

"One thing more," she said; "Don John did not send you down to tell this news to the court without warning. He meant that I should know it before any one else. You have told me—now go away and do not tell others."

Adonis hesitated a moment. He wished to do Don John's bidding if he could, but he knew his danger, and that he should be forgiven if, to save his own head, he did not execute the commission. The Princess wished an immediate answer, and she had no difficulty in guessing the truth.

"His Highness sent you to find Doña Dolores," she said. "Is that not true?"

"It is true," replied Adonis. "But," he added, anticipating her wish out of fear, "it is not easy to find Doña Dolores."

"It is impossible. Did you expect to find her by waiting in this corner! Adonis, it is safer for you to serve me than Don John, and in serving me you will help his interests. You know that. Listen to me— Doña Dolores must believe him dead till to-morrow morning. She must on no account find out that he is alive."

At that moment the officer who had offered to get information for the dwarf returned. Seeing the latter in conversation with such a great personage, he waited at a little distance.

"If you have found out where Doña Dolores de Mendoza is at this moment, my dear sir," said Adonis, "pray tell the Princess of Eboli, who is very anxious to know."

The officer bowed and came nearer.

"Doña Dolores de Mendoza is in his Majesty's inner apartment," he said.

CHAPTER XX

Dolores and Ruy Gomez had passed through the outer vestibule, and he left her to pursue his way towards the western end of the Alcazar, which was at a considerable distance from the royal apartments. Dolores went down the corridor till she came to the niche and the picture before which Don John had paused to read the Princess of Eboli's letter after supper. She stopped a moment, for she suddenly felt that her strength was exhausted and that she must rest or break down altogether. She leaned her weight against the elaborately carved railing that shut off the niche like a shrine, and looked at the painting, which was one of Raphael's smaller masterpieces, a Holy Family so smoothly and delicately painted that it jarred upon her at that moment as something untrue and out of all keeping with possibility. Though most perfectly drawn and coloured, the spotlessly neat figures with their airs of complacent satisfaction seemed horribly out of place in the world of suffering she was condemned to dwell in, and she fancied, somewhat irreverently and resentfully, that they would look as much out of keeping with their surroundings in a heaven that must be won by the endurance of pain Their complacent smiles seemed meant for her anguish, and she turned from the picture in displeasure, and went on.

She was going back to her sister on the terrace, and she was going to kneel once more beside the dear head of the man she had loved, and to say one last prayer before his face was covered for ever. At the thought she felt that she needed no rest again, for the vision drew her to the sorrowful presence of its reality, and she could not have stopped again if she had wished to. She must go straight on, on to the staircase, up the long flight of steps, through the lonely corridors, and out at last to the moonlit terrace where Inez was waiting. She went forward in a dream, without pausing. Since she had freed her father she had a right to go back to her grief. But as she went along, lightly and quickly, it seemed beyond her own belief that she should have found strength for what she had done that night. For the strength of youth is elastic and far beyond its own knowledge. Dolores had reached the last passage that led out upon the terrace, when she heard hurrying footsteps behind her, and a woman in a cloak slipped beside her, walking very easily and smoothly. It was the Princess of Eboli. She had left the dwarf, after frightening him into giving up his search for Dolores, and she was hastening to Don John's rooms to make sure that the jester had not deceived her or been himself deceived in some way she could not understand.

Dolores had lost her cloak in the hall, and was bareheaded, in her court dress. The Princess recognized her in the gloom and stopped her.

"I have looked for you everywhere," she said. "Why did you run away from me before?"

"It was my blind sister who was with you," answered Dolores, who knew her voice at once and had understood from her father what had happened. "Where are you going now?" she asked, without giving the Princess time to put a question.

"I was looking for you. I wish you to come and stay with me to-night—"

"I will stay with my father. I thank you for your kindness, but I would not on any account leave him now."

"Your father is in prison—in the west tower—he has just been sent there. How can you stay with him?"

"You are well informed," said Dolores quietly. "But your husband is just now gone to release him. I gave Don Ruy Gomez the order which his Majesty had himself placed in my hands, and the Prince was kind enough to take it to the west tower himself. My father is unconditionally free."

The Princess looked fixedly at Dolores while the girl was speaking, but it was very dark in the corridor and the lamp was flickering to go out in the night breeze. The only explanation of Mendoza's release lay in the fact that the King was already aware that Don John was alive and in no danger. In that case Dolores knew it, too. It was no great matter, though she had hoped to keep the girl out of the way of hearing the news for a day or two. Dolores' mournful face might have told her that she was mistaken, if there had been more light; but it was far too dark to see shades of colour or expression.

"So your father is free!" she said. "Of course, that was to be expected, but I am glad that he has been set at liberty at once."

"I do not think it was exactly to be expected," answered Dolores, in some surprise, and wondering whether there could have been any simpler way of getting what she had obtained by such extraordinary means.

"He might have been kept under arrest until to-morrow morning, I suppose," said the Princess quietly. "But the King is of course anxious to destroy the unpleasant impression produced by this absurd affair, as soon as possible."

"Absurd!" Dolores' anger rose and overflowed at the word. "Do you dare to use such a word to me to-night?"

"My dear Dolores, why do you lose your temper about such a thing?" asked the Princess, in a conciliatory tone. "Of course if it had all ended as we expected it would, I never should use such a word—if Don John had died—"

"What do you mean?" Dolores held her by the wrist in an instant and the maddest excitement was in her voice.

"What I mean? Why—" the Princess stopped short, realizing that Dolores might not know the truth after all. "What did I say?" she asked, to gain time. "Why do you hold my hand like that?"

"You called the murder of Don John an absurd affair, and then you said, 'if Don John had died'—as if he were not lying there dead in his room, twenty paces from where you stand! Are you mad? Are you playing some heartless comedy with me? What does it all mean?"

The Princess was very worldly wise, and she saw at a glance that she must tell Dolores the truth. If she did not, the girl would soon learn it from some one else, but if she did, Dolores would always remember who had told her the good news.

"My dear," she said very gently, "let my wrist go and let me take your arm. We do not understand each other, or you would not be so angry with me. Something has happened of which you do not know—"

"Oh, no! I know the whole truth!" Dolores interrupted her, and resisted being led along in a slow walk. "Let me go to him!" she cried. "I only wish to see him once more—"

"But, dearest child, listen to me—if I do not tell you everything at once, it is because the shock might hurt you. There is some hope that he may not die—"

"Hope! Oh no, no, no! I saw him lying dead—"

"He had fainted, dear. He was not dead—"

"Not dead?" Dolores' voice broke. "Tell me—tell me quickly." She pressed her hand to her side.

"No. He came to himself after you had left him—he is alive. No—listen to me—yes, dear, he is alive and not much hurt. The wound was a scratch, and he was only stunned—he is well—to-morrow he will be as well as ever—ah, dear, I told you so!"

Dolores had borne grief, shame, torment of mind that night, as bravely as ever a woman bore all three, but the joy of the truth that he lived almost ended her life then and there. She fell back upon the Princess's arm and threw out her hands wildly, as if she were fighting for breath, and the lids of her eyes quivered violently and then were quite still, and she uttered a short, unnatural sound that was more like a groan of pain than a cry of happiness.

The Princess was very strong, and held her, steadying herself against the wall, thinking anything better than to let her slip to the floor and lie swooning on the stone pavement. But the girl was not unconscious, and in a moment her own strength returned.

"Let me go!" she cried wildly. "Let me go to him, or I shall die!"

"Go, child—go," said the Princess, with an accent of womanly kindness that was rare in her voice. But Dolores did not hear it, for she was already gone.

Dolores saw nothing in the room, as she entered, but the eyes of the man she loved, though Inez was still beside him. Dolores threw herself wildly into his arms and hid her face, crying out incoherent words between little showers of happy tears; and her hands softly beat upon his shoulders and against his neck, and stole up wondering to his cheeks and touched his hair, as she drew back her head and held him still to look at him and see that he was whole. She had no speech left, for it was altogether beyond the belief of any sense but touch itself that a man should rise unhurt from the dead, to go on living as if nothing not common had happened in his life, to have his strength at once, to look into her eyes and rain kisses on the lids still dark with grief for his death. Sight could not believe the sight, hearing could not but doubt the sound, yet her hands held him and touched him, and it was he, unhurt saving for a scratch and a bruise. In her overwhelming happiness, she had no questions, and the first syllables that her lips could shape made broken words of love, and of thanks to Heaven that he had been saved alive for her, while her hands still fluttered to his face and beat gently and quickly on his shoulders and his arms, as if fearing lest he should turn to incorporeal light, without substance under her touch, and vanish then in air, as happiness does in a dream, leaving only pain behind.

But at last she threw back her head and let him go, and her hands brushed away the last tears from her grey eyes, and she looked into his face and smiled with parted lips, drinking the sight of him with her breath and eyes and heart. One moment so, and then they kissed as only man and woman can when there has been death between them and it is gone not to come back again.

Then memory returned, though very slowly and broken in many places, for it seemed to her as if she had not been separated from him a moment, and as if he must know all she had done without hearing her story in words. The time had been so short since she had kissed him last, in the little room beyond: there had been the minutes of waiting until the King had come, and then the trying of the door, and then the quarrel, that had lasted a short ten minutes to end in Don John's fall; then the half hour during which he had lain unconscious and alone till Inez had come at the moment when Dolores had gone down to the throne room; and after that the short few minutes in which she had met her father, and then her interview with the King, which had not lasted long, and now she was with him again; and it was not two hours since they had parted—a lifetime of two hours.

"I cannot believe it!" she cried, and now she laughed at last. "I cannot, I cannot! It is impossible!"

"We are both alive," he answered. "We are both flesh and blood, and breathing. I feel as if I had been in an illness or in a sleep that had lasted very long."

"And I in an awful dream." Her face grew grave as she thought of what was but just passed. "You must know it all—surely you know it already—oh, yes! I need not tell it all."

"Something Inez has told me," he replied, "and some things I guess, but I do not know everything. You must try and tell me—but you should not be here—it is late. When my servants know that I am living, they will come back, and my gentlemen and my officers. They would have left me here all night, if I had been really dead, lest being seen near my body should send them to trial for my death." He laughed. "They were wise enough in their way. But you cannot stay here."

"If the whole court found me here, it would not matter," answered Dolores. "Their tongues can take nothing from my name which my own words have not given them to feed on."

"I do not understand," he said, suddenly anxious. "What have you said? What have you done?"

Inez came near them from the window, by which she had been standing. She laid a hand on Dolores' arm.

"I will watch," she said. "If I hear anything, I will warn you, and you can go into the small room again."

She went out almost before either of them could thank her. They had, indeed, forgotten her presence in the room, being accustomed to her being near them; but she could no longer bear to stay, listening to their loving words that made her loneliness so very dark. And now, too, she had memories of her own, which she would keep secret to the end of her life,—beautiful and happy recollections of that sweet moment when the man that seemed dead had breathed and had clasped her in his arms, taking her for the other, and had kissed her as he would have kissed the one he loved. She knew at last what a kiss might be, and that was much; but she knew also what it was to kneel by her dead love and to feel his life come back, breath by breath and beat by beat, till he was all alive; and few women have felt that or can guess how great it is to feel. It was better to go out into the dark and listen, lest any one should disturb the two, than to let her memories of short happiness be marred by hearing words that were not meant for her.

"She found you?" asked Dolores, when she was gone.

"Yes, she found me. You had gone down, she said, to try and save your father. He is safe now!" he laughed.

"She found you alive." Dolores lingered on the words. "I never envied her before, I think; and it is not because if I had stayed I should have suffered less, dear." She put up her hands upon his shoulders again. "It is not for that, but to have thought you dead and to have seen you grow alive again, to have watched your face, to have seen your eyes wake and the colour come back to your cheeks and the warmth to your dear hands! I would have given anything for that, and you would rather that I should have been there, would you not?" She laughed low and kissed away the answer from his lips. "If I had stayed beside you, it would have been sooner, love. You would have felt me there even in your dream of death, and you would have put out your hand to come back to me. Say that you would! You could not have let me lie there many minutes longer breaking my heart over you and wanting to die, too, so that we might be buried together. Surely my kisses would have brought you back!"

"I dreamed they did, as mine would you."

"Sit down beside me," she said presently. "It will be very hard to tell—and it cannot be very long before they come. Oh, they may find me here! It cannot matter now, for I told them all that I had been long in your room to-night."

"Told them all? Told whom? The King? What did you say?" His face was grave again.

"The King, the court, the whole world. But it is harder to tell you." She blushed and looked away. "It was the King that wounded you—I heard you fall."

"Scratched me. I was only stunned for a while."

"He drew his sword, for I heard it. You know the sound a sword makes when it is drawn from a leathern sheath? Of course—you are a soldier! I have often watched my father draw his, and I know the soft, long pull. The King drew quickly, and I knew you were unarmed, and besides—you had promised me that you would not raise your hand against him."

"I remember that my sword was on the table in its scabbard. I got it into my hand, sheathed as it was, to guard myself. Where is it? I had forgotten that. It must be somewhere on the floor."

"Never mind—your men will find it. You fell, and then there was silence, and presently I heard my father's voice saying that he had killed you defenceless. They went away. I was half dead myself when I fell there beside you on the floor. There—do you see? You lay with your head towards the door and one arm out. I shall see you so till I die, whenever I think of it. Then—I forget. Adonis must have found me there, and he carried me away, and Inez met me on the terrace and she had heard my father tell the King that he had murdered you—and it was the King who had done it! Do you understand?"

"I see, yes. Go on!" Don John was listening breathlessly, forgetting the pain he still suffered from time to time.

"And then I went down, and I made Don Ruy Gomez stand beside me on the steps, and the whole court was there—the Grandees and the great dukes—Alva, Medina Sidonia, Medina Cali, Infantado, the Princess of Eboli—the Ambassadors, everyone, all the maids of honour, hundreds and hundreds—an ocean of faces, and they knew me, almost all of them."

"What did you say?" asked Don John very anxiously. "What did you tell them all? That you had been here?"

"Yes—more than that, much more. It was not true, but I hoped they would believe it I said—" the colour filled her face and she caught her breath. "Oh, how can I tell you? Can you not guess what I said?"

"That we were married already, secretly?" he asked. "You might have said that."

"No. Not that—no one would have believed me. I told them," she paused and gathered her strength, and then the words came quickly, ashamed of being heard—"I told them that I knew my father had no share in the crime, because I had been here long to-night, in this room, and even when you were killed, and that I was here because I had given you all, my life, my soul, my honour, everything."

"Great God!" exclaimed Don John starting. "And you did that to save your father?"

She had covered her face with her hands for a moment. Then suddenly she rose and turned away from him, and paced the floor.

"Yes. I did that. What was there for me to do? It was better that I should be ruined and end in a convent than that my father should die on the scaffold. What would have become of Inez?"

"What would have become of you?" Don John's eyes followed her in loving wonder.

"It would not have mattered. But I had thrown away my name for nothing. They believed me, I think, but the King, to spare himself, was determined that my father should die. We met as he was led away to prison. Then I went to the King himself—and when I came away I had my father's release in my hand. Oh, I wish I had that to do again! I wish you had been there, for you would have been proud of me, then. I told him he had killed you, I heard him confess it, I threatened to tell the court, the world, all Spain, if he would not set my father free. But the other—can you forgive me, dear?"

She stood before him now, and the colour was fainter in her cheeks, for she trusted him with all her heart, and she put out her hands.

"Forgive you? What? For doing the bravest thing a woman ever did?"

"I thought you would know it in heaven and understand," she said. "It is better that you know it on earth—but it was hard to tell."

He held her hands together and pressed them to his lips. He had no words to tell her what he thought. Again and again he silently kissed the firm white fingers folded in his own.

"It was magnificent," he said at last. "But it will be hard to undo, very hard."

"What will it ever matter, since we know it is not true?" she asked. "Let the world think what it will, say what it likes—"

"The world shall never say a slighting word of you," he interrupted. "Do you think that I will let the world say openly what I would not hear from the King alone between these four walls? There is no fear of that, love. I will die sooner."

"Oh, no!" she cried, in sudden fear. "Oh, do not speak of death again to-night! I cannot bear the word!"

"Of life, then, of life together,—of all our lives in peace and love! But first this must be set right. It is late, but this must be done now—at once. There is only one way, there is only one thing to be done."

He was silent for a moment, and his eyes looked quickly to the door and back to Dolores' face.

"I cannot go away," she cried, nestling to him. "You will not make me go? What does it matter?"

"It matters much. It will matter much more hereafter." He was on his feet, and all his energy and graceful strength came back as if he had received no hurt. "There is little time left, but what there is, is ours. Inez!" He was at the door. "Is no one there upon the terrace? Is there no servant, no sentry? Ho, there! Who are you? Come here, man! Let me see your face! Adonis?"

Inez and the dwarf were in the door. Dolores was behind him, looking out, not knowing what he meant to do. He had his hand on the dwarf's arm in his haste. The crooked creature looked up, half in fear.

"Quick! Go!" cried Don John. "Get me a priest, a monk, a bishop,—anything that wears a frock and can speak Latin. Bring him here. Threaten his life, in my name, if you like. Tell him Don John of Austria is in extreme need, and must have a priest. Quick, man! Fly! Your life and fortune are in your legs! Off, man! Off!"

Adonis was already gone, rolling through the gloom with swinging arms, more like a huge bat than anything human, and at a rate of speed none would have guessed latent in his little twisted legs. Don John drew back within the door.

"Stay within," he said to Dolores, gently pressing her backwards into the room. "I will let no one pass till the priest comes; and then the world may come, too, and welcome,—and the court and the King, and the devil and all his angels!" He laughed aloud in his excitement.

"You have not told me," Dolores began, but her eyes laughed in his.

"But you know without words," he answered. "When that is done which a priest can do in an instant, and no one else, the world is ours, with all it holds, in spite of men and women and Kings!"

"It is ours already," she cried happily. "But is this wise, love? Are you not too quick?"

"Would you have me slow when you and your name and my honour are all at stake on one quick throw? Can we play too quickly at such a game with fate? There will be time, just time, no more. For when the news is known, it will spread like fire. I wonder that no one comes yet."

He listened, and Inez' hearing was ten times more sensitive than his, but there was no sound. For besides Dolores and Inez only the dwarf and the Princess of Eboli knew that Don John was living; and the Princess had imposed silence on the jester and was in no haste to tell the news until she should decide who was to know it first and how her own advantage could be secured. So there was time, and Adonis swung himself along the dim corridor and up winding stairs that be knew, and roused the little wizened priest who lived in the west tower all alone, and whose duty it was to say a mass each morning for any prisoner who chanced to be locked up there; and when there was no one in confinement he said his mass for himself in the small chapel which was divided from the prison only by a heavy iron grating. The jester sometimes visited him in his lonely dwelling and shocked and delighted him with alternate tales of the court's wickedness and with harmless jokes that made his wizened cheeks pucker and wrinkle into unaccustomed smiles. And he had some hopes of converting the poor jester to a pious life. So they were friends. But when the old priest heard that Don John of Austria was suddenly dying in his room and that there was no one to shrive him,—for that was the tale Adonis told,—he trembled from head to foot like a paralytic, and the buttons of his cassock became as drops of quicksilver and slipped from his weak fingers everywhere except into the buttonholes, so that the dwarf had to fasten them for him in a furious hurry, and find his stole, and set his hat upon his head, and polish away the tears of excitement from his cheeks with his own silk handkerchief. Yet it was well done, though so quickly, and he had a kind old face and was a good priest.

But when Adonis had almost carried him to Don John's door, and pushed him into the room, and when he saw that the man he supposed to be dying was standing upright, holding a most beautiful lady by the hand, he drew back, seeing that he had been deceived, and suspecting that he was to be asked to do something for which he had no authority. The dwarf's long arm was behind him, however, and he could not escape.

"This is the priest of the west tower, your Highness," said Adonis. "He is a good priest, but he is a little frightened now."

"You need fear nothing," said Don John kindly. "I am Don John of Austria. This lady is Doña Maria Dolores de Mendoza. Marry us without delay. We take each other for man and wife."

"But—" the little priest hesitated—"but, your Highness—the banns—or the bishop's license—"

"I am above banns and licenses, my good sir," answered Don John, "and if there is anything lacking in the formalities, I take it upon myself to set all right to-morrow. I will protect you, never fear. Make haste, for I cannot wait. Begin, sir, lose no time, and take my word for the right of what you do."

"The witnesses of this," faltered the old man, seeing that he must yield, but doubtful still.

"This lady is Doña Inez de Mendoza," said Don John, "and this is Miguel de Antona, the court jester. They are sufficient."

So it chanced that the witnesses of Don John of Austria's secret marriage were a blind girl and the King's fool.

The aged priest cleared his throat and began to say the words in Latin, and Don John and Dolores held their clasped hands before him, not knowing what else to do, and each looked into the other's eyes and saw there the whole world that had any meaning for them, while the priest said things they but half understood, but that made the world's difference to them, then and afterwards.

It was soon done, and he raised his trembling hand and blessed them, saying the words very softly and clearly and without stumbling, for they were familiar, and meant much; and having reached them, his haste was over. The dwarf was on his knees, his rough red head bent reverently low, and on the other side Inez knelt with joined hands, her blind eyes turned upward to her sister's face, while she prayed that all blessings of life and joy might be on the two she loved so well, and that they might have for ever and unbroken the infinite happiness she had felt for one instant that night, not meant for her, but dearer to her than all memories or hopes.

Then as the priest's words died away in the silent room, there was a sound of many feet and of many voices on the terrace outside, coming nearer and nearer to the door, very quickly; and the priest looked round in terror, not knowing what new thing was to come upon him, and wishing with all his heart that he were safe in his tower room again and out of all harm's way. But Don John smiled, while he still held Dolores' hand, and the dwarf rose quickly and led the priest into the study where Dolores had been shut up so long, and closed the door behind him.

That was hardly done when the outer door was opened wide, and a clear, formal voice was heard speaking outside.

"His Majesty the King!" cried the chamberlain who walked before Philip.

Dolores dropped Don John's hand and stood beside him, growing a little pale; but his face was serene and high, and he smiled quietly as he went forward to meet his brother. The King advanced also, with outstretched arms, and he formally embraced Don John, to exhibit his joy at such an unexpected recovery.

Behind him came in torch-bearers and guards and many of the court who had joined the train, and in the front rank Mendoza, grim and erect, but no longer ashy pale, and Ruy Gomez with him, and the Princess of Eboli, and all the chief Grandees of Spain, filling the wide bedchamber from side to side with a flood of rich colour in which the little constellations of their jewels shone here and there with changing lights.

Out of respect for the King they did not speak, and yet there was a soft sound of rejoicing in the room, and their very breathing was like a murmur of deep satisfaction. Then the King spoke, and all at once the silence was profound.

"I wished to be the first to welcome my dear brother back to life," he said. "The court has been in mourning for you these two hours, and none has mourned you more deeply and sorrowfully than I. We would all know the cause of your Highness's accident, the meaning of our friend Mendoza's strange self-accusation, and of other things we cannot understand without a word from you."

The chair in which Don John had sat to read Dolores' letter was brought forward, and the King took his seat in it, while the chief officers of the household grouped themselves round him. Don John remained standing, facing him and all the rest, while Dolores drew back a little into the shadow not far from him. The King's unmoving eyes watched him closely, even anxiously.

"The story is short, Sire, and if it is not all clear, I shall crave your Majesty's pardon for being silent on certain points which concern my private life. I was alone this evening in my room here, after your Majesty had left supper, and I was reading. A man came to visit me then whom I have known and trusted long. We were alone, we have had differences before, to-night sharp words passed between us. I ask your Majesty's permission not to name that man, for I would not do him an injury, though it should cost me my life."

His eyes were fixed on the King, who slowly nodded his assent. He had known that he could trust his brother not to betray him, and he wondered what was to come next. Don John smiled a little as he went on.

"There were sharp words," he said, "and being men, steel was soon out, and I received this scratch here—a mere nothing. But as chance would have it I fell backward and was so stunned that I seemed dead. And then, as I learn, my friend Mendoza there came in, either while we fought, or afterwards, and understood—and so, as I suppose, in generous fear for my good name, lest it should be told that I had been killed in some dishonest brawl, or for a woman's sake—my friend Mendoza, in the madness of generosity, and because my love for his beautiful daughter might give the tale some colour, takes all the blame upon himself, owns himself murderer, loses his wits, and well-nigh loses his head, too. So I understand the matter, Sire."

He paused a moment, and again the King slowly nodded, but this time he smiled also, and seemed much pleased.

"For what remains," Don John continued, "that is soon explained. This brave and noble lady whom you found here, you all know. I have loved her long and faithfully, and with all my heart. Those who know me, know that my word is good, and here before your Majesty, before man and before Heaven, I solemnly swear upon my most sacred word that no harm has ever come near her, by me, or by another. Yet, in the hope of saving her father's life, believing and yet not believing that he might have hurt me in some quarrel, she went among you, and told you the tale you know. I ask your Majesty to say that my word and oath are good, and thereby to give your Majesty's authority to what I say. And if there is any man here, or in Spain, among your Majesty's subjects, who doubts the word I give, let him say so, for this is a grave matter, and I wish to be believed before I say more."

A third time the King nodded, and this time not ungraciously, since matters had gone well for him.

"For myself," he said, "I would take your word against another man's oath, and I think there is no one bold enough to question what we both believe."

"I thank your Majesty. And moreover, I desire permission to present to your Majesty—"

He took Dolores' hand and drew her forward, though she came a little unwillingly, and was pale, and her deep grey eyes gazed steadily at the King's face.

"—My wedded wife," said Don John, completing the sentence.

"Your wife!" exclaimed the King, in great surprise. "Are you married already?"

"Wedded man and wife, Sire," answered Don John, in tones that all could hear.

"And what does Mendoza say to this?" asked Philip, looking round at the veteran soldier.

"That his Highness has done my house a great honour, your Majesty; and I pray that my daughter and I be not needlessly separated hereafter."

His glance went to Dolores' triumphant eyes almost timidly, and then rested on her face with a look she had never seen in his, save on that evening, but which she always found there afterwards. And at the same time the hard old man drew Inez close to him, for she had found him among the officers and she stood by him and rested her arm on his with a new confidence.

Then, as the King rose, there was a sound of glad voices in the room, as all talked at once and each told the other that an evil adventure was well ended, and that Don John of Austria was the bravest and the handsomest and the most honourable prince in the world, and that Maria Dolores de Mendoza had not her equal among women for beauty and high womanly courage and perfect devotion.

But there were a few who were ill pleased; for Antonio Perez said nothing, and absently smoothed his black hair with his immaculate white hand, and the Princess of Eboli was very silent, too, for it seemed to her that Don John's sudden marriage, and his reconciliation with his brother, had set back the beginning of her plan beyond the bounds of possible accomplishment; and she was right in that, and the beginning of her resentment against Don John for having succeeded in marrying Dolores in spite of every one was the beginning of the chain that led her to her own dark fate. For though she held the cards long in her hands after that, and played for high stakes, as she had done before, fortune failed her at the last, and she came to unutterable ruin.

It may be, too, that Don John's splendid destiny was measured on that night, and cut off beforehand, though his most daring fights were not yet fought, nor his greatest victories won. To tell more here would be to tell too much, and much, too, that is well told elsewhere. But this is true, that he loved Dolores with all his heart; that the marriage remained a court secret; and that she bore him one fair daughter, and died, and the child grew up under another reign, a holy nun, and was abbess of the convent of Las Huelgas whither Dolores was to have gone on the morning after that most eventful night.

F. Marion Crawford – A Short Biography

Francis Marion Crawford was born in Bagni di Lucca, Italy on 2nd August, 1854, the only son of the American sculptor Thomas Crawford and Louisa Cutler Ward. His aunt was Julia Ward Howe, the American poet, most famous for the words to 'The Battle Hymn of the Republic'.

After his father's death in 1857, his mother remarried to Luther Terry, with whom she had Crawford's half-sister, Margaret Ward Terry.

Crawford's education began at St Paul's School, Concord, New Hampshire and then went on to Cambridge University, the University of Heidelberg and finally the University of Rome.

In 1879, Crawford went to India to study the ancient language of Sanskrit and to edit Allahabad, The Indian Herald.

Returning to America in February 1881, he enrolled at Harvard University for a year to continue his studies in Sanskrit. Crawford had no real career path at this time although for two years he contributed to various periodicals, mainly The Critic.

Early in 1882, Crawford established a close, lifelong friendship with Isabella Stewart Gardner, a noted and eccentric heiress from Boston who over the years built up a large and eclectic collection of art.

Crawford lived most of his time in Boston with his Aunt Julia and Uncle Sam. The family were concerned by his lack of ambition, prospects in general, and his financial ones in particular.

His mother had hoped he might train in Boston for a career as an operatic baritone based on his private renditions of Schubert lieder. With that in mind it was, in January 1882, that George Henschel, the conductor of the Boston Symphony Orchestra, was called in to assess young Crawford's talents. Henschel was direct and to the point. Crawford would 'never be able to sing in perfect tune'. His Uncle Sam, knowing that Crawford was keen on literary pursuits, proposed that his years in India might be good source material to write about. Crawford agreed. He set to work. Uncle Sam also set about developing contacts with a number of New York publishers.

Events moved very quickly. By December of that year Crawford had completed his first novel, 'Mr Isaacs', based on modern Anglo-Indian life flavoured with a touch of Oriental mystery. It was an immediate success. Crawford set about writing a second novel and the result was 'Dr Claudius' in 1883.

In October 1884 he married Elizabeth Berdan, the daughter of the Civil War Union General Hiram Berdan. The marriage would produce two sons; Harold and Bertram, and two daughters; Eleanor and Clara.

Crawford, buoyed by his excellent start, now decided to return to Italy and to live there permanently.
The couple initially went to Sorrento and lived at the historic Hotel Cocumella during 1885 before moving permanently to Sant' Agnello, where the purchase of the Villa Renzi would now be rededicated as Villa Crawford.

As a writer Crawford had more than his fair share of detractors but, perhaps due to the physical distance between author and these detractors, they did not distract from his prolific output.

Each year seemed to bring a new F. Marion Crawford novel. His popularity was evident although some works, such as 1896's offering 'Adam Johnstone's Son', was described by his left-wing English contemporary, George Gissing, as "rubbish". Over half of his novels are set in Italy. He also wrote three long historical studies of Italy and was nearing completion on a history of Rome in the Middle Ages when he died.

His 'Saracinesca' series are considered his best works. The third in the series, 'Don Orsino' (1892) was told against the background of a real estate bubble and is especially effective. The volume immediately after was 'Corleone' (1897), and the first major treatment of the Mafia in literature.

Crawford himself was fondest of 'Khaled: A Tale of Arabia' (1891), a story of a genie who becomes human. 'A Cigarette-Maker's Romance' (1890) was dramatized, and had considerable popularity on the stage as well as in its novel form.

Towards the end of the 1890's Crawford ventured down another path with his writing. He began his historical works. 'Ave Roma Immortalis' was published in 1898, followed by 'Rulers of the South' (1900), and 'Gleanings from Venetian History' (1905). Most were re-titled with longer more explanatory titles for the American market. Within them all his careful and precise knowledge of the local Italian history together with his literary talents combined to great effect.

Whilst on an American Lecture tour in the winter of 1897-1898 Crawford was researching and gathering technical information for his historical work 'Marietta' (published 1901), that describes glass-making in late medieval Venice. Whilst visiting a glass-smelting plant in Colorado he suffered a severe lung injury when he inhaled toxic gasses. This would eventually contribute to his death a decade or so later.

Crawford's commercial popularity and appeal at the time was such that in 1901, the American Macmillan firm began a deluxe uniform edition of his novels as his works came up for re-printing. In 1904 the P. F. Collier Company in New York was authorized to publish a 25-volume edition (which was later expanded to 32 volumes).

In 1902 he wrote a stage play 'Francesca da Rimini', that was produced in Paris by his friend and legendary actress Sarah Bernhardt.

Towards the end of his life Hollywood had begun to realise that his works were a valuable source of stories and ideas and several were turned into movies and continued to be so for decades after his death.

Crawford also had a gift for pulling off excellent short stories. Several, such as 'The Upper Berth' (1886), 'For the Blood Is the Life' (1905, a vampiress tale), 'The Dead Smile' (1899), and 'The Screaming Skull' (1908), are among the most anthologized classics of the horror genre. After his death several collected volumes were published from various sources.

After most of his fictional works had been published, most had the view that he was a gifted narrator; and his books of fiction, were full of historic vitality and energy as well as dramatic characterization. He was widely popular among readers to whom literature was more for escapism than a confrontation with reality or pages of subjective analysis. In 'The Novel: What It Is' (1893), Crawford was both resolute and disarming in defending his literary approach, self-conceived as a combination of romanticism and realism, defining the art form in terms of its marketplace and audience. The novel, he wrote, is "a marketable commodity" and "intellectual artistic luxury" that "must amuse, indeed, but should amuse reasonably, from an intellectual point of view .... Its intention is to amuse and please, and certainly not to teach and preach; but in order to amuse well it must be a finely-balanced creation ...."

Francis Marion Crawford died at Sorrento on Good Friday 1909 at Villa Crawford of a heart attack.

F. Marion Crawford – A Concise Bibliography

Novels

Mr. Isaacs: A Tale of Modern India (1882)
Dr. Claudius (1883)
To Leeward (1884)

A Roman Singer (1884)
An American Politician (1884)
Zoroaster (1885)
A Tale of a Lonely Parish (1886)
Saracinesca (1887)
Marzio's Crucifix (1887)
Paul Patoff (1887)
With the Immortals (1888)
Greifenstein (1889)
Sant' Ilario (1889); sequel to Saracinesca
A Cigarette-Maker's Romance (1890)
Khaled: A Tale of Arabia (1891)
The Witch of Prague (1891)
The Three Fates (1892)
Don Orsino (1892); sequel to Sant' Ilario
The Children of the King (1893)
Pietro Ghisleri (1893)
Marion Darche (1893)
Katharine Lauderdale (1894)
The Upper Berth (1894); with "By the Waters of Paradise"
Love in Idleness (1894)
The Ralstons (1894); sequel to Katharine Lauderdale
Casa Braccio (1895); related to Katharine Lauderdale and The Ralstons.
Adam Johnstone's Son (1896)
Taquisara (1896)
A Rose of Yesterday (1897)
Corleone (1897)
Via Crucis (1899)
In the Palace of the King (1900)
Marietta (1901)
Cecilia (1902)
Man Overboard! (1903)
The Heart of Rome (1903)
Whosoever Shall Offend (1904)
Soprano (1905); U.S. title: Fair Margaret.
A Lady of Rome (1906)
Arethusa (1907)
The Little City of Hope (1907)
The Primadonna (1908); sequel to Soprano/Fair Margaret
The Diva's Ruby (1908); sequel to The Primadonna
The White Sister (1909)
Stradella (1909)
The Undesirable Governess (1910)
Wandering Ghosts; British title: Uncanny Tales.

Non-fiction

Our Silver (1881)
The Novel: What It Is (1893)
Constantinople (1895)

Bar Harbor (1896)
Ave Roma Immortalis (1898)
Rulers of the South (1900; 1905 in the U.S. as Southern Italy and Sicily and The Rulers of the South)
Gleanings from Venetian History (1905; in the U.S. as Salvae Venetia and in 1909 as Venice; the People and the Place)

Drama

In the Palace of the King (1900) with Lorrimer Stoddard.
Francesca da Rimini (1902) The piece was adapted into an opera by Franco Leoni in 1904.
Evelyn Hastings (1902) Unpublished typescript discovered in 2008.
The White Sister (1909) with Walter C. Hackett.

Filmography

A Cigarette-Maker's Romance, directed by Frank Wilson (UK, 1913, based on the novella)
The White Sister, directed by Fred E. Wright [it] (1915, based on the novel)
In the Palace of the King [it], directed by Fred E. Wright [it] (1915, based on the novel)
Whosoever Shall Offend, directed by Arrigo Bocchi (UK, 1919, based on the novel)
Il cuore di Roma, directed by Edoardo Bencivenga (Italy, 1919, based on the novel)
A Cigarette-Maker's Romance, directed by Tom Watts (UK, 1920, based on the novella)
Saracinesca [it], directed by Gaston Ravel (Italy, 1921, based on the novel)
Sant' Ilario [it], directed by Henry Kolker (Italy, 1923, based on the novel)
The White Sister, directed by Henry King (1923, based on the novel)
In the Palace of the King, directed by Emmett J. Flynn (1923, based on the novel)
Son of India, directed by Jacques Feyder (1931, based on the novel Mr. Isaacs)
The White Sister, directed by Victor Fleming (1933, based on the novel)
The Screaming Skull, directed by Alex Nicol (1958, named after the short story)
The White Sister, directed by Tito Davison (Mexico, 1960, based on the novel)